SUN CITY

GUY ALLEN

This is a work of fiction. All characters,
incidents, and dialogues are products of the author's
imagination.

ISBN- 978-0-9938107-0-1

Author's Notes to the Second Edition

This version of Sun City is the result of detailed re-editing of the original manuscript.

This is third book in my Dusty Sherant series. Although Sun City was written as a stand-alone novel, it has been suggested that the initial book in the series, Amyot, should be read first. Some of the characters in Amyot also appear in Sun City, and occasional references are made to events in that previous story.

Guy Allen
New Westminster, BC
September, 2019

1

Sunrise was at 6:47. It was a beautiful day, the kind of morning when avid golfers dip into their repertoire of excuses for reasons why they would be unable to take part in the workaday world.

The boys were on the course, ready to go at 6:45. Dan was the first to arrive; he was always the first. He paid special attention to sunrise times and precise calculations of the exact number of minutes it would take the sun to completely clear the horizon, thus providing enough light to proceed with their game. It was more than a game to Dan; it was one of the main reasons he enjoyed his life in the retirement years. This was a good day for Dan; everyone had showed up at the proper time. He was pleased to see Tim and Louie were properly attired with a complete compliment of expensive clubs. Tim's son Tony was filling in for Jeremy, who was out of town again. Dan was not pleased to look on this young man with his garish clothes.

The first hole was a par 4, 346 yards to the pin with a sharp dogleg to the right about 200 yards out. The lack of rain and constant sun for the past month had baked the ground to rock hardness. Rather than experience disappointment, the boys were encouraged that a good drive might reach the green with extra bounces on this cement-like surface. The fairway was narrow with numerous sand traps and areas of rough gravel along the borders. Two small ponds with their complements of aquatic vegetation and small amphibians broke the continuity of the green expanse. Louie put his drive on the dogleg in the middle of the fairway, fifty yards beyond the first pond. Dan and Tim, whose powerful drives were often a topic of the 19th hole beer and brag sessions, both cleared the rough areas on the right border and came to rest within an easy chip shot of the green. Tony tried to match his father's shot, but with a mighty swing, proceeded to hook his ball into a sand trap along the left border.

His companions waited patiently while Tony planted his feet firmly in the sand and set up for his second attempt.

"Why don't you throw it out on the grass and count two," his father suggested.

"No way. I'm getting out of here in one."

Tony's first attempt, a mighty swing, cut a foot-long furrow in the sand and lobbed the ball six inches up the slope, where it immediately rolled back to rest in its original spot. Exasperated, he set up again. His second stroke deepened the furrow as it glanced off a buried object causing the club to fly out of his grip, narrowly missing his spectators. The ball remained in its original spot.

"What the hell is going on?" He exclaimed as he bent down to have a look. "There's something down here."

As he scraped the sand away, a human finger was exposed. When he had carefully cleared away more sand, an entire human hand, severed at the wrist, was revealed.

Tim used his cell phone to put in a 911 call, which summoned the police and ended the golfing activities for the day. They retrieved their balls and walked back to the clubhouse to inform the manager of this new development.

"Get everyone off the course, and wait until the police arrive," was the official order broadcast over the loudspeakers to the other golfers.

Their second hole was a non-event. The boys grumbled their way around the clubhouse until the police arrived.

The next couple of hours were spent drinking coffee and complaining while the trap was dug out and thoroughly examined. A backhoe was brought in and directed to systematically dig up the remainder of the pits on the course. In the meantime a scuba diver made a thorough search of all the ponds. Needless to say, golf was over for the day.

"Why didn't you just kick sand over it so we could have gotten on with our game? They'll probably be digging up this course for the next week," Louie said.

Tim was watching the activity on the course. He turned to Louie and asked, "Isn't that your bowling friend, the cop, out there?"

Louie had a look and agreed it was. "I'll go and see if I can find out what's going on."

When he returned to the clubhouse, he announced to the assembled group. "They figure they will be at this most of the day, but we should be able to play the day after tomorrow. They also want to come in and ask us a few questions."

Then he added to his companions. "He couldn't tell me much, but evidently that hand was all they found. Also, it appears to have been surgically removed, and the tips of the fingers have been sliced off. There was no blood around it."

"It sounds to me like whoever did this wanted it to be found but not identified. Maybe it's a warning to someone," Dan observed.

The three officers came into the clubhouse a few minutes later and proceeded to question the group, attempting to determine if anyone could shed some light on the mystery.

"Do any of you know if one of the locals has been reported missing?"

No one was aware of any missing resident.

"People come and go in Sun City all the time," someone observed. "With all the snowbirds showing up for the winter, there's no way to keep track."

Dan thought for a minute then said, "Jeremy Prince's wife told me last week that his uncle had gone out prospecting in the hills, and they were worried since they hadn't heard from him in over a month."

"Thanks. We'll check it out."

After the police had gone, and the group was breaking up, Louie remarked with a smile, "You know, when I saw all the trouble Tony was having getting out of that trap, I felt kind of sorry for him. I was going to go over and offer to lend him a hand."

The police contacted Kellie Prince that afternoon. With Jeremy on another problem-solving trip to the mine, Kellie figured it was up to her to have a look at this severed hand and determine if it belonged to Fred. She was apprehensive as she entered the Medical Examiner's lab. Her anxiety wasn't diminished by the ambiance of the room, with its covered corpses stretched out on the metal tables and the jars of assorted body parts lining the walls. She just wanted to get the ordeal over with as quickly as possible.

As usual, with events concerning Uncle Fred, she had been conditioned over the years to expect the worst and was seldom disappointed. His total unpredictability and strange habits had not changed as he passed his eightieth birthday. At this advanced age, he was now considered eccentric rather than strange. His physical and mental abilities had shown no signs of diminished capacity, and his ability to bed younger women gave him hero status among the geriatric set. He had gotten into an argument with his nephew over some mining claims, which Jeremy had staked. As a result, he had packed up and moved out of their caseta over a month ago.

Her first look at the hand, however, assured her this was not one of Fred's appendages. Jeremy's uncle was a big man, well over six feet, packing two hundred plus pounds on his frame. As expected, his hands were also large.

The severed hand was from a much smaller person.

"It almost looks like a woman's hand," Kellie remarked to the attendant.

"Could be," he replied. "We haven't done a DNA analysis or had an expert look at it yet. We should know in a couple of days."

Although somewhat relieved, she still had serious concerns over Fred's whereabouts.

GUY ALLEN

2

Fred Prince was definitely still alive and well.
He had spent a week prospecting for gold with his
friend Rafael in the mountains near Tucson. They
had covered most of the open ground in the area
without success, so they returned to the city. After
pulling out of MacDonalds, they drove around
trying to decide what to do next, whether to look at
some lapsed claims to the east or just pack it in for a
week or so. Then they sighted the little man's truck.

"He's a long way from home," Fred observed.
"I wonder what he's doing over here."

"Didn't you say you thought the area north of
here was where his gold claims are located? He's
probably on his way out there."

"Sounds right. We have a pretty good idea
where they are."

"I'm going to follow him. Are you coming
along?" Rafael asked.

"No. I'm going home and get some rest. I'm

getting too old to go roaming around the countryside chasing that little weasel."

Rafael had decided that following the little man seemed like a good idea at that time. If he could find out exactly where he was going, it would save them a lot of searching for his claims. He had tracked him into some wild country to the north, where the little man drove down a dry wash and parked. But now, huddled in his thin blanket far from home in the cold desert air, it didn't seem like such a great move. Maybe he should have listened to Fred and waited. They could have planned it for the next day and driven up into the mountains at their leisure and just looked for his truck.

"A stupid idea," he thought. "Here I am freezing my butt off while he's got his little girlfriend to keep him warm. I wish I had scrapped the whole idea and driven back to Mesa."

There was just enough light from the moon sliver to make out the outline of the little man's truck. It was parked along the dry creek bed just below Rafael. It hadn't moved in six hours, but he knew the little man was probably asleep inside. He decided to get closer.

Just as he wriggled up to the top of the ridge for a better look, he heard the drone of a small plane in the distance. Scuttling back into the mesquite, he picked a spot where he had a clearer view of the valley but hopefully was hidden from above.

As the sound of the engine got louder, the growing speck from the south materialized into a small single-engine aircraft. It came in low, dipped down into the valley and leveled out at about fifty feet, slowing almost to a stall. Rafael was on the wrong side of the draw to see who opened the cabin door. All of a sudden, two packages with small parachutes were ejected and floated to earth. The pilot gunned the engine, and the aircraft ascended into the night sky as it circled to the south and disappeared.

Then nothing. Rafael was totally confused. He had not expected anything like this. He had followed the little man hoping to find his claims, where all that gold was supposed to be found. Fred had told him about the gold the little man was bringing to his home in Sun City. The little man had tried to keep it a secret but was exposed when his wife tried to pay for some clothes at a local store with small nuggets and gold dust. The storekeeper was a friend of Fred and had told him the story.

"Maybe the gold is in those packages," Rafael thought. "I could get to them before he does, but he probably has a gun, and I don't."

Rafael waited patiently for the little man to rush out and retrieve the packages, which were within a hundred feet of the truck, but there was no movement until an hour had passed. Rafael was getting tired of waiting and feeling the pain from lying on the cold ground, when the truck started up and moved slowly up beside the parcels. The little man got out, threw the packages in the back and drove off up the valley.

Rafael scampered back to his Jeep to follow the little man's truck. The rising sun was providing enough light and the country was mostly clear of vegetation, allowing him to stay far enough behind so as not to be spotted. He had no trouble following the trail of dust.

It was almost noon when the dust trail suddenly disappeared. Rafael quickly pulled off the trail and parked behind a large rock. He took out his binoculars and searched the landscape for any signs of movement. The truck was nowhere in sight. He thought of tracking on foot but immediately saw the danger in that decision. He decided to wait and had no sooner settled in, when he saw the dust cloud appear again, this time coming in his direction. The little man's truck passed close enough below that he could see the packages were no longer resting in the back. This was also confusing. If the packages contained gold, why would he leave them out here in the middle of the desert? He waited until he saw the dust disappear to the west before he ventured forth. He followed the track the little man had made into the maze of hills. It was easy to trace the faint outline of the tire marks, which ended suddenly in a small blind canyon, where the truck had evidently turned around and followed its own track out. A thicket covered one side, backed up against a steep cliff. The other side was solid rock. Rafael was confused. He got out and walked back and forth along the line of shrubs. Near the end of the thicket he felt a light waft of cool air, which ended as suddenly as it had begun. He walked back to the spot and felt the light cool breeze on his face again. It was evidently coming from inside the thicket. He tried to peer through the bushes, but the growth was too thick. As he attempted to part them, he found the bushes were not rooted, but had been piled carefully to hide a narrow entrance into the wall. He moved enough of the brush aside so that he could slither through. The portal led to a short tunnel that swung to the right, opening into a small room. It was a natural cave with no indication of any past mining activities. Shining his flashlight about the room, Rafael spied the two packages sitting on a rock ledge toward the back. He picked up one and was surprised at how light it was, as he had been expecting them to contain gold. He hefted the other one and came to the same conclusion. These mysterious parcels certainly did not contain gold. His curiosity was beginning to germinate into fear, as he had no idea what was going on. He just wanted to get out of the cave and away from this area as quickly as possible. The temptation to open one of the parcels was strong, but the fear of whatever he had stumbled into was greater.

He hesitated, but then in a moment of courage, he grabbed the packages and headed for the tunnel entrance. At the bend, he heard voices outside. He stopped and backed into the room, as he could see someone pushing his way through the thicket. Two men came into the room giving Rafael nowhere to run. He tried to go by them, but they grabbed him and dragged him out into the open. Two other men were standing by a Hummer parked beside his Jeep. He tried in vain to struggle loose.

The last thing Rafael felt was the needle in his arm.

Rafael had no idea where he was. As he slowly regained consciousness, he was aware of strange smells and the terrible throbbing pain in his arm and head. He was lying on a hard flat surface. As he tried to rise to a sitting position, he felt the straps stretched around his body, holding him down. Something wrapped around his head totally blocked his vision.

He lay there helpless. He struggled to reach across his body with his right hand to locate the source of the intense pain in his left arm, which was wrapped in bandages. To his total shock he discovered his left hand was gone. What had happened? The last thing he remembered was the two men grabbing him in the cave and dragging him outside. It was too much. As he tried to sort it out, the pain in his head shoved him back into unconsciousness.

The next thing he knew someone was shaking him. He was somewhat relieved to discover the restraining straps had been removed, and he was able to sit up. The blindfold still covered his eyes. He tried to reach up and remove it, but his arm was quickly grabbed and tied to the table.

"We will leave that on. It is to your advantage if you want to live for you to not see our faces or be able to recognize us. We don't wish to cause you any more pain, but you must do exactly what we tell you."

The voice was deep with a heavy accent. The man spoke slowly and with authority.

"Where am I, and what have you done to me?" Rafael asked.

"You have done a very bad thing by trying to rob us, and we have punished you. Those packages in the cave are our property. You tried to take them away. Fortunately, we arrived in time to prevent you from making a fatal mistake."

"I didn't know who they belonged to. I just found them in the cave."

"Do not make things worse for yourself by lying. We know you followed our courier from the time he left Tucson. You did not see us, but we were with you all night. We have punished you much in the way of my ancestors. When they captured a thief, they chopped off his hand. We are not that barbaric. We simply had your hand removed by a qualified doctor. You should thank us for foregoing the brutal practices of my countrymen. If you disobey us, the next time we won't be so generous. You will find a note in your pocket with the name and address of a doctor across the border in Nogales. Go and see him if that arm needs more treatment. And, if you tell anyone, anyone at all, what has happened, or the location of that cave, your beautiful wife, Miranda, and your two daughters will suffer much pain before they die."

Rafael was about to respond, but he again felt the pain of the needle in his side and the soft envelope of sleep surrounding him.

When he regained conscious, he was no longer bound or blindfolded. He was sitting in his jeep somewhere in the desert. His first thought was that he must have dreamed it all until he looked at his hand, or rather where his hand used to be. Only a carefully bandaged stump remained. Rafael felt the presence of the missing appendage, but it was gone forever. He had no idea where he was or even how long he had been there. He looked around, but nothing was familiar. He dug around for his cell phone without success. He realized his captors must have taken it.

Rafael just wanted to get away from wherever he was and go home. The problem was, he didn't have any idea in which direction to go. It was a cloudy day, but there was just enough sun to estimate a compass direction. He had spent enough time with Fred to learn useful things, like using his watch and the sun to find north and work it out from there. Fortunately, they had left his pocket watch, which he dug out of his jeans and figured out which way to go. The painkiller was wearing off, and the hand, or where the hand used to be, was beginning to throb.

"I don't know what they gave me, but its effects are wearing off fast. I've got to get away from here and find my way home. My best bet is to just travel south. Sooner or later, I'll hit a major east-west highway or the Mexican border. I need to get some strong pain killers fast."

Two hours of back roads and rough trails brought him to an intersection with Highway 93 somewhere northeast of Surprise. Now at least, he knew where he was. When he hit the city limits, he pulled into the first gas station and called Miranda from a pay phone. He was greeted with, "Where have you been for the last three days? I was just about ready to call the police. I tried to reach Fred, but as usual, he doesn't answer his cell."

"I'm just outside Surprise. I'll be home in a couple of hours. Please don't try to reach Fred or talk to anyone before I see you."

"What do you mean, Rafael? That sounds weird."

"I know, but don't worry. I'll explain when I see you."

Rafael didn't know what he was going to do. The warning not to talk about what had happened was real and seriously scared him. He was too afraid to disobey their orders. On the other hand, he had to give Miranda some explanation for the injury. He knew anything he told his wife would be common knowledge to everyone they knew by morning. The problem boiled down to coming up with some plausible account for his missing hand, which was not going to generate suspicion and a whole bunch of questions.

He thought up a number of explanations, but by the time he got to Mesa and drove into the Mobile Home Park, he had it all worked out. It was a pretty flimsy story, but he thought she would accept it. As expected, Miranda freaked out when she saw the damage to her husband's body.

"What happened?" She asked the minute he walked in the door.

Rafael started out slowly, concentrating on getting the words right.

"Well, I was out prospecting up in the hills near Flagstaff. I was driving along an old mining trail when a log that had fallen across the road blocked my way. I decided to cut through it with my chainsaw. I had forgotten to sharpen the saw before I left, and it was so dull it got stuck, bucked out and came down on my arm. It went right through the bone. I wrapped my shirt around what was left of my arm to slow the blood flow and managed to drive to a clinic in the city, where they cleaned and stitched it up. They gave me some stuff to kill the pain and sent me home."

Miranda was sympathetic but dubious.

"Where's your hand? What did you do with it? Didn't they try to sew it back on?"

"I don't know. They tried to put it back, but it was chewed up too much. There was nothing else they could do. It is really important for you to not tell anybody about this, at least for a while, and please don't ask me any more questions. I need to stick around here until the wound heals, but I have to have some strong painkillers right away. Do you think you can get your kid brother to bring me something out of Mexico? I don't want to have to go to a doctor for a prescription."

Against her better judgment, she agreed.

3

Dusty Sherant firmly believed that any time his phone rang after midnight; it would not be a harbinger of good news. Experience had taught the lesson well. Consequently, he usually unplugged the machine before he went to bed, and if he forgot, and it rang, he never answered it. He felt that all crises, imminent disasters, threats on his life, and stupid questions from drunken friends could be handled more efficiently during daylight hours. So, when a call came in at 3:15 AM, he rolled over and ignored it. Unfortunately, he wasn't home in his bed, and it wasn't his phone. Lucie picked it up, said hello, jabbed him in the ribs, and announced, "It's for you. It's Jeremy."

"It can't be for me. At 3 in the morning, I don't know any Jeremys, and besides, how would he know I'm here?"

"Everyone we know is aware you're here, even the people I work with who enjoy pointing out I'm shacked up with someone without a job and to whom I am not legally married."

Dusty took the phone and asked, "Jeremy, why are you phoning me in the middle of the night? It better be to tell me you have a terminal illness, or that I've won the lottery."

"Uncle Fred is missing. We haven't heard from him in over a month, and we can't find him anywhere."

"Jeremy, ever since we've known Fred Prince, he has spent major portions of his life missing, and we have spent much of our lives looking for him. That's always been part of his charm, his total unpredictability and lack of concern for any form of social protocol. How is this time different?"

"I don't know. Most of the time it's the same old story, but this time Kellie has a bad feeling about it. It's not like when he and your dad used to go on those week-long drinking sprees, and we had to find them and drag them home. We always knew where they were and what they were doing. This has been too long, and Uncle Fred was acting weird and very secretive about his plans before he left. He just said he'd see us in a couple of weeks, and he was gone."

"C'mon, there has to be more to it than that, and you say Kellie is concerned. What about you? How worried are you? Don't get me wrong, I have the greatest respect for Kellie's intuition, and her methods of making you do things you don't want to do, but I sense you are not telling me everything."

"Yeah, there is more, but I can't get a handle on it. I guess I've been a bit rough on him. He and I got in an argument over some claims I staked. He thinks they are worthless and doesn't understand the reasons why I staked them. Also, he's got some sort of a map supposedly pointing the way to lost treasure up north of Tucson. He was about to tell us the story behind the map, but I kind of made a joke about it, and he got all quiet and refused to discuss it further. The next morning he left. He was acting strange, even stranger than usual. I'm at a loss as to what to do next."

"Just back up a minute. Why did you stake some claims with no apparent value?"

"That is just Fred's opinion."

"Fred's been in this prospecting business forever. He taught us the game. If anyone can see value in a mining prospect, it is Fred. So, what's the real reason for staking them?"

"It's the old story," Jeremy replied. "I set up a new company, and I put these claims in to raise the seed money, and only Fred thinks they are worthless. I have an engineering report indicating potential and recommending further work. Anyway, we were wondering if you and Lucie could come down and help us look for him."

"Is that 'we' both of you, or does she have a gun to your head?"

"Go easy, will you. She's on the other phone, and you're pissing her off."

"You don't ever give up trying to push my buttons, do you?" Kellie put in. "I do think something weird is going on. If you can find your way down here without getting lost or sidetracked by a pretty face, I'd like you to help find him. Lucie once told me, when she was trying to come up with something positive to say about you that you have good investigative skills, but I guess that was when she still thought you were a normal human being."

"No, she has never had that delusion, but I don't know about making the trip to Arizona, although it would be a great chance to escape our

Canadian winter. Are you sure you've tried everything? What are the cops doing about it? Have you checked all the bars, hospitals, morgue, jails, brothels, and mental institutions? How about a girlfriend? Fred usually has some lady on the string."

"We did most of that," Jeremy replied, "but I just filed a missing person report with the police this evening. They had Kellie down to the medical examiner's office to see if she could identify a hand they found in a sand trap on the golf course. They had heard from someone that I was looking for Fred and thought it might be his hand. It wasn't, but I figured I'd better make a formal report. I hadn't done it before because I thought he'd probably show up and climb all over me for calling in the cops."

"They found a what?"

"A human hand, surgically removed with the finger tips cut off."

"Jeez. What kind of people do you have down there?"

"Come on down and find out. You'll probably fit right in with the rest of the weirdos," Kellie said.

"You realize those kind of remarks aren't helping your case. Hang on for a minute you two. I need to talk to Lucie."

Dusty thought about it for a minute then turned to Lucie.

"You heard both ends. What do you think?"

"Two things come to mind. I get a sense he's overreacting to a situation that is not as serious as he imagines on one hand, but also that he's is not that anxious to find his uncle. I agree with you Kellie is pushing him. You know yourself, she is a tough gal and usually gets what she wants, but I also trust her take on the situation."

"I sensed that also. Jeremy and I have always been close to Fred. He was our mentor while we were growing up, and he has baled Jeremy out of more messes than I can count. This apparent apathy about his uncle bothers me, and you're right, Kellie is one smart lady, and she is truly concerned. That alone adds a lot of creditability to the problem."

"Jeremy is your best friend and has been all your life. You and Kellie have been buddies ever since Amyot. If the situation was reversed, they would come to your aid without a second thought."

"I know, and you're right. It's time I got off my butt, go down there and see what can be done. Fred and I tend to think alike, and I would probably have a better chance of tracking him down. Do you want to go?"

"I can't right now. You know I have finally got my business on a paying basis, and I need to keep it afloat. I have three important investigations to wind up before I can get free. If things work out, maybe I'll come later, but I want you to go and help your friends. They need you. Will you do it?"

"Are you that anxious to get rid of me? If so, I'll leave tomorrow."

"Maybe that is part of it. Before you go, we need to talk. Do you want to get into it now, or try and get some more sleep?"

"Is this about us?" Dusty asked. "You're getting serious, and it's starting to scare me."

"Yes, this is serious. I guess I need to know where we're going and whether this will continue to be an off-again, on-again relationship like it has in the past."

"I don't know, Lucie. That has always been your choice, and I have gone along with it. You laid out the rules right from the start. You wanted to avoid any commitments and feelings of being tied down, and as far as I'm concerned, it has been a great relationship. Do you feel different now?"

"I'm beginning to. My biological clock has run out, and I realize in a couple of years, I'll be fifty. I guess I am experiencing the need for some kind of permanence in a relationship and in my life. Taking my retirement from the RCMP and starting my own investigation business has been a life-altering event. I feel I want to settle down and grow old with someone I can rely on and who cares about me. I gave up any idea of having kids years ago because my career seemed more important. I still feel that was the right decision, but now I am looking for something more. I just don't know if you are capable of that kind of a relationship. All the time we have spent together has been superficial. It was the way we both wanted it, but I still have the feeling you don't know me anymore."

Dusty was quiet for a few minutes before he replied. "This is a bit unsettling. I had no idea you were feeling this way. Maybe you have put out a few clues, but I definitely have missed them. I did believe I knew how you felt."

"You are seldom aware of how I feel. Sometimes I wonder if you know anything about me, or what I care about. Getting you interested in things about me other than my body is just as difficult as me trying to crack through that shield you put up to shut out the rest of the world. For a long time I have put your indifference down to the terrible hurt you suffered from Elena's treachery, but I can't do that anymore. You have to get over her and get on with your life. I know you loved her, but like Kellie told me once, you two were lovers but never friends. Before you and I can have anything meaningful, you have to get past your hurt and learn to care again."

"Maybe you're right. I feel Elena destroyed any chance I might have for a future loving relationship. I've tried to get past it, but it's like climbing a high wall that never ends, so I've given up trying. I guess I don't know who you are and what you want. I obviously haven't tried hard enough to find out. I've always tried to keep it simple between us. Right now, that's all I can do in any relationship. I hope this feeling will change someday, but most of the time I doubt if I can ever go down the serious road again."

"I know," Lucie replied, "and that's why I want you to go away for a while. I think we both have a lot to think about, and hopefully, this will give us the chance to sort it out."

To Dusty, it was a road he had traveled before Elena. The words were different, but the context was the same: commitment. The one time he had let his guard down, it had ended in disaster. He knew that, even though he was over fifty, he was nowhere near ready to settle down and do the pipe and slippers routine. Somehow, he had imagined Lucie to be immune from that scenario as well. She was right. It was time to be apart and resolve these issues in his mind and between them.

4

Dusty found it interesting that the major concerns in his life, the ones he would worry about for weeks, usually turned out to be just minor events, which had resolved themselves by the time a decision had to be made. On the other hand, spur of the moment choices were often life-changing. So it was on that crisp December afternoon.

He left Lucie's condo in Saskatoon on a cold crisp Saskatchewan morning. The drive to Calgary was the usual boring trek across the prairie. He opened up his apartment in the Alberta city and dealt with the phone messages and bills, which had accumulated over the past three months. The phone and electricity had been cut off due to nonpayment, and he decided not to reconnect. Since he planned to drive to Arizona, he figured he might as well spend the entire winter away from the cold, snow and Lucie.

The trip to the Coast took another day. He crossed the border in record time without the myriad of questions and was on his way south on I-5. Noon brought him to the Oregon border.

The first time he had driven this route, it had been exciting. Even the second trip was interesting, the third, not so much. After that, each trek had been an exercise in sanity retention. Logically, he should stay with the plan and endure it again, but Dusty's actions were seldom based on logic or careful planning. So he reasoned, why start now? Abruptly, he turned east on Highway 26, eliciting the finger from a frustrated traveler, whom he had cut off.

As he drove east on 26, the warm coastal air gave way to a cold, steady rain, which quickly turned to snow as the road gained elevation. By the time he reached the Mount Hood ski area, his wipers were working frantically to clear the profusion of large, wet flakes, which were rapidly accumulating. The road was becoming packed with slush, which was quickly turning to ice.

"Maybe I should have stayed on I-5 after all," he thought.

In spite of Lucie's remarks, he was thankful he had decided to take his old Landrover for the trip. She had continually made suggestions that he should rid himself of this old vehicle, which belched smoke, always smelled and continually demanded repairs. He had countered with the observation that she, in return, should divest herself of her smelly old dog, which was always farting and regularly being taken to the Vet. He regretted the analogy as soon as it passed his lips, but it did effectively end a dialogue that was going nowhere.

By the time he had passed the summit, he had winched three cars from the ditch.

The first two skiers drove off after offering

money then thanks when Dusty refused the cash.
The last car, a fifteen-year-old Toyota, wasn't going
anywhere. Its nosedive into a depression by the side
of the road had been stopped short by a fallen tree.
The front was crumpled, and coolant continued to
stain the snow, as Dusty wrapped a chain around the
rear bumper. The lady driver stood by with her
hands on her hips as he pulled her ride back up on
the road.

As they stood surveying the damage, she said,
"I guess I'd better call a tow truck to drag this thing
out of here."

She tried her cell phone, but there was no
signal. Dusty had no better luck with his device
even though it was supposed to be able to tap into a
signal anywhere.

"I'll get back to civilization and try again from
someplace where people use these things on a
regular basis. Which way are you going?"

"East and south," he replied. "I was hoping to
make it to Bend by nightfall."

"That would work if I can catch a ride with
you."

"Sure. Grab your stuff and pile in."

"Just a minute," she said, as she pulled a small
pistol from her handbag and fired three shots into
the motor of her car. "I've been wanting to do that
ever since I got this piece of junk. They do it to
horses, why not cars?"

She then dragged a suitcase and duffel bag
from the trunk and threw them, with her skis, into
the back of the Landrover.

Dusty's first impression of this bundled-up
female was of a young lady in her twenties. As she
peeled away outer garments in the warmth of the
truck, she appeared to age about twenty years.

"My name's Misty," she announced, as they headed east along the snow-packed corridor.

"Dusty Sherant," he replied. "It's too bad we had to meet under such unfortunate circumstances."

"You came along and helped a lady in distress. That's not unfortunate for me. I really appreciate it."

Their ride to Bend was pleasant in spite of the storm and hazards of the road.

Dusty pulled into the first motel on the outskirts of town.

"I'm going to book in here for the night, but I'll drive you to wherever you want to go."

"No, this looks okay," she replied. "I'll split you on the cost of something with two bedrooms."

Dusty registered them as Mr. and Mrs. Sherant of Calgary to go with his Alberta plates.

"Are you ready for your new home, Mrs. Sherant?"

"Jeez, that's scary."

"Don't worry. There are no strings attached. I figured it would avoid a lot of questions."

"I understand, but too bad about the strings."

When Dusty awoke the next morning, it took a few seconds to figure out where he was, and the identity of this beautiful lady in bra and panties perched on the edge of his bed. Misty was gesturing wildly, as she tried to explain her car problem to someone on the other end, who obviously wasn't getting it.

Dusty wore no pajamas, and his clothes were on the other side of the room. Waiting until her attention was averted; he jumped out of bed and scooted across to the bathroom. When he emerged after his morning routine, she was dressed, with

coffee and food spread out on a small table.
"I hit the continental breakfast out in the lobby.
I got you coffee and a couple of Danish."
"How come you were sitting on my bed half-
naked when I woke up?"
"I had to phone for a tow truck, and you have
the only phone book in this place. Did I bother
you?"
"Absolutely, and thank you. Did you have any
luck getting a tow?"
"No. I think I woke up the village idiot. I'll
have to try someone else."
"Here, let me get in touch with Triple A and
see if I can get a line on a reliable local outfit that
will do the job."
Three calls later, Misty had it arranged that a
local company, Consolidated, would pick up the
Toyota and haul it to the wreckers. All they needed
was a transferred ownership and her credit card
information.
"I gathered from that conversation that you are
not getting it repaired," Dusty observed.
"No, just like you can't bring a dead horse back
to life. I'll be glad to see the end of it. I just miss the
joy I would have experienced pushing it off a cliff
somewhere."
"So, where do you go from here, and how do
you get there?"
"I'm headed for home, Sun City, in Arizona."
Dusty didn't answer. He began packing his
gear and hauled it out to the truck. His mind was in
conflict as to whether he should reveal to her that
his destination was the same. If he did, he was stuck
with her for the next three days. He liked the lady,
but he wasn't sure he wanted to deal with her for
that length of time. On the other hand, she could be

a welcome relief to the boredom of the remaining trip. In the end, he decided to offer her the ride. When he came back in the room, she was packed and ready to head out.

"Well, it just so happens that I'm heading for Sun City also. You can tag along if you promise not to shoot me if I piss you off."

"That's a tough decision. As long as you don't get stuck in a ditch, you should be okay. It took you a while to make that offer. Do I frighten or bore you that much?"

"You scare the hell out of me, but I guess I can take the chance."

Highway 97 south from Bend was an adventure in black-ice driving. The old Landrover held the road at fifty but had a tendency to fishtail on the slippery sections. Consequently, it was a slow trip. A blanket of snow masked the ice at the higher elevations, increasing the hazards of traveling at greater speeds.

"Dusty, this is kind of scary," Misty observed. "How many miles do you think we can make today?"

"I don't know. The roads will be a lot better south of Klamath Falls. We can stay there, or see how far we can get before dark."

"I've got a suggestion and a proposal for you. I have a timeshare, which has a resort at a ranch just outside of Klamath Falls. We can stay there if you're willing to drive a bit more out of the way. Besides, all this stress is starting to make me bitchy."

"Alright, but remember my decision is based partly on fear. You're the one with the gun."

Misty's directions brought them to the resort office, where they were able to get a condo unit with two bedrooms and a fully equipped kitchen. At the store they selected a bottle of wine and the ingredients for a pasta meal, which Misty prepared as soon as they settled in. After dinner they sat out on the deck, which overlooked an expanse of pasture bordered by a ring of trees on three sides.

"This is beautiful," Dusty observed.

After a few minutes, Misty replied, "Would you like to stay here an extra day if this unit is available?"

"Yes, but I thought you were in a hurry to get home."

"I was, but that doesn't seem so important now. I was under the impression it was you who was in a rush. You never did tell me why you picked Sun City as your destination, and don't tell me it was so you could get me home safely."

"No. My friend down there phoned and said he needed my help in finding his uncle. He's evidently been missing for a couple of months. I don't think it's that serious, but it gave me an excuse to have a winter holiday in a warm place."

"Who is your friend? I might know him. I know, or know of most everyone down there."

"Jeremy Prince."

"Sure, I know Jeremy and Kellie, and Fred, as well. What's the deal with Fred missing?"

"I don't know. Jeremy wouldn't tell me much over the phone."

Misty was silent for a few minutes then said, "I was kind of attracted to Jeremy and flirted with him, but he never responded, although I could tell he was interested. I think Kellie keeps him on a short leash. I also had a brief fling with Fred. He is a sweet old man."

"I'll tell you, Misty; I've known Kellie for over

fifteen years. She is the toughest chick I have ever met, and I never heard anyone describe Fred as sweet."

"I can believe that. I'm no pushover, and she scares me sometimes, but I like her. She says what she thinks. Anyway, what's the deal with her and their businesses? I understand it's got something to do with oil wells or mines up in Canada."

"It's complicated," Dusty replied. "Kellie's father, Martin Angleton, who is richer than God, owns this resource company, which Jeremy theoretically manages. I suspect, however, it is Kellie who makes most of the corporate decisions."

"What about the other Company, which has all those silver properties in Arizona and Mexico?"

"He just told me about his new venture a few days ago. I don't know much about it. Where did you hear about it?"

"Fred Prince told me about it. He was concerned that Jeremy was making a mistake in forming the company."

"I'm planning to check it out with Jeremy. What do they call the Company?"

"It's something like Arimex or Mexari. That's it, Mexari Silver."

It was close to midnight when Misty headed off to bed. Dusty stayed outside to finish the last of the wine.

5

The next morning Misty awakened him with a fresh cup of brewed coffee. The sun was streaming in, and the sounds of a large flock of birds at the feeder outside his window helped erase the last vestiges of sleep.

"Do you always sleep in this late?" She asked.

"Not usually, but I stayed up late last evening sipping the last of the wine and listening to the sounds of the night. This is probably the most restful place I've experienced for a while. I had to savor it while it lasts."

"Well, we don't have to rush off if you're not in a hurry. I contacted the office. We can have this place for another night."

It was a beautiful late autumn day. Pastel shades of green, red, and gold marked the limits of their view from the deck as they consumed Misty's breakfast offerings. She had prepared a feast of hotcakes and eggs with a side of bacon.

"We need to get out and do some walking to

work this off," he said.

They set out on a long hike following some of the riding trails, which wound through the fields and woods. This was followed by the lunch she had packed to be eaten beside the river. In the afternoon they explored the Activity Center and finished their excursion with a swim in the indoor pool and an extended soak in the adjacent hot tub. Dusty's treat was dinner at the local restaurant.

"What a great day," Misty observed, as they curled up on the sofa in front of the TV. "I will remember this one always. You are a great traveling companion."

They retired to their separate rooms, but in the middle of the night, Dusty was awakened, as Misty crawled under the covers. As he reached for her, she said softly, "No, please just hold me."

The next morning, with the sun again streaming through the window and the birds singing, they made love.

As they sat at the table after another of her bountiful breakfasts, she said, "Before we leave, we need to have a talk. There are a few things you should know about me. First of all, I am married. My husband, Paul, is considerably older but cares very deeply for me. Unfortunately, he is physically unable to express his affection and has been this way since we met. He is aware I have lovers and accepts it because he wants me to be happy. I love him and am totally open with him. I could never do anything to hurt him or sneak around behind his back. You are going to meet many people in Sun City and will probably hear a number of stories about me. Some of them will be true, but many will be false, especially from women who wish to hurt me. I have been what you might call, selectively promiscuous. Wives of the men I have been with hate me and will do anything they can to get back at me. I don't blame them. I would probably be the same. I'm sorry if all of this is a shock to you, particularly after what we had this morning, but I feel you should know what to expect."

Dusty put his arm around her and held her close.

"I'm not concerned about who you've been or what you have done, or even how you live your life now. All that matters to me is that I've enjoyed these days we've had, and I like spending time with you. It's not over as far as I'm concerned. I hope we can continue this relationship in Sun City."

"I hoped you would feel that way. I want us to be friends."

The last three days of the trip were spent on the road.

The first day was an eight-hour drive into central California. They took No. 97 across the Oregon border then continued on I-5 to Fresno, where they booked into a Super 8 for the night.

"This is a comedown from last night's accommodation," Dusty observed.

"That's okay. Another hour of bouncing along in your truck would have completely worn through my natural sunny disposition."

The nest day was a mixture of heavy cloud and drizzle. They took a leisurely six hours to cover the shorter run to Las Vegas and took a room at Circus Circus.

Still fresh from the abbreviated trip, they hit a few casinos on the Strip, eventually staggering back to their room at three in the morning, bone-tired and a few dollars poorer for their efforts.

"I don't think I've ever won, gambling in this

town, but I guess I'll never quit trying." she observed.

"That's why the jokesters call it 'Lost Wages'. The casinos would be out of business fast if people started to win on a regular basis."

They slept until noon the next day before driving the final short hop through the desert to Sun City.

Dusty pulled up in front of Misty's house on the west side of the City and helped her pull her gear from the back of the Landrover.

"When will I see you again?" He asked.

"I don't know. I have your cell number and will call you. I try to be as discreet as I can, but sometimes it doesn't work. I assume you will be staying with Jeremy and Kellie."

"I guess so, although I haven't discussed it with them yet. If that doesn't work out, I'll pick up a rental here for at least a couple of months. I'm going over there now and see what's going down. Call me in a day or two, and I'll let you know what's happening and where I'm going to be staying."

Dusty programmed Jeremy's address into the GPS and made his way through the maze of streets to their home. Jeremy opened the door and greeted him as he was coming up the walk.

"I was expecting you a couple of days ago. What happened?"

"I took my time and made a couple of side trips. The country is beautiful this time of year, and besides, my old truck can't go at the pace of your Lexus."

"We were concerned something had happened to you. Kellie called Lucie, who told us you had left a few days ago, and she hadn't heard from you and had no idea where you were. She sounded a bit pissed. Are you two okay?"

"Who knows, and right now I'm at the point I don't really care."

They went into the living room, where Kellie welcomed him with a big hug.

"I am sure glad to see you. I had visions of you doing something stupid and ending up in the hospital or jail," she said. "Now that you are here, maybe you can help us find Fred and learn what's going on."

"Like I said before," Jeremy countered, "I don't think this is such a big deal. Fred will show up when he gets good and ready, just like he always has."

"Well, you are probably right, but since I'm down here, I'd like to see him. It's been a few years, and it's time. So, tell me the whole story."

"Fred lived with us in the caseta up to three months ago. He's been the same Fred we've known since we were kids, taking off on wild business ventures and hooking up with strange partners and even stranger women. He's been having a great time since he moved down here. Sometime last summer he got a hold of a map, claimed he bought it from an old prospector over at the Mesa swap meet. He said it showed where some bags of gold, which were robbed from a stagecoach back in the eighties, were buried. The map was pretty crude. It looked like a kid had drawn it. I guess I made fun of it and hurt his feelings. The map had nothing to show what part of the country it covered or any identifiable landmarks. He got a bit huffy, stomped out, and took off for about a week. For some reason, he had the idea the gold was hidden north of Tucson and he decided he was going to see if he could pin it down. Around that time I was starting negotiations on some silver and copper prospects here and across the border. The Mexican properties still have reported reserves of native silver. When I told Fred about it, he told me I was wasting my time and money. He offered to have a look at the Arizona claims, but he had irritated me to the point I refused to tell him where they were located. He also said the area in Mexico, which I was in the process of acquiring, was mined out years ago. I showed him some of the samples the owners had sent me, but he refused to be impressed. I'll get them for you. They look pretty good."

When Jeremy left the room, Dusty looked to Kellie. He had noticed the strange expression on her face all through the discourse, and the fact she had added nothing to the conversation disturbed him. Before he could question her, Jeremy returned.

"This is great stuff, almost pure native silver," he said as he handed the samples to Dusty.

"It comes from the state of Chihuahua, where mines dating back to the sixteen hundreds are located. I'm still having discussions with the owners, and I have to fly down to Mexico City tomorrow morning to further consolidate our deal."

"This is definitely ore material," Dusty observed. "What's the grade and tonnage of the reserves?"

"I don't know. There has been no recent work or written assessments. None of the ore has been bulk assayed, and the geologist doing the prospectus is unable to calculate reserves. I have some old maps and reports, but they are pretty much out of date. Once I get a deal firmed up, we'll go in and evaluate. Anyway, Fred went down there without me knowing. When he returned, he told me he didn't think there was much ore left, but when I questioned him, he was vague about where he went. I don't think he was at the right location. And it could be sour grapes because I didn't get excited about his treasure map."

"No. That is not Fred's nature. He is too easygoing. I've never known him to hold a grudge or stay angry for very long," Dusty countered.

"I don't know. He turned eighty last year. I think he's starting to lose it. Anyway, I formed a company to take on these properties as well as the ones I staked here in Arizona. The local claims are supposed to have had sub-economic gold and silver values when the price of the metals was much lower."

"Do you want me to go down to Chihuahua and check them out for you?"

"Maybe, if I get the deal put together. The owners are dragging their feet on signing, but I think I can wrap it up this time. We'll talk when I get back in a few days."

"I moved Fred's stuff out of the caseta for you to stay there," Kellie put in. "It's small, but there's a bed, a bathroom, and a tiny kitchen. You should be okay. Let me know if you need anything."

Dusty unpacked and settled himself in the little house. It was just the right size for one person. Two people trying to live there would be a crowd.

His mind went back over the evening's conversation, and he was bothered. It wasn't anything definite he could put his finger on. It was just a feeling. He was concerned about the apparent deterioration of the relationship between Jeremy and his uncle. He fell asleep hoping it would sort itself out in the light of day.

6

At six AM there was a light knock on the caseta door, and Kellie immediately barged in. She was in her nightgown with the signs of sleep still etched in her face.

"Are you awake?"

"I am now," Dusty mumbled, as he sat up and planted his feet on the floor. "What's going on?"

"I know it's kind of early for you. If I remember right, you don't get up until noon unless you really have to, or your current lover kicks you out, but I need to explain why I couldn't say anything to you last night in front of Jeremy. I waited until he left for Sky Harbor to fly down to Mexico early this morning. We have to talk."

"You're the third beautiful woman that has said that to me in the last week. It's starting to freak me out, but since you woke me up in the middle of the night, the least you can do is provide coffee and breakfast. Let me get some clothes on, and I'll come over to your house."

When they had finished the morning meal,

Dusty said, "I did figure from last night that something else is coming down. I wondered then why you had so little to say, but I figured I'd wait until you were ready to tell me."

"Yeah, I thought you'd get that impression. We've known each other too long for me to believe you would buy into Jeremy's story completely."

"What's happening, Kellie? I got the strong feeling Jeremy didn't want me down here, even after phoning in the middle of the night urging me to come."

"That was mostly my doing. I'm seriously worried about Fred, and I couldn't leave it alone. I hassled Jeremy into calling you. I'm sorry, but I'm also worried about what my husband has gotten himself into. He won't tell me much about his new venture. I'm afraid he's involved in something way over his head."

"Don't worry about Fred. If he is in trouble or courting danger again, I will find him and help him sort it out. God knows he has bailed me out enough times. As far as Jeremy is concerned, he is a big boy. He should be smart enough to look after himself."

"Yes, I know, but Fred practically raised Jeremy, or so he has told me. I don't know why he isn't more concerned. And Dusty, Jeremy has changed. You two haven't seen each other for at least four years. He's not the same person you grew up with."

Dusty thought for a few minutes then replied, "Kellie, Jeremy has been my best friend ever since we had a playground fight in the third grade. His memories of his childhood have been, shall we say, selective. Fred was his hero, way more interesting and caring than his own conservative parents, who devoted their lives to their careers and making money. Fred and my dad, Shelly, were drinking buddies. The only difference was that Fred would have one or two drinks then go, whereas Shelly would stay until they kicked him out, or I dragged him home."

"Well, I think I should tell you what you didn't hear last night. Earlier this month when they found this human hand buried in a sand trap at the golf course, Jeremy freaked out, thinking it might be Fred's. After all, his uncle had been gone for over a month by then after promising us he would be back in a couple of weeks. Since we had received no word from him during that time, both of us were worried. I went down to the Lab and saw the hand. I could tell it was way smaller than Fred's. When I told this to Jeremy, he lost interest in looking for him."

A few days before the hand was found, I had gone over to the Mesa Swap Meet looking for some Mexican pottery, and I ran into Fred and his friend Rafael. We went for coffee. He wouldn't say much about where he had been or what he was doing, and he was insistent I not tell Jeremy that I had seen him. I'm still not sure why, but he was acting mysterious. He confessed that the treasure map was a phony. The weird part was he had drawn it himself to convince anyone, including Jeremy, that he was looking for buried treasure. I finally got it out of him that he and Rafael were looking for Lonnie Trame's gold claims. They had an idea where the claims were, but they hadn't found them. You haven't met Lonnie yet. He lives here in Sun City. Presumably, he makes his living panning gold from some claims north of Tucson. Every couple of weeks he comes home with a sack of gold dust. He kept it very hush-hush until his wife tried to pay for some clothes with the dust, and Fred found out about it. Lonnie Trame is just a little guy, but he is as dangerous as he is miserable. I warned Fred about him, but he didn't seem too worried. He figured they could track Lonnie when he was going to his claims."

"So, what were they planning, to jump the claim or just go in and take his gold?"

"He wouldn't say. I had trouble even getting that much out of him."

"Do you think Fred would be upset if I came looking for him?"

"I don't know. Like I said, he's acting weird, but I think he would be happy to see you."

"So, he didn't tell you where he was staying, or give you anything that would help to locate him?"

"No. He said he would call me, but he hasn't as yet."

"Didn't you ask him straight out for an address or phone number?"

"Of course, but he was vague. He just sort of waved his hand and said he was staying down south for a while. As far as a phone is concerned, Jeremy gave him a cell phone last Christmas with a bunch of minutes. He never used it, and left it here when he moved out."

"That definitely sounds like someone who doesn't want to be pestered with visitors, or keep in touch, or has something to hide. What about his buddy, this Rafael? Did you get a last name, or whether he was local?"

"No. We were only together for about ten minutes, but when we parted, I did get the impression that Rafael lived nearby. Fred said he had come in to Mesa to make sure Rafael didn't get ripped off selling some nuggets he had found. He was going to drop him off before he headed out."

"So, all we have is that Fred is somewhere in Arizona, probably south of Mesa, and we have no obvious way of getting in touch with him. Rafael had brought gold to the swap meet to sell, and chances are he probably lives in Mesa or close by. Maybe I should concentrate on finding him first. What does he look like?"

"He'd be about my age, mid-thirties. He is five-six or seven, small-boned and wiry and looked to be in good physical shape. He has a full head of black hair pulled into a ponytail. I thought at first he was pure Mexican, but his facial bone structure was more native, probably part Apache or Navajo. He is a handsome fellow; I did find him attractive. I got the impression he is married and has some kids. I know that isn't much to go on, but it's all I can tell you. How do you plan to locate him?"

"Well, Lucie used to tell me that in her police work, especially when I was helping her on that Moose Jaw job, you go for the obvious first. In this situation that would entail checking out all the Rafaels in the Mesa area and spending time where he was last seen, the swap meet. I have no idea how to locate someone with just their first name. There has to be a whole bunch of Rafaels in this part of the world. I don't even want to go down that road. The second part has more potential for success. I will go down to the swap meet, hang around, talk to some of the vendors and check out all the buyers of gold. I'll need a couple of nuggets to get their attention. I guess we're trying to find a Rafael in a haystack."

"When are you going to Mesa?" Kellie asked.

"I might as well get started today. Do you want

to go with me in case he shows up?"

"No. We would just end up arguing and insulting each other."

"I know, but don't you miss it?"

"No. I think I'm getting too old and mellow to spar with you."

"Okay. I can see you aging, but you will never be mellow."

"Thanks. Now I know I don't want to go. Jeremy says you are welcome to use the Lexus while he's away. You can put your truck in the garage."

"Is this because of his overwhelming generosity, or does he figure my old truck sitting out in front is lowering your property values?"

Kellie smiled. "It's probably a bit of both."

"And, as long as you're confessing all your secrets, what's with this Mexican silver deal? I agree with Fred that most of those mines are either worked out or controlled by large Mexican, Canadian or American mining corporations. I have no doubts Fred was checking out the right claims. He's been in this business too long to make that kind of mistake. I trust his judgment in evaluating prospects."

"I don't know, and I can't seem to find out much. I've asked Jeremy to take me down there so I could do some sampling and meet the people he was doing business with. I suggested that Dad could check them out, but he keeps putting me off. It's beginning to bug me."

"Jeremy should know what he's doing, but I agree with your suspicions about doing business down there. You need to trust him in this. I think he's trying to prove to you and your old man that he can be successful without any Angleton help. You know you have a knack for destroying people's confidence."

"How would you know? I never even made a dent in yours."

"Just keep believing that. Anyway, it bothers me that Fred wasn't impressed. He is usually very supportive."

"Yes. That bothered me too. I tried to talk to Fred, but he refused to discuss it."

"It sounds like I will eventually have to go down there. I hope this isn't another case of bailing Jeremy out of a mess."

"Dusty, you said I was the third lady in a week who said she needed to talk to you. I know you and Lucie are having problems, but who was the other one?"

"I wondered when you were going to ask that. You know her. It was Misty Corolli. She rode down here with me."

"Jeez, you do play with fire. Sure, I know her. How did you two get hooked up?"

When Dusty recounted the events of the trip, Kellie replied, "That sounds like Misty. She tried to get Jeremy into bed last year."

"She only told me that she was attracted to him."

"Did she tell you I threatened to kill her and Jeremy if they ever hooked up?"

"No. I think she left that part out, but what's the deal with her husband? Is he actually aware of her adventures and accepts them?"

"Oh, I'm sure he knows, but I doubt he's happy with her lifestyle. Just be careful, Dusty. She has a lot of old boyfriends around here that have never gotten over her."

"I'll keep that in mind."

7

Dusty knew that a trip to the Mesa swap meet, as an attempt to locate Rafael or Fred was a shot in the dark. What he didn't realize was the trouble he was going to have finding his way there. Kellie had proceeded to give him detailed directions, which he tuned out after the third left turn. She even tried to trace it out on a map without success.

"You're not getting this, are you? For someone who can find his way anywhere in the wilds, you are hopeless in the city."

"I know, but I have the feeling I would end up where I started if I tried to make sense of all these instructions you just dumped on me. I'll be better off plugging the address into the GPS and let modern technology guide my way."

However, he didn't anticipate the next problem. The battery in the GPS was dead, and the cigarette lighter in the truck used to charge it hadn't worked for years. This was suddenly discovered when he arrived on the outskirts of Mesa and tried to turn it on. He had no idea where to go and wished he had paid more attention to Kellie's directions. It took four stops at various service stations to swallow his pride and ask for guidance. He finally arrived at the swap meet just after noon. The place was packed, and he had to drive around the parking area twice before spotting a space being vacated. Unfortunately, he had missed the breakfast special leaving him only four hours to find something to eat and attempt to locate Rafael or Fred.

Dusty had expected a dingy old building with a few dozen booths peddling the results of garage cleaning and collections of shiny geegaws from China. Instead, four long rows in covered buildings with a total of over fifteen hundred booths greeted his arrival. The variety of merchandise being offered was impressive. He wished he had the time to stroll leisurely along the aisles, checking out the many interesting items for sale. However, he realized he was going to have to move fast up and down the rows, ignoring most of the booths and focusing his attention on those buyers and sellers of gold if he was to have any hope of talking to someone who had done business with Fred or Rafael. To his surprise, in spite of the popularity of gold jewelry and nuggets, there weren't that many vendors of these items. Although they were interested in the nuggets he had brought, they offered him much less than he had originally paid for them, and they were no help in his quest. One old geezer, who was peddling pieces of fool's gold, cemented to neck chains and rings, thought he remembered a man of Rafael's description with nuggets to sell the previous week. When Dusty mentioned that he was probably with a large older fellow, and described Fred, the man became agitated.

"I remember him. He called me down for trying to pass my iron pyrite collection off as gold. I told him I made no claim these were gold. That's why we call it 'fools' gold, but he was a rude old bugger, and hustled the young fellow away before we could talk a deal on the nuggets. I never got their names, and I don't want to see either one of them again."

Dusty spent the rest of the afternoon going up and down the aisles, and had covered most of the area by the time the four o'clock closing rolled around. There was too much distraction to speed it up. A half-hour was lost talking to a pretty senorita selling homemade candy and pastries. While most of the vendors were packing up, he wandered down the last row, convinced the whole trip was wasted time. Near the end of the final aisle, tucked away in a small booth, was an ancient lady of mixed blood tidying up her collection composed mostly of Apache tears, opals, and a few small gold nuggets. Dusty looked over her display until she finished with a well-dressed lady who was looking for some expensive pearls.

"Do any of my treasures interest you?" She asked.

"Right now, you are the treasure that interests me."

The old lady smiled and said, "That is the nicest thing anyone has said to me today. Thank you, but I sense you are looking for something in return."

"I confess that is true. I am trying to learn the identity of a man who has been known to sell nuggets here. His first name is Rafael, but I don't know his last name, or where he lives. He may have been with an older fellow, a big man with long hair and a beard."

"I know him, the big man. That's Fred. They were here about a month ago. I bought a couple of small pieces of gold from the young fellow. Most of his stones were common, but these two I purchased had unique shapes, which I could see being fashioned into interesting broaches. I have to keep records of all transactions for tax purposes, so it should be here in my book. Give me a few minutes while I look it up."

She rummaged around in the trunk of her old car until she came up with a battered ledger. "Here it is, Rafael Teija. It was three weeks ago. I don't have an address, but Fred and I kind of made a connection, so he gave me Rafael's phone number if I ever wanted to get in touch with him. I never bothered. I figured if he was interested, he could come and see me. He still hasn't showed up again."

She wrote the number on a piece of paper and handed it to Dusty.

"Here is my card with my number," Dusty replied. "If Fred does hook up with you, have him give me a call. We go back a few years, and I haven't seen him for a while."

"I will, but I doubt if I'm going to see that old man again."

Dusty managed to stretch the normal hour-long trip back to Sun City into three by getting lost at least a half dozen times.

When he finally got back to the caseta, he just wanted to sack out for the rest of the day, but instead, he called Rafael's number.

"Hola."

"Is this the home of Rafael Teija?" Dusty asked.

"Yes."

"May I speak with him?"

"Rafael is sleeping. Who is calling?"

"My name is Dusty Sherant. I'm trying to locate Fred Prince. I understand Rafael knows Fred, so I'd like to find out from him how I can get in touch with Fred. Who am I talking to?"

"I am Miranda, Rafael's wife. Fred is not here. He lives somewhere south. We haven't seen him. That is all we know."

Dusty could see that he was getting nowhere. However, he did detect a note of fear in the young woman's voice. She didn't wish to talk to him, but he wanted to keep her on the line in case she might open up. His senses told him that she was being polite, but was afraid of something.

"Look, Miranda, I don't want to bother Rafael if he is sleeping or wants to be left alone. I just need some help in locating Fred. I'll give you my phone number and will welcome any help you folks can give. You may call me at anytime, and if Fred gets in touch with you, please give him my number and ask him to call me."

Before she hung up, she agreed, but Dusty could still feel the fear in her voice. He decided to call again the next day and try and talk to Rafael.

At least the trip wasn't a total loss. He did bring home a nice shirt and some homemade candy.

Just as he was lying down, Kellie knocked on the door a few minutes later.

"I saw you pull up and am anxious to see if you actually found the swap meet and had any luck in locating Fred or Rafael. Besides, I cooked up a big pot of pasta with alfredo sauce. Jeremy phoned a few minutes ago to say he will be delayed a couple more days putting his deal together, and I hate to eat alone. So, you're invited for dinner. It sounds like his negotiations down there aren't going as smooth as he had hoped. I would sure like to know what is going on. Do you think you can get him to level with you? "

"Kellie, if he wouldn't let Fred in on the deal, I doubt if I can get much out of him. We'll just have to trust that he doesn't screw things up too badly."

"Okay, I guess I can live with that for a while. I just hope this whole thing doesn't blow up in his face. Oh, and another thing, he wonders if you will fill in for him in his weekly tennis match on Monday."

"Sure, I can do that. Has he got a spare racquet I can use? I didn't bring one."

"There are about eight or ten of them in the garage. He buys a new one each year, hoping it will improve his game. You can take your pick."

"Has his game gotten any better? I'd hate to think he has finally gotten to the point where he could beat me."

"I don't think so, but when I tell him it's not the racquet that is the problem, he gets all defensive and points out that since I don't play the game, how would I know? Your game Monday should be interesting. Two of the players, Lonnie and Dan, are Misty's former lovers, and the third is her husband. At least, you all will have something in common. I may come over and watch the fireworks."

When they sat down to eat, Dusty related his meeting with the elderly lady at the swap meet and his subsequent phone conversation with Miranda.

"Rafael's last name is Teija. His wife sounded frightened about something, and I got the feeling she didn't want to talk to me."

"Do you think it would help if I called her? She might open up to a woman."

"No harm in trying. So far, I've got nothing."

He listened in on the extension as Kellie dialed the number. Again, it was Miranda that answered the phone. She was barely responsive to Kellie's questions. When she hung up, Kellie thought for a minute then agreed, "That lady is definitely scared of something. I wonder if it ties in with Fred's disappearance. I'm beginning to imagine all kinds of things and get bad feelings about this."

"Well Kellie, I learned to trust your intuition a long time ago. So, what do we do? I'm lost as to our next move."

"I don't know. I don't think it would do any good to find their address and go there and confront them. It might make things worse."

"Yes. I agree. I guess if we're going to find Fred, we need to try something else. Did he make any friends or have any other contacts here in Sun City while he was staying with you?"

"Well, he did spend some time with Misty. He took her out for dinner a couple of times. Other than her, he was one of a bunch that would meet at the bar once or twice a week, but I never met any of them. He didn't spend much time with us or tell us much about his private life. I can't think of anyone else."

"I guess I can talk to Misty and see if she has any ideas about how to contact him. Maybe he has called her in the last couple of days. "

8

Dusty awoke to an irritating alarm clock, a bare thirty minutes before he was to appear in proper attire on the tennis court. He had a strong suspicion as to the identity of the person who had programmed the treacherous little machine to disturb his sleep. He hardly recognized the unshaven mess in the mirror. He had no tennis shorts; just an old pair of sweats, and the only shoes that even came close was a scruffy pair of runners he used for hiking through the bush.

"Oh, what the hell," he muttered, "Maybe I can add a little grunge to the scene."

He skidded his truck into a parking spot next to a spotless Mercedes beside the courts just as the previous players were walking off. They were all dressed in white: white shirts, shoes, shorts, and caps. Three of them also had white racquets with white strings. The fourth man was packing a blue racquet and seemed somewhat embarrassed by his slip from protocol. They looked at Dusty and his ride with a mixture of surprise, contempt, and anger. One of the crew made a move to approach the truck until he saw Dusty emerge and stare him down.

Jeremy's tennis friends were waiting as he walked on the court. Obviously surprised at this strange apparition in their midst, they proceeded to introduce themselves.

"I'm Paul, Paul Carolli. Jeremy called me last night to tell us you would be taking his place. Welcome to our group. They shook hands, and Dusty thought, "So this is Misty's husband." He was looking at a man well into his seventh decade, short and overweight, bordering on obese. His features were true to his race, a prominent nose, swarthy complexion, and a rapidly disappearing hairline.

A taller man held out his hand and announced, "My name is Dan Seabourne. I would also like to welcome you. It's always a challenge to have some new blood in the mix."

The third member of the party was a small, wiry man with ferret-like features.

"I'm Lonnie. I hope you're a better player than Prince, but by the look of you I would guess that tennis isn't your game."

"I haven't played for a few years, but I think I've got enough game for you."

Dusty picked up the quick flash of anger, which he had expected.

Kellie had cautioned him that Lonnie had a short fuse and a hot temper. She had suggested he not needle the man, but Dusty couldn't resist pushing the buttons to see the reaction.

The first set teamed Dusty with Dan against Paul and Lonnie. Dan won the coin toss and elected to serve. As they walked back to the line, he confided in Dusty.

"Paul can't run very well, so we have agreed to give him two bounces, and I try to keep my shots to him close enough so that he can reach them. Lonnie is a different story. He is fast and has a good shot. He is also quick to anger over the slightest thing. Any disagreement over a line call really gets him going, and his game deteriorates as a result. I seldom take advantage of that weakness, as I like to keep the match going as peaceful as possible."

And, the first set was peaceful. Dusty and Dan eked out a 6 – 4 win. Lonnie played close to the net, and anytime he got a soft overhead, he hammered it at Dusty or Dan. Dan seemed unruffled by the attacks, but Dusty was beginning to grow tired of this unbridled aggression.

The second set pitted Paul and Dusty against Lonnie and Dan. With Paul serving at 2 – 3 and game point, his second serve just caught the back of the box and was called, "Out," by Lonnie.

Dusty walked slowly to the net and announced, "That ball caught the line, and the point is ours."

"Bullshit," screamed Lonnie. "I saw it out, and it's our call, not yours."

"That's right, it's your call, but your call was wrong. If you can't see them better than that, you should let your partner make the calls."

"Are you calling me a liar?"

"No, Lonnie, I'm calling you a lousy sport. You wanted the ball to be long, so you called it that way."

As Dusty walked back to the baseline, Lonnie was in full anger mode and started after him, but Dan was in his way. He grabbed Lonnie and held him until he calmed down.

The set continued relatively peaceful until Dan's first serve at 5 – 4 to Dusty. It was a strong flat serve to the back of the box. Dusty caught it just right with a hard forehand topspin return. The ball barely cleared the net and caught Lonnie in the throat before he could react. He went down but was on his feet immediately. He ran around the net, grabbed Dusty by the shirt, and pushed him against the net post.

"You did that on purpose. You aimed that ball straight at me," he screamed.

"My aim is nowhere near that accurate. You were simply in the way of my shot. Now, I suggest you let go of me."

"What are you going to do about it?" He snarled as he pushed Dusty harder against the fence.

"I'm going to beat the crap out of you if you don't let go right now. Do you really want to get into it?"

By this time, Paul and Dan had walked over, grabbed Lonnie by the arms, pulled him away, and began talking him down. Finally, he let go, walked to the bench, collected his gear, and left the court without a further word.

"I'm sorry fellows. Dan, you warned me about his temper. So did Kellie, but I guess I couldn't resist pushing him over the edge. People like him piss me off so bad, I have to retaliate."

"Did you purposely aim that shot at him?" Paul asked.

"I don't have anywhere near that kind of control, but I will admit I hit it in his general direction."

"No big deal," Dan observed. "It's not the first time. A few weeks ago, he got into it with his stepson. They were throwing punches when we pulled them apart. I can usually keep him under control unless he really loses it."

"Why don't we go over to the Nineteenth Hole. I'll buy you guys a beer," Paul offered.

By the fourth beer, the event had been pretty much talked out. The one conclusion they all agreed on was that Lonnie was an asshole. Whether this was an inherited trait or one he had learned and cultivated throughout his life, was not determined.

"Time for me to go," Dan announced. "Dolly gets cranky when I'm late for one of her gourmet meals. She is a less-than-talented cook, and one of the toughest parts of our relationship is faking enjoyment of these culinary creations. At least she hasn't poisoned me yet. Dusty, Dolly and I would like to play some mixed doubles next Saturday. I promise not to bring Lonnie along. Would you be available to team up with my sister for a match?"

"Sure, as long as none of you try to beat me up."

Paul and Dusty sat in silence, nursing their drinks, and admiring the sunset. It was a beautiful quiet evening. Dusty felt the time was right to bring up the subject that had been on his mind since meeting Paul, but Misty's husband beat him to it.

"Misty told me all about your trip. I appreciate you rescuing her and helping her out. And yes, she has described the relationship that evolved between you. I hope it doesn't bother you to talk about it."

Dusty was surprised at the openness of the man in talking about his wife's affair. He was at a loss as to how to react and chose his words carefully before answering.

"Paul, I don't feel a need to apologize or explain my actions. I was helping a young woman stuck up in the mountains with a car that was done.

I don't usually hook up with strange ladies in that manner, but later when I found out our destinations were the same, I offered to bring her here. I didn't know she was married when we spent the night together. She didn't tell me until the next morning, but I don't think it would have been different even if I had known. It seemed like a natural development in our brief relationship."

"I understand all of that," Paul replied. "There is no blame or accusations involved here. I brought it up so that you can understand my situation. I can guess it has been bothering you since we met. I have been fighting cancer since I was in my fifties. It steadily got worse, until about ten years ago; my condition had advanced to the point I had to have prostate surgery. The good news was that they got all of the malignancy, but as a result, I couldn't get my flag to fly. Three years ago, I met Misty and discovered I cared for her very much. It was a dilemma. I didn't want to lose her, but I was afraid my resultant physical condition would mean an end to the relationship, so we made a deal. As long as she would be upfront with me about her affairs and sexual adventures, I would look after her and provide a comfortable home and lifestyle. She was alone and barely able to look after herself, so she agreed to stay and care for me. She had originally come from a family of West Virginia coal miners and spent most of her early life in poverty, with an ongoing struggle for a decent life up to the time I met her. She had worked at a whole range of jobs, mostly for men who took advantage of her. When we met, she was an employee and part-time mistress to a crooked Chicago politician. I felt, and still feel it is a reasonable price to pay for her companionship, and I would hope love. Most of her affairs have been short-lived, arranged to fill her physical needs at the moment. Only one relationship, with old Fred Prince, has given me cause for concern. It lasted over six months. I think she was beginning to fall for that crazy old man. He and I had developed a friendship, and when he learned of my concern, he decided to break it off before it evolved any further. He came to me with his decision and to discuss how to end it without hurting her. That was about two months ago, and soon after, he left Sun City without a forwarding address. He didn't tell anyone where he was going, even me, because he knew she would find him if anyone around here knew where he was. Now she has met you. She sees in you a free and kindred spirit, not a serious friend or lover, but a person to enjoy and have fun with. I hope we can be friends as well. All I ask is don't hurt her. In spite of her bravado, she is basically a shy, sensitive girl."

Dusty was quiet for a few moments. He could see the tears beginning to form in the older man's eyes. He sensed the man was undergoing an internal struggle trying to balance these aspects of his relationship with his wife.

"Paul, I could never intentionally hurt her. My lack of sensitivity has sometimes caused pain in the past to people I cared about. The only time in my life I took a relationship seriously, even to the point of planning marriage, I was hurt very badly by a treacherous lady. I vowed never to leave myself vulnerable to anything like that again. You can be assured that my relationship with Misty will never evolve beyond a healthy friendship."

"I thank you for that," Paul replied.

9

Dan Seabourne was a man of habit: dependable, predictable, and seldom straying from his daily rituals. But, when he did, the results were usually interesting. He knew what he wanted out of life – he always had, and through superior intelligence, strict attention to detail and unflinching determination, he was able to succeed in everything he tried, and he tried just about everything. As a result, he had made his first million by the age of thirty. His success with the opposite sex was equally impressive. His tall good looks attracted a wide range of beauties, so when he courted and married Dolly, it was a surprise to most of his acquaintances. Dolly was plain in appearance, in mannerisms, and in just about every category society uses to grade members of her gender, but Dolly fit well into Dan's lifestyle. He wasn't looking for a mate who could draw attention away from him. She didn't ask questions and supported him in all his projects. On the few occasions, when he temporarily strayed from the marriage, Dolly forgave him, although after twenty years of wedded bliss, she was oblivious to most of his escapades. She had finally evolved a life of her own.

Each morning at sunrise, Tuesday through Saturday, found Dan setting up to drive the first hole at one of the many golf courses in Sun City. For six months, he hadn't missed a day. It was the dry season, so rain had not been a problem until today. At tee off time it was coming down by the bucket. He showed up at his usual time and waited patiently, huddled in his rain cape, hoping for the downpour to let up. His scheduled companions for the round, Louie, Tim, and Jeremy, made no effort to make an appearance, or even notify each other of their intentions. After all, a sane man could see it was not a day for golf. Dan, though generally considered sane, however, had not even entertained any of these thoughts. It was Tuesday, it was daybreak, and that meant golf. Making adjustments in his plans was not an option under any conditions. After half an hour of staring at the leaden blanket that stretched across the sky, Dan reluctantly plodded to the clubhouse.

The restaurant area was sprinkled with little groups of disheartened players, sullenly nursing their Starbucks. As usual, the buffet was adorned with the usual assortment of breakfast delicacies. But, for Dan, it was too early for the morning meal. That was only properly taken after eighteen holes of strenuous play. He acknowledged the greetings of friends and was almost tempted by offers to join them for pancakes and eggs. It would have set the pattern of his day back on track, even if the hour was wrong.

On a whim, he decided to return home early

and have a surprise breakfast with Dolly. He smiled as he thought how even such a simple act would rock her world. She had given up pestering him to spend more time with her. He always countered by informing her that he was very busy, and, after all, didn't he devote every Sunday in escorting her to church and taking her for a fine dinner afterward. Evidently, she did not consider this a sufficient level of devotion. She was becoming a pain in the neck, but, what the hell, most of the time she minded her own business.

As he parked in front of the house, he observed that her car was still in the garage. She was home; although he had no idea where else she might be at this time of the day. When he walked into the kitchen, she wasn't there, but he heard the sounds of movement upstairs.

"She must be cleaning up," he thought. "I'll go up and surprise her."

As he reached the top of the stairs, the noise was louder. Slowly, he opened the bedroom door to a scene of frenzied passion. Dolly; completely naked was entangled with a young man, also without clothes. As they thrashed around; completely absorbed in each other, she was shrieking and crying out in the pangs of intense pleasure. They were unaware of their visitor. Dan watched their physical antics for a minute then softly closed the door and went quietly downstairs to his den. He thought about the scene he had just witnessed with a smile unfolding on his face. He unlocked his gun cabinet and retrieved his twenty-gauge shotgun. He checked the mechanism and examined the well-oiled barrel for any signs of rust or discoloration. Then he loaded the clip with bird-shot shells with No. 6 pellets. He cradled the gun in his arms and stomped up the stairs, kicked the door open and banged it shut. The young man was reclined serenely on the bed, lighting a cigarette. Dolly, her body, glistening with sweat, was curled up beside him, desperately trying to catch her breath.

"Norman, it appears you have invaded my house and violated my wife. I think it is time you got dressed and left," Dan said in a calm voice.

"What are you going to do if I don't go? Are you going to shoot me? No, I think I'll stick around and have another run at this old girl. She's pretty good at this," he replied.

"No, I don't think so. In fact, I doubt if you will even have time to finish your cigarette. You have to the count of three to gather your clothing and leave."

"And what if I don't go."

"That would not be a good idea, but you have the option to stick around and find out."

"ONE" Dan walked over to Norman's side of the bed.

Slowly, Norman rolled out of bed and looked around for his clothes.

"TWO" He slid the bolt back and injected a shell into the barrel.

The boy quickened his pace, pulling on his socks and underwear.

As Dan yelled, "THREE," he stood beside the boy, held the gun to his head, and fired a shell into the skylight directly above them.

The silence was broken by the sounds of falling glass and Norman losing control of two major bodily functions.

He scrambled frantically around the floor, trying to stuff both feet in one pant leg. He finally gave up and stumbled out of the room, carrying as many of his clothes as he could find.

"Give our regards to your mother," Dan said as the boy hurried past him through the doorway. "We'll send the rest of your clothes over to her when we find them."

After they heard the front door close, Dolly sat up in bed and said; "I guess you know what that was all about."

"Yes, I kind of figured it out as payback for my affair with Misty two years ago. I wondered when you were going to get back at me. So, are we even?"

"We're even. Why don't you come to bed and we'll resolve it completely."

"That will have to wait. I'm not into playing on a wet deck. Why don't you take a shower with lots of scrubbing in the right places and we'll see what happens, and we need to use the other bedroom, it stinks too much in here."

That afternoon Dolly collected Norman's clothes and stuffed them in a paper sack. Norman lived with his mother and step-father, Lonnie Trame on the other side of Sun City. Since it was only a few blocks out of his way, downtown, Dan agreed to deliver them to Norman's home.

"What have we got here?" Mildred Trame asked when she opened the door.

"Your son's clothes. It seems he had to leave our place in a rush this morning. You might want to take them outside before you open the bag."

"Oh, I wondered about him charging in here half-dressed this morning. Now, I understand. I'm surprised your wife would succumb to my son's charms. How do you feel about what happened?"

"I can live with it. Just tell Norman that if he

comes around again, he may not get away so easily."

Mildred was quiet for a moment then, making strong eye contact, said, "How would you like to get even?" She moved closer to him, their bodies almost touching. "We could go upstairs, and I assure you I can make it worth your while. You deserve payback."

Dan looked down at the small woman facing him. With her little girl's body and features, although considered quite plain-looking, she had a strong, earthy sexual attraction that was difficult to ignore. He found her offer surprisingly enticing.

"That is very tempting," he replied, "but my life is complicated enough for me right now."

"Well, remember, this as an open offer. Anytime you are feeling lonely or used, or just want to screw, give me a call. I guarantee you won't be disappointed."

Dan drove into the city, wondering if he had made one of the smarter decisions in his life, or passed up on an enjoyable mistake. He found it unfamiliar, being faced with a situation where the correct decision wasn't obvious. If it was a mistake, he could take comfort in the fact that it could easily be rectified at a later date.

When Norman returned home that evening, he slammed the screen door and announced his arrival with, "Hey Mom, I'm home".

"You can cut the Mom crap; Lonnie is gone for a couple of days. I was hoping you could follow him this trip and find his stash, but you were too busy screwing the prim and proper Mrs. Seaborne. And, speaking of your recent adventure, there's a little present for you in the back yard. Dan Seaborne came by with your smelly clothes. It must have

been quite a circus over there this morning," she
smiled.

"It's not funny. I thought he was going to blow
my head off with that shotgun. It was so close I still
can't hear right. That is one scary dude," Norman
replied with rising anger.

"Oh, I think it is funny. I would have loved to
see you trying to get your smelly clothes on and get
out of there at the same time."

"Well, let's see how fast we can get yours off,"
he replied as he grabbed the bottom of her dress and
jerked it quickly off over her head. He picked up
her naked body and tossed her on the sofa. In an
instant, he was out of his pants and had plunged
himself inside her.

Mildred screamed at the instant pain then
wrapped herself around him as they moved in their
familiar rhythmic motion.

"I'm getting sick of this charade of playing
your son. I'm beginning to believe that Lonnie is
getting suspicious. When are we going to end this
game?" He asked as they lay together.

"As soon as you can find the source of
Lonnie's gold and I can figure out a way of
emptying his bank accounts. I want out of here as
bad as you do, but I need to get his debit card,
account number, and password. So far, all I have is
the name of one of the banks and the number of his
account. The rest will be tougher, but I don't think
he suspects anything. If he does, he'll close
everything and disappear. We have to clean him out
before that happens."

"Can't you take the card from his wallet when
he's asleep? He'll think he's lost it and get a
replacement."

"Sure, and he'll cancel the old one when he

does."

"You're right, as usual. We don't want that to happen. You need to wait to get his card after you have his password, and I know where to find the gold, which I think I have finally figured out a way to locate. I bought a tracking device, which I'll hide in his truck then when he takes off. I can keep out of sight and follow him to his gold claims."

10

Dusty got the call on his cell just as he was preparing for bed Wednesday night.

"Is this Mister Dusty Sherant?"

The female voice was soft and hesitant, but somehow familiar with its slight accent. When he assured the lady whom she was speaking to, she went on, "It's Miranda Teija. You called me looking for Fred Prince. I need to talk to you."

"Go ahead; I'm listening," Dusty replied, anxious to keep her on the line.

"No, not now. Rafael is out for a short walk. He doesn't want me talking to anyone. I don't have long. He will be back soon. It is important. I think his life is in danger. Will you meet me at my mother's home next Sunday afternoon?"

Dusty agreed and copied down the address in Peoria. He tried to question her further, but she quickly hung up.

He thought about the call and its implications. He wanted to discuss it with Kellie but decided it was too late to tell her of the new development. By morning he wished he had confided in her when he discovered Jeremy had returned home. For some reason, he was hesitant in discussing the Rafael situation with his friend. Until Kellie told her husband of running into Fred and Rafael, he felt leery of bringing the subject to his attention. Jeremy had always had a tendency to ridicule people who were concerned about things that didn't particularly interest him. It was a character flaw that Dusty had taken advantage of in their younger days, resulting in Jeremy unwittingly taking the blame for actions he had been tricked into.

When Dusty opened the caseta door the next morning to take his morning walk, Jeremy was standing there about to knock.

"Great. I caught you before you left. Come on over for breakfast."

"I wasn't planning on going anywhere today, except maybe to the gym or pool, but thank you; I'd enjoy a hot breakfast."

As they walked over to the main house, Dusty remarked, "You're looking full of life. Mexico must have agreed with you. Did you have a good trip?"

"I got the deal put together. It actually happened. I couldn't believe it. I worried about it all week and was still concerned when I flew down. The negotiations were tough, but I got the deal finalized and signed before I left."

"That's great. Tell me about it."

As they sat down to the meal, Jeremy sketched out the results of his negotiations.

"These hombres agreed to transfer their silver properties into my company, Mexari Silver, for a majority block of stock. They also get the contracts for the exploration and development work for the service companies, which they own."

"These are the properties which Fred doesn't like. Is that right?" Dusty asked. "Have you had an engineering report done on them?"

"Yes, these as the ones he bad-mouthed, but like I told you, I don't put much credence into what Fred thinks anymore. I haven't received any final reports yet, but they have a geologist down there visiting all the prospects and preparing a study. I had a look at his preliminary findings. I had to get it translated, but it seemed okay."

"Can I have a copy? I'd like to go over it."

"Sure, but the deal is done. Even if you pick holes in it, which you usually do, it's a completed deed. Whatever negative aspects you find, I'll have to live with."

"Okay, Jeremy, I hear you. I'll stay out of it if you want. I'm not trying to rock your boat or bring you down. I just naturally get concerned about all mining deals. I operated in Vancouver too long to trust any mining stock promoters."

"I know that, but the beauty of this is I have lined up the investors to pay for the work in Mexico. Since this is a private company, I can just as easily use some of the funds to finance exploration and development on the Arizona claims, which I vended in."

"And, you say you had to give up a majority interest in the company. So, these Mexican partners of yours have control of your company. They call the shots. Is that right?"

"Well..., yes, but I'm president, and they have agreed that I make the decisions on what work is to be done and how the money is to be spent. Their only condition is that all the exploration and development work on the Chihuahua properties is to be performed by their service companies."

"Do you have a written and signed agreement confirming those discussions?"

"No, but it was their idea that I run the show."

At this point, Kellie asked, "Jeremy, who are your investors, and on what basis are they providing further funding? What do you know about their backgrounds or reputations?"

It was evident Jeremy was bothered by his wife's question. She had asked for this information before. And, being Kellie, the subjects were never asked in a sweet, gentle manner. She was too used to getting what she wanted through the power of her personality.

After a moment, he replied, "These are friends and business associates of Paul Carolli. He pledged their contributions based on my Arizona properties and the proposed deal with the Mexicans. I don't plan to name names so your father can hire a bunch of detectives to dig into their lives. This Company and the people involved are none of his business. I don't want him meddling in my affairs. My only obligation to him is to look after that damn Amyot mine of his."

Aware of Jeremy's rising level of irritation, Dusty decided to change the subject and relate the confrontation with Lonnie on the tennis court.

"I kind of thought something like that might happen when I asked Kellie to get you to fill in for me. I've known you for too long to think you would put up with his crap. It's too bad you didn't punch him out. It might make him think twice about controlling his temper. The rest of us have agreed to put up with it to a point, which, in my opinion, he passed a long time ago. We tend to feel sorry for him living with that bitch of a wife and her creepy son."

As Dusty walked back to the caseta, the thought struck him. Jeremy had not mentioned the disappearance of his Uncle Fred once.

An hour later, after Jeremy had cooled down, he came over to see Dusty.

"Sorry about getting a little testy this morning. Kellie's frequent questions about Mexari are beginning to bug me. It's not her. I love and trust her, but she wants to bring her damn father in on it. I do not need that arrogant bastard up my ass. It's been bad enough running his Company up in Canada."

"I get you. Kellie and her Dad are close. Up at Amyot, he depended on her opinions in making his decisions. It's something you have to live with if you care for her. If you want my advice, which you probably don't, but stick to your decisions if you believe in them, and ignore any Angleton suggestions to the contrary."

"Thanks, Dusty. I needed to hear that. I know you have figured out that I'm not as confident in all this as I try to appear. What is bringing this to a head is that Kellie and I have to fly to Toronto for her dad's seventy-fifth birthday. It's going to be some big, plushy catered deal, and I'd give anything to get out of it, but that's not going to happen."

With the rest of the day to himself, Dusty called Misty to see if she would be interested in meeting him for lunch.

"I'd love to get together, but I promised to make lunch for Paul. Why don't we meet at the Rec. Center around three? I've been wanting to spend some time by the pool working on my tan."

Dusty was waiting at the entrance when she walked over. She was a vision to behold in her skin-tight white shorts and matching halter-top.

"You get more beautiful every time I see you."

"Well, thank you, sir. Are you going to veg out by the pool with me?"

"Maybe in a while, first I want to do a workout in the weight room. I need some exercise."

"Don't tire yourself out. I'll be happy to provide you with some pleasant exercise later."

"I'll keep that in mind."

Later they met at the pool, went for a swim, stretched out in the deck chairs, and talked until the sun began to hide behind the clouds in the western sky.

"Let's go over to your place and see if we can build something nourishing to eat," she suggested.

"That could be a challenge with the meager contents of my fridge."

They walked over to her pink golf cart with a ribbon identifying it as 'Misty's Limousine.'

Dusty looked it over and remarked,"Aren't you concerned driving around the streets of Sun City in this thing with a man who is not your husband?"

"No. Nothing I do surprises the folks around here anymore."

Misty rolled out of Dusty's bed around eleven. She kissed him and said, "I'd like to go home while it's still today. This has been great. We'll do it again soon."

He walked her out. They kissed again before she drove off in her 'Limousine.'

Dusty settled back into the soft warmth of sleep looking forward to his meeting with Rafael's wife and, hopefully, finding Fred Prince.

11

Joel knew he was going to have to kill her. He could see no other way. In his heart, he still cared for her, but the situation was impossible. Maybe he had always known that someday it would come to this.

The shock of seeing her again the other day had brought back all the old memories and fears. She was so beautiful. As he stretched out on the lounge by the waterfall, his mind went back to that one wonderful summer they had together. He had managed to avoid the annual dreary three months at the lake cottage by committing to teaching the summer semester. It was a summer of love, filled with soft, warm days like today. The sound of a breeze blowing through the trees and the water babbling over the rocks brought him back to the present. Those memories were to be cherished but were clouded by the fear that Janet would someday find out, and he would lose everything.

Losing her and the kids would be welcome, but he had gotten too used to their standard of living and the extras that her inheritance had provided, and he was very loath to let that go.

On one level he had never expected to see Misty again, but somehow he had always felt and hoped their paths would cross. She had dropped out of his life that autumn as suddenly as she had appeared the previous spring. One final passionate night of love and it was over. No explanation or words of goodbye, she was just gone, and he had not seen nor heard from her until now.

He could see no other way of resolving his problem. He had thought that maybe he could talk to her and persuade her not to reveal their secret. But, the danger would always be there, a slip of the tongue or an innocent conversation, which got back to Janet, would end it all. He was married to a very suspicious woman who felt he should be accountable to her for all his actions. No, relying on Misty's promise of silence would be too risky.

The thought of the actual act of taking her life was distasteful. After all, he had cared for her, even loved her in his own way.

Much as he wanted to; he couldn't go back home. Janet had been planning and urging him to undertake this move to Sun City for years, continually pestering him to take early retirement so that they could go. He had held out as long as he could, but when the school enforced mandatory retirement at age sixty-five, he had no further valid excuse. Eagerly, she had flown down, picked the neighborhood, the most expensive, of course, and purchased the largest house available without any consultation with him. On her return, she had informed him he could come with her or stay up north and freeze on his own. On the other hand, she had put up all the money for the house and was paying all the bills. And, it had been a wonderful place to live until now, when the past returned to haunt him.

Sitting in the restaurant's outdoor patio, he observed Misty walking along the gravel path to the gym. She had that same sexy walk, a swing without a porch, his friends used to call it. And, she was still as beautiful, not the dewy freshness of a girl just out of her teens, but the sensual beauty of a mature woman.

She had seen him a couple of days ago, looked right at him, but her eyes told him she hadn't made the connection. After all, he was twenty-five years older, thirty pounds heavier, practically bald, with a full beard. He looked nothing like the tall, dark middle-aged man that had swept her off her feet.

Sadly, as she disappeared down the walk, he knew there was no other way. It was just a matter of how and when.

On a hunch, he followed her at a distance. If he was going to go through with this, he needed a plan, and a plan required all the information he could gather about her present life.

The recreation complex was a multifunctional facility with an Olympic-size swimming pool on one side and a workout room with machines and weights on the other. Both rooms were surrounded by floor to ceiling glass walls. Between them, a recessed entrance opened into a foyer, where all members were required to register. Behind the building, within a gated enclosure was a large outdoor lounging area, where the sun worshipers were baking their bodies. Spotted throughout the enclosure were a series of small wading pools, spas, and another large pool.

At the entrance, she walked briskly to a man

resting on one of the benches. As she approached, he got up and embraced her in a manner that told Joel that this was a person of importance to her. Whether it was a husband or a lover, he intended to find out, although he expected the latter. Another piece was dropping into the puzzle.

He settled himself in an alcove where his presence was not easily observed. Though hidden, it gave him a view of the indoor pool as well as the fitness room. Also, he could see portions of the outside area.

"Let's see where they go," he thought. Within a few minutes, the man entered the fitness area. He was of medium height, fine-boned, slim, but in excellent physical condition with well-defined muscles.

On a whim, Joel entered the building and approached the registration desk. The clerk was busily booking an elderly couple into a Silver Sneakers class.

"Can I help you?"

A young lady clerk had materialized from a back room.

"Yes," he replied. "A gentleman I once knew entered the building a short time ago. I have been trying frantically, without success I might add, to remember his name. Perhaps you can help me and check your sign-in book."

"Well, we've registered a lot of folks this afternoon. I don't know. Maybe, if you described him, I might remember."

After hearing his description, she thought for a moment then replied, "That sounds like the guest Mrs. Carolli signed in about twenty minutes ago."

"I don't know a Mrs. Carolli, but the time frame sounds about right."

"Really, I thought everyone around here knew Misty Carolli. Let me see," she said, thumbing through the book,

"Oh yes, Misty, I've heard of her, but I wouldn't know her to see her," he lied.

"Her guest registered as Dusty Sherant. He doesn't appear to be a member. I could page him if you'd like."

"No, that's okay. That's the name," Joel replied. "Thank you so much for your help."

"This is beautiful," he thought as he walked out of the building. "Her last name is now Carolli, so I will assume there is a Mr. Carolli somewhere. And she has a boyfriend. This has the makings of a perfect triangle for the police to sort out when they find her body."

As he walked around to the back of the enclosure, he observed Misty stretched out beside the pool, leafing through a magazine and wearing the skimpiest bikini he had seen in some time. She still had that fantastic body that brought a lump to his throat. To think he had possessed that beautiful creature for a whole summer. The rest of his life paled miserably in comparison. The prospect of what he had to do suddenly generated a wave of sadness, but he forced it to pass. He wouldn't waver from protecting this life of comfort he had built.

He waited for another hour until Misty and Sherant exited the building together and walked over to the golf cart parking area. They climbed into a bright pink cart with a bow across the back, proclaiming it to be 'Misty's Limousine.'

Fortunately, Joel had parked near enough, so that by the time he reached his car, they were still in sight proceeding out of the lot. He followed close enough to keep them in view, but hopefully not too close to be noticed. They proceeded down Oasis Drive and then made a couple of turns into secondary streets, finally pulling up in front of a small caseta. Sherant took out his keys and opened the door.

As they went inside, Joel parked down the street in front of a couple of foreclosure houses, where he had a clear view of the small house. He turned the radio on low and settled back to wait.

The next thing he knew, a large sweeper moving along the other side of the street awakened him. The clock on the dash showed a few minutes after eleven. He could see Misty's Limousine still parked in the driveway. After a few minutes, she emerged from the caseta, embraced and kissed Sherant then walked to her cart. He ducked down low as she passed his car, heading back toward Oasis Drive. When she had rounded the corner, he turned the key to start the motor. It turned over slowly and finally caught on the third try.

"The radio must have drained the battery," he thought, and then smiled. "All I needed was to walk over and knock on Sherant's door and ask him to help me start my car."

Quickly, he did a U-turn and backtracked his way out of the side streets, hoping to spot the little cart. He saw her just as she pulled on to Oasis and headed west.

East Sun City was a medium-priced neighborhood. Houses in this area normally sold for three to four hundred thousand, although now with all the foreclosures, a two-bedroom model could be picked up for just over two hundred. He passed through increasingly more affluent areas as he moved to the far western edges of the City, where properties were still in the one to two-million-dollar range. This was the area where Janet bragged to anyone who would listen that she had paid over two million of her own money in cash for their home.

Misty turned on to Mesquite Canyon Drive, entered the cul-de-sac, and continued onto the driveway of a dark, two-story mansion. He parked along the opposite side of the street just as she was reaching for the code box beside the garage door. Quickly he grabbed his binoculars from the glove box. Fortunately, it was a moonlit night, and he could see her punching in the code. Her hand partially hid the numbers, but he could tell she pressed four digits, the middle two being a six and a three.

He realized, looking at the home address, her code was the house number.

"This could be useful," he thought as the garage doors opened and closed after she had parked the cart and turned on the lights in the house.

Logic told him this was an excellent time to complete his mission. She was probably alone in the house, and he could quickly get inside. He would just have to wait until she was asleep. Two thoughts prevented him from proceeding. He knew he would have to psyche himself up with pills and booze before he could go through with it. The other potential problem was Janet. She would be all over him, asking him where he had been and what he had been doing this late. She wasn't stupid. His behavior coupled with the murder of a beautiful woman in their neighborhood would probably arouse her suspicions.

"This had better wait until a safer time," he thought.

Later that night, he lay awake beside his snoring wife. Sleep had become more difficult since

Misty had impacted his life again. However, handling Janet's interrogation of his whereabouts was getting easier all the time. Years of lying to her had become second nature to the point that she had no idea of what went on in his life. Just as long as she kept paying the bills, it worked fine. He simply told her that he had run out of gas while driving to the bookstore and that he had to walk half a mile to a service station. Whether she believed it or not mattered little as long as she shut up with the questions.

"Maybe he was going about this the wrong way and had picked the wrong woman to eliminate from his life. He looked over at his sleeping mate. How he would like to be rid of her, although he knew he could never get away with it unless he could cause her to expire from natural causes. The prospect made him smile. As an added bonus, it would get him rid of those kids and their wretched offspring.

He couldn't sleep. He lay for a while with his eyes open, pondering the alternative courses of action. Getting rid of Misty would be less desirable, but with a lower chance of getting caught. On the other hand, eliminating Janet would be great, but tougher, and he would be the main suspect.

Knowing that any further attempts at sleep would be futile he slid quietly out of bed and crept downstairs for a drink and some web-surfing, He dug his bottle of Johnny Walker out from under the planter in the front yard, where he had hid it from Janet's prying eyes and poured himself a tumbler-full of the amber liquid. Carefully, he replaced the bottle and smoothed the dirt away. He always got a rush when he dipped into this forbidden pleasure.

He googled the name Corolli. Most of the hits were meaningless, but one caught his eye, a profile of Paul Carolli. The former union organizer from Chicago was now living in Sun City. The narrative went on to say that Carolli was born in 1941 in Chicago. He was married to the former Misty Sewell, his third wife. The page also showed what was obviously a much younger man dressed in tennis gear holding a racquet.

"I need a more current picture of this guy," he thought. "He should be in the current Community Association pamphlet."

He was beginning to feel sleep coming on but finally found the pamphlet in the bottom of his desk drawer. The book contained listings, pertinent information, and pictures of current members. Janet had bought their house after publication; hence, they were not included. As he expected under the C's, there was a picture of Paul and Misty, arm in arm.

"He looks old enough to be her grandfather," he thought, examining the image of this short, fat, balding man.

"Looks like Misty married for the same reason I did."

Finishing his drink, he said to himself, "I guess I can sleep now."

12

Sunday morning Dusty set out with his GPS charged and ready to find Miranda's mother's house. Jeremy and Kellie had flown out of Sky Harbor on Friday for Toronto. Dusty had driven them to the airport, and while Jeremy was checking their bags, Dusty told Kellie of Miranda's call.

"Just don't scare the girl any more than she already is," was Kellie's advice.

Dusty had no trouble finding the house, a modest two-story frame in a working-class neighborhood. A beautiful young Hispanic lady answered his knock and ushered him quickly into the house.

"I am Miranda," she said as she led him into the sitting room, "and this is Rosa, my mama. She made me call you to come here."

"Go on. Tell heem bout Rafael," Rosa urged.

"My husband would be very angry if he knew I was here talking to you, but I worry about him. He won't leave the house or see any of his friends. He is terrified of something ever since the accident. He doesn't want our children or me saying anything about it."

Dusty could sense the fear growing in her voice as she seemed to be picking her words very carefully. Tears filled her eyes, and she rapidly wiped them away.

"My husband was a brave man, but now he is not. Something is very wrong."

"What happened in his accident?" Dusty asked.

"He cut his hand off with a chainsaw. He said he went to a clinic, but they couldn't put his hand back on," she sobbed.

"Ees not right," Rosa put in. "He should go to hospital to get hand put back. He lose hand."

Dusty was visibly shaken, but all of a sudden, a few things started making sense.

"Is this true, Miranda? Did Rafael not keep his hand after it was cut off?"

"He said he passed out, and when he awoke it was gone."

"How did he stop the bleeding and wrap it up?"

"He wouldn't talk about it."

"Do you believe that is what happened?"

"He is my husband. He does not lie to me?"

Dusty was quiet for a few moments, trying to decide what to tell these two ladies. This was not helping him find Fred, but at the moment it seemed more important.

"I want you two to listen to what I have to tell you. Right now, the police in Sun City have a human hand that was found at a local golf course. They don't know who the hand belonged to, but they are running tests on it in an attempt to find its owner. The hand was not cut off by a chainsaw but was surgically removed by someone, probably a doctor, who knew what he was doing. Did you not read about this in the newspaper or hear it on TV?"

"No. Rafael stopped the newspaper and won't let us watch the news."

"Well, I believe it is Rafael's hand the police are testing."

"Course eet ees," Rosa added. "You tell Rafael go to police and tell them ees his hand."

"No mama, he is too frightened and will be angry with me."

"It's up to you what you do," Dusty said. "I will take no action on it. You and Rafael must make the decision. Just remember, the police will eventually sort this out, and Rafael can't hide forever. Just let me know what you decide."

Dusty was so deep in thought as he walked down the street toward his truck that he wasn't aware of the black Hummer that pulled up slowly beside him until it was too late.

The passenger door opened quickly, a large man jumped out and ran toward him. He had just enough time to whirl around and catch the man in the side of the head with his elbow. The big man was stunned for an instant, just enough time for Dusty to deliver two swift kicks, one to the kneecap, the other to the groin. The man folded and went down on the pavement. Before Dusty could leave the scene; however, the driver had come around the front of the vehicle, grabbed him, and pinned him to the side door. The man was powerful. All Dusty's attempts to break free were in vain. The driver held him long enough for his partner to get to his feet and deliver a series of blows and kicks to Dusty's body. He could feel a rib snap, and blood filled his mouth before he dropped to the ground.

"Maybe this will teach you to stay out of our business," the driver growled as his partner continued to deliver kicks to Dusty's back and side.

Just as quickly as they had arrived, the two men jumped into the Hummer and were gone. Dusty lay without movement until two locals, who had been watching the scene from a house across the street, came to his aid. They looked down at him for a moment then asked if he wanted them to call 911. Dusty was conscious but in considerable pain. He tried to get up, but his legs buckled, and he went down again.

"No, just help me to my truck."

With a man on either side, they practically carried him to his vehicle. He dug around in his pockets for his keys and was able, with their help, to pull himself inside the cab. He thanked them, and then sat there trying to figure out what to do next. He knew he needed help, but where? Jeremy and Kellie were gone. Misty was the only other person he knew well enough to ask. He called her cell, and she answered on the first ring.

"Misty, I need your help. I've been beaten up pretty bad. Can you meet me at the caseta? I'm driving over from Peoria and should be there in about an hour."

"What happened? Are you sure you can drive? I can come and get you."

"No. I think I can make it, but bring some medical stuff: bandages, antiseptic, and things like that."

"I'll be there," Misty replied. "I have a friend who is a nurse. I'll see if she can come with me."

The drive back to Sun City was torture. An extreme effort was required every time he had to lift his foot to apply the brake. Of course, he managed to hit every red light on Bell Road. Each breath he took was accompanied by a sharp pain in his side. His mind seemed to be trying to slip into unconsciousness to avoid the discomfort, and he found himself drifting across lanes as his focus slipped. When he pulled up to the caseta, he saw Misty with a tall younger woman waiting on the driveway. He stopped the truck and slumped forward against the wheel. Misty rushed over and opened the driver's door.

"What happened to you?" She asked as she helped him out of the truck.

She grabbed the keys from the ignition, and with the other girl's help, they opened the caseta door, led him inside and helped him stretch out on the bed. The blonde girl put some water on to boil as Misty introduced her.

"This is Anna Seaborne, Dan's sister. As I said, she's a nurse over at Del Webb. Anna has agreed to patch you up the best she can."

Dusty had taken little notice of Anna until that moment. He had only observed her from the back as a tall, well-built lady with ash blonde hair. When she turned around, the effect was shocking. The expected beauty from the front was seriously flawed by a jagged scar running from just below her left eye, across her mouth to her chin. She didn't smile as she greeted him, but Dusty could see the gentleness in her eyes and could feel the tenderness in her actions as she bathed his wounds.

"You should go to a hospital or at least a clinic. I can't tell how much internal damage you have."

"Anna, I'm a Canadian, and I don't have any health care down here. I can't afford a stay in your hospital. Whatever you can do to put me back together will be most appreciated. I do need something strong for this pain."

"Okay, I will have to put some stitches in those cuts, and I think I have some codeine pills. I need to run home and get my kit."

As soon as Anna had gone, Misty demanded to know what happened.

"I can't tell you all of it, as it could put some other people in danger, but let me say that it's part of my mission to find Fred. It's all connected to one of his friends who I thought could lead me to him. Unfortunately, it hasn't worked out so far. I probably took this beating for nothing. It's made me more concerned about what has happened to Fred."

"Okay, I won't pry. I used to have a number for Fred's cell, but it quit working when he left Sun City. I tried to find out where he went at that time but had no luck. At least I didn't get physically beat up, but it was tough on my emotions. I grew to love that old man."

When Anna returned, she toted a doctor's bag into the room.

"First thing I have to do is sew up those major cuts. Unfortunately, I don't have anything to put you out short of a rap on the head, and I think you've had your quota of those today. Also, I need some antiseptic."

"There is a bottle of vodka in the shower stall. Will that work?"

"Absolutely! Are you ready for this?"

"No, but go ahead anyway."

The feeling of the sutures just added another level of pain to his body. A shot of vodka taken internally matched each one poured over a cut. Dusty was impressed with the speed and precision of Anna's work. When she was finished, she checked his body for any broken bones or extremely sore spots and set out some pills for the pain.

"It looks like at least one, maybe two broken ribs and possible damage to your kidneys. If you start passing blood, call Misty or me right away to get you to Emergency. Will you promise that?"

Dusty reluctantly agreed.

"That scar on your chest tells me this isn't your first experience with this kind of violence."

"Somebody tried to finish me off with a hunting rifle a few years back. It seems like I make enemies without even trying."

"Look after yourself. I don't like losing friends as soon as I meet them. Just be as active as your body allows. I'll look in on you tomorrow afternoon."

"So will I," Misty winked as the girls left.

Dusty lay back on the bed thinking about this sweet, gentle lady that had tried to heal his damaged body. There was something special about her. He felt a hint of those old feelings he had about Elena before she destroyed them with her treachery. He looked forward to Anna's promised visits. With these thoughts floating around in his head, the combination of the pills and the booze put him away until noon the next day.

Anna arrived at two to check his condition and change bandages. She also brought some stronger painkillers, which she warned him not to take with alcohol.

"I'm working the evening shift, so I've only have a few minutes. Is there anything else you need? I can come Wednesday about this time if you would like."

By Wednesday, Dusty was mobile with much less pain. He had gone for a short hike in the neighborhood in the morning and was sitting on the patio with a coffee when Anna arrived.

"I brought you some fruit and healthy food. I checked your fridge last visit, and there was very little in there that was recognizable. What have you been eating?"

"Crackers, cheese, peanut butter, and coffee."

"Yuch! It's time to get you healthy."

They spent the next hour getting to know each other. To Dusty, it was refreshing to talk to a gentle, non-judgmental lady. None of the defending his lifestyle, as it had been with Lucie, or the verbal combat with Kellie, or even the continual expectations of sex with Misty. This lady seemed to accept him for who he was.

"Can I ask you a personal question, which I don't want you to answer if it is too uncomfortable?"

"You're referring to the scar?"

"Yes."

"It no longer bothers me to talk about it. It happened when I was sixteen. I was riding my horse on my uncle's ranch up in Wyoming. We came to a fence, which he usually jumped, but this time, he didn't. He stopped short, and I fell off. A strand of barbed wire caught me across the face. It was my only injury, but it's stayed with me all my life. I was a spoiled little bitch before it happened, and it changed me, made me think seriously about myself. I figured it was nature's way of paying me back for the person I had been."

"I sense in your voice and see in your eyes that what you are telling me does bother you. I'm sorry for asking."

A single tear ran down her cheek.

"Don't be sorry," she said. "Somehow, I felt it was important to tell you."

"Have you talked to anyone about having a plastic surgeon work on it?"

"Yes, one of the doctors at the hospital has a friend in private practice that he wants me to see. Unfortunately, it's not covered by my medical insurance, and I can't afford to pay for it myself. My brother has offered to cover it, but it's my problem, and I have to sort it out."

By Saturday, when Kellie returned home, Dusty was almost back to feeling normal, except for the occasional grimace from the pain of the broken rib, and the multicolored bruises. When he told her what had happened, she didn't reply for a few minutes.

"Dusty, what have we gotten ourselves into? I'm beginning to get really scared, not just for us, but more so about what has happened to Uncle Fred. Are you sure this wasn't just a random mugging?"

"I'm sure. They told me to stay out of their business. What I can't figure out is, what exactly is their business, and how did they know I would be there. Miranda was insistent on the phone that I meet her at her mother's house. Maybe they followed her there, saw me, and guessed I was somehow involved. I don't know."

Kellie sat for a minute, then reached forward and took his hands.

"Dusty, maybe these people have planted bugs in Miranda's home and phone, and possibly her mother's as well. It's one explanation that makes sense."

"That could well be it. We need to get in touch with Miranda and see if she is willing to have someone come and debug everything, or...," he paused, "we could just drop the whole thing and do nothing."

"Can you walk away from it?"

"No."

"I didn't think so. I know you too well. You need revenge."

"You're right. I do. What we have to do is get communication with Miranda that can't be bugged. I suggest you go to her mother's house tomorrow after lunch. Miranda will probably be there. Don't go in the house, but talk to her outside or in your car. Tell her what we think about the bugs. We give her a new cell phone with some minutes, which she is to use when calling us or anyone about Rafael. She is to keep the phone on her person at all times. I doubt if Rafael would permit anyone coming in to debug the house, so this has to be the best alternative. Will you do it?"

"Sure, but why don't you want to take it to her?"

"Those goons may be keeping an eye on her, and would be on me as soon as I showed up. By the way, where's Jeremy. I think it's about time you brought him up to date about what's going on."

"He had to go up to the mine at Amyot to try and settle a labor dispute. He and my father had a bit of a faceoff after the birthday party. Dad told him to spend more time doing his job looking after the Company and leave his little project down here for me to take care of. Jeremy was furious and came that close to quitting. I had to calm him down and tell my father to back off. It was not a fun time. I don't think Jeremy would be interested in doing anything or even hearing about this. He also doesn't seem concerned about his uncle. When he gets back, I'll lay it all on him and see how he reacts."

Kellie drove to Peoria the next day and cruised

the streets around Rosa's home looking for the black Hummer. Satisfied that it wasn't in the immediate vicinity, she parked in front of the house, walked up, and knocked on the door. When Miranda answered, Kellie asked her softly to come outside and close the door. When the girl hesitated, Kellie mentioned that she had a message from Dusty Sherant. Miranda followed her to the Lexus and got inside. In the privacy of the car, Kellie told her of the beating and their conclusion that her home and phones had listening devices and that the men whom Rafael feared could hear all their conversations. Miranda was visibly shaken by the news and readily accepted the new cell phones for her and her mother. She promised to keep in touch after Kellie was adamant that they made all calls outside the homes, and that they do not answer incoming calls on the cells until they were outside.

13

Lonnie Trame knew another delivery was due soon, as they usually ran every two weeks. Each day he scanned the want ads in the Republic for his notice. It was in the Sunday issue. The ad read, 'Aurumographer wanted. Phone: 042-3023'.

Lonnie dug out the codebook to translate. The drop was scheduled for the 4th at 2:30 in the morning at location 2, which Lonnie determined to be a prearranged spot near Superstition Mountain. The deposit location 3 was a cabin on the outskirts of Superior. The fact that the ad had been placed also meant his payment for the last job had been made and was waiting for him to pick it up.

Norman had purchased and installed a radio transmitter under the rear bumper on Lonnie's truck and was just waiting for his next trip to turn it on. Monday morning, Lonnie started rustling around in the garage, putting his gear together for the journey. Norman sneaked into the garage while Lonnie was having breakfast and activated the bug.

When Lonnie took off along Highway 60, heading northwest, Norman followed him. He stayed back far enough in his Subaru so as not to be seen but in range of the transmitter. Just over an hour later, Lonnie drove into the town of Wittenberg, pulled up in front of the Bank of America, went in and requested access to his safety deposit box.

Norman located Lonnie's truck, drove by it and parked around the corner. He got out, walked to the bank, and peered through the glass. He saw Lonnie hand a key to a girl then follow her into a back room.

Lonnie was eager to get his hands on the little sack of gold dust, his payment for the last delivery, but when he opened the box, his anticipation turned to anger. The box contained only a note. He handed the box back to the girl and stormed out of the bank. He sat in the cab of his truck and read the note.

'We do not pay for sloppy work. You were followed on the last delivery. You are fortunate that we were able to procure the packages and punish the man that tried to steal them. We seriously advise you to be more careful, or you will suffer.'

"This is crap," Lonnie thought. "Nobody was following me. These bastards are trying to scare me and weasel out of paying."

He immediately took out his cell and dialed his contact in Sun City.

"What the hell are your friends trying to pull? They're refusing payment for that last delivery. All I got was this snarky note telling me I was followed."

"Calm down. You don't want to threaten these people or get them mad. You remember that hand that was found at the golf course? That belonged to the man they caught tracking you and trying to steal that last shipment. The hand was left down here as a warning to us to be more careful. Just follow orders and make sure no one is on to you."

Lonnie resigned himself to the fact there was nothing he could do. The next drop was scheduled in a week. He might as well spend the time with Ellerie.

The night before Lonnie left, Mildred had pulled his three bank cards from his wallet, copied the numbers, and put the cards back. She found his checkbooks in his desk, took a cheque from each and returned the books. Norman had told her that he knew a young computer nerd who could probably hack in and find the passwords. Once she had the passwords, she could access the accounts. He had set it up for the kid to come over as soon as Lonnie was gone.

"How did you get the kid to do this? It's illegal, isn't it?"

"That was no problem. I told him my mother would go to bed with him and teach him to be a man."

"Seriously, you told him that? How old is this kid?"

"I don't know, fifteen or sixteen."

"Are you crazy? They can throw me in jail for having sex with a minor."

"Well, you're going to have to show him such a good time that he won't want to tell anyone."

Jerome showed up the next afternoon. He looked to be all of twelve years old: small, scrawny and sporting a face pitted with acne. When asked, he assured Mildred he was sixteen.

"Are you sure you want to do this? Do you know we could both end up in jail?" she asked.

"I guess so," he replied timidly, but once he got on the computer, he was in complete control.

"These cheques will give me the name of the bank and the account number. Then I'll need to dig in there and find the passwords."

When Mildred returned with a Coke for him, he had the passwords written on a scratchpad.

"That was quick. How did you do that?"

"Most people copy passwords somewhere in case they forget them. One of the obvious places I look is on the back of the computer. This time it paid off."

He turned the machine around and showed Mildred where Lonnie had copied the information. On the paper was written,

WF Audust

C Agplate

BA Pbbars

"I don't get it," she said. "What do all those letters mean?"

"It's easy. For the second set of words, the first two letters are symbols for metals, so for the Wells Fargo account, the password is golddust. The Chase account password is silverplate, and the password for the Bank of America account is leadbars. Anyway, we'll try them and see if they get us in."

Jerome was able to bring up all three accounts, which contained a total of just over half a million dollars.

"Wow!" The young man exclaimed. "Your husband has a lot of money."

Mildred had no idea Lonnie had socked away that much cash. She was overwhelmed by the urge to get her hands on it.

"How can I withdraw it?" She wondered. "Do I go down to the ATM machine? No, I would need his cards to access the ATM. Do I forge his name to a cheque?"

She decided to risk asking the boy how she could withdraw the money.

"You would have to either forge his name to a cheque or initiate a bank transfer to an account you control in another bank, preferably in another country."

"Could you do it?"

"No. It could get me in a lot of trouble."

"Well, you think about it for a minute. I'll be right back."

When Mildred returned, she was naked. She sat on Jerome's lap and began to undress him. The boy began to shake. She stood him up, removed the rest of his clothes, and led him to the sofa. Afterward, they lay side by side until he was ready again.

"Now, will you help me figure out how to get that money?"

Norman was well hidden, as he watched Lonnie emerge from the bank and return to his truck. He drove to the edge of town and then continued for a couple of miles to the northwest on gravel roads. His destination was a small farmhouse, hidden by a grove of trees beside the road. Lonnie pulled into the driveway, got out, and used a key to unlock the door and enter. Norman drove past the house and parked on a small side road at a point that afforded him a clear view of the building and yard. He settled in to wait. Finally, in the late afternoon, Lonnie came out into the back yard, followed by a young dark-skinned woman and a small child. They sat in the lawn chairs drinking beer and talking until dark. When Norman could barely make out their images, they returned to the house. An hour later, the lights in the house went out. Norman decided that Lonnie wasn't going anywhere that night, so he decided to find a cheap motel and come back the next morning. When he did, the truck was still there.

The pattern repeated itself for the next six days. The eternal waiting was getting on Norman's nerves. Lonnie never left the property, although he and the young woman spent considerable time outside. On the morning of the seventh day, Norman arrived at his view spot and observed Lonnie packing his truck, obviously making preparations to leave. The woman gave him a long, lingering kiss as he got into the truck. His route took him through town then back down Highway 60. Norman assumed he was going home when he passed the city limits of Surprise, but Lonnie kept right on driving through Phoenix, Mesa, and beyond on 60 to the southeast.

"I'm getting tired of this," Norman thought, "but I might as well stay on him. Maybe this time he'll lead me to his gold mine."

Jerome was hooked. He had explained to his parents that Mrs. Trame was helping him with his homework in return for teaching her about computers. Since it wasn't entirely a lie; his feelings of guilt lessened with each session of sexual instruction. He had researched for a solution of Mildred's dilemma as to how to get her hands on the money. His fear of her withdrawing her services spurred him on to find an answer.

"You are going to have to learn to forge your husband's name to cheques. Since these are not joint accounts, there is no way the banks will transfer the money for you without his signature. If you'd kept his debit cards, you could have used them on the ATMs, but only for small amounts each day. I think you need to set up some bank accounts in Mexico in a name that is unfamiliar to your husband. Forge the cheques made out to this new name for large amounts, say half the balance, and deposit them in the Mexican accounts. Don't clean his accounts out; leave half the money there. That could give you more time. As soon as the money clears, you can empty your accounts and put the money somewhere in your name."

"This is illegal, isn't it?"

"Absolutely! You could go to jail, and what scares me, even more, is that they could lock me up if they found out I helped you. I hope you won't tell anyone what I've done. I suggest you go and stay in Mexico, or anywhere but here. Eventually, your husband will sort it out with the help of the police, unless he acquired all that cash illegally. Then I doubt if he would go to the cops. This is as far as I want to get involved."

"I don't know how to thank you," Mildred replied. "Oh, yes, I do. Come upstairs to the bedroom for a special treat, one you will never forget."

Norman called home every night to let her know what was happening with Lonnie and find out how she was doing with the boy's help. His last call was Saturday night. Lonnie returned home Monday in a sour mood and refused to discuss his trip with her. He was noticeably without an additional supply of gold. Mildred had taken no further action on the bank accounts. With Lonnie home, she decided to wait until his next trip to put her plan into action. She phoned Jerome's cell and left the message that her husband was home and for him to stay away until he heard from her again. That evening, Lonnie got a call from Paul Carolli. The message was simple.

"You need to get over here right away."

14

They lay side-by-side Sunday evening, their
sweaty naked bodies glistening in the moonlight
that was streaming through the window. Neither
said a word until Janet had finished her cigarette.
"It was a beautiful funeral with all those
flowers. I was surprised that so many people
showed up. There must have been over fifty at the
service. We hadn't met that many people since we
moved down here. Joel certainly didn't go out of his
way to make new friends or even bother meeting
our neighbors. So, I suppose, all those people
crowded into the church were just curious folks
from the community."
She got up, walked over to her dresser, and
grabbed another chilled bottle of wine from the ice
bucket.
"Would you like some more wine?"
"Sure."
"I couldn't understand why you didn't want to
go. You sure knew him well, at least back in those

days."

"That's exactly why I didn't go. I didn't see any point to it. Except for Lara, I'd like to forget everything about that relationship," Misty replied. "After all, he was your husband. As far as anyone knows, we had no connection."

"I know you were very clear in telling me that, but I could have used some moral support."

"I thought you didn't give a damn. Anyway, that should have come from your kids. Hell, they didn't even show up for their father's funeral. I thought it was kind of strange."

"Well," Janet replied. "I expected that. They had no feelings for their dad; they hardly knew him. He never could relate to them and didn't get involved in any of their activities. Even though I was married to him, I failed to see why you were attracted to him that summer."

"I know. It was the classic case of the distinguished older professor and the impressionable young student. Even from that first summer, when we became lovers, he never showed up at the lake to be with you or the kids."

"You know I went to great lengths to keep him away from the cottage. I had some great summers with all those young fellows keeping me warm at night, and then you spending all those days you skipped out of classes to be with me. You can see why I encouraged your little affair. It was wonderful. I always dreaded September, when I would have to come home and live with him again."

"What I resented was you using me to keep him in town," Misty responded. "I was just too starstruck. He could be charming and very smooth when he wanted to get a young female student into bed."

"It wasn't that bad. You got a lovely daughter out of the deal and my continued financial support for you two over the years. One thing I have to warn you about; I would be very unhappy if you had an affair with another woman. I expect you to be true to me. I don't care how many guys you screw, just stay out of other women's beds. I believe you owe me that much for all I've done for you over the years."

"I know, and I've appreciated it, but that sounds like a threat. I don't think it wise to threaten me. You know I treasure my freedom."

"It's not a threat. I don't know what I'd do if you were unfaithful to me. Just be thankful you don't have to worry about Joel anymore."

"That is a relief. Just seeing him down here brought back all the old feelings of disgust and loathing I developed for him over those two months. I got a bit freaked out when he followed me over to Dusty's and then all the way home. I had no idea what he was planning, but it gave me a bad feeling. I know he died of a massive heart attack, but what brought it on? Was he concerned I was going to tell you about our affair? Those things are usually stress-related, aren't they? He must have been on some kind of medication."

Janet was quiet for a few minutes, and then replied, "He was. I don't know what happened; perhaps the shock of finding you living here was too much for his heart. You know, he tried to keep your affair secret all these years. I got a kick out of the irony of it, seeing as I knew about it all the time. I sure as hell am not going to mourn him. He was a jerk, and I doubt if anyone will miss him."

"Was Joel's heart attack the result of too much medicine or not enough? I was wondering because

Paul has a similar problem and I'd like to keep him alive for a while."

"The doctor said it was from too much," Janet replied.

Misty lay quietly for a few minutes then rolled out of bed and began pulling on her clothes. She walked into the bathroom to clean up. Inadvertently, she opened the medicine chest and was surprised at the array of prescription medicines lining the shelves. The one medication she did recognize from Paul's collection was digoxin. She opened the bottle to see it was almost full. The label indicated the prescription was dated two weeks ago, and it was for fifty pills. Misty thought about it. Since Joel died four days ago, there should be forty pills left on normal dosage. Since he overdosed, Misty expected a much smaller number remaining. There were, however, forty-two pills left. It didn't make sense. If he overdosed, there should be way fewer pills.

"Are you going to be in there forever?" Janet asked.

She was getting up when Misty returned to the bedroom.

"I'd better get home and get all sexied up. Paul is taking me out for a late dinner at a fancy club downtown. I'll see you on the weekend."

She finished dressing, put on some makeup, and started for the bedroom door. Her discovery in the bathroom bothered her, but she put it out of her mind, as she anticipated the upcoming evening.

After Misty had gone, Janet sat for a long time at her dressing table thinking about Misty's question and going over the events of the past year. Her plan had worked perfectly. For the last fourteen months, she had taken three or four pills from each of Joel's digoxin prescriptions. Since he often missed a day or two each month, he didn't notice the discrepancy. When Misty reported that Joel had spotted and followed her, she knew it was time to act. He was unpredictable. She was afraid he would overreact and put Misty's life in danger. Misty was too important to her, so she had to get rid of him. She was well aware that stress put a heavy burden on his heart, and he tended to over-medicate to counteract it. She had also perfected methods of causing him stress by continually making him accountable for his every action. The stage was set. She badgered him constantly the day after his surveillance of Misty. He took an extra pill. For dinner, she ground up four more pills in his stew. Her final stroke of genius was the foxglove tea, which she had prepared from those pretty little plants in the garden. She mixed a concentrated batch of this brew into his bottle of Johnny Walker, which he had hidden under a planter in the front yard. She conveniently went to a movie that evening. When she returned home around midnight, her dead husband was stretched out on the bedroom floor. She called 911 in a practiced state of panic. The paramedics tried to revive him without success.

Everything was going so well, but she knew she would have to be careful whom she talked to, and what she said, especially to Misty. She tended to be a bit careless when she was with her lovers. Janet longed to confide in her, and at the same moment, knew how dangerous that would be. Who knows what she would say in the throes of passion with one of her male partners.

The first thing to do, the most important, was to thoroughly clean the place of all traces of Joel. She dressed in her gardening clothes, then went immediately to the front yard and retrieved his bottle of Johnny Walker from under the planter. She emptied the contents down the sewer, washed out the bottle then smashed it and threw the pieces of glass into a water hazard on a nearby golf course. Next, she dug up the flask of foxglove tea she had prepared and disposed of it in a similar manner. For a final touch, she emptied Joel's bottle of prescription digitalis into the garbage, wiped the empty bottle clean and replaced it in the medicine cabinet.

"Poor Joel," she thought. "He just didn't know how to medicate himself properly."

15

Lonnie drove to Paul's home immediately after
receiving the call. Paul was standing in the alcove
as he pulled up. He walked over to the truck,
opened the passenger side door, and got in.

"We have a serious problem. The Arab called
and demanded we go to your last delivery point
right away. I don't know why; he refused to say any
more. We better get a move on; he sounded real
angry."

"That's the cabin down at Superior. I just came
from there after leaving the packages. This whole
job is really getting to be a pain in the ass. What the
hell is his problem now? I didn't get paid for the
last delivery. It's beginning to piss me off. "

"That was because you screwed up. Were you
followed on this trip, like last time?"

"Hell no, I kept my eyes open the whole way
up to Wickenberg and back."

"Why did you go to Wickenberg?"

"To pick up the payment they cheated me out

of, and to spend some time with my girlfriend."

"Lonnie, you're pushing the edge. You don't want to get these people mad at you. They don't mess around."

"Who the hell are they? I've never had contact with them. How do I know it's not just you calling the shots?"

"Look, I don't know who they are either. I get my orders from this one who calls himself 'the Arab', but he scares me. You saw what they did to that fellow who followed you out of Tucson."

"Well, I don't like it, but I'll hang in with it for a while. I guess we'd better go and see what this is all about."

Neither man spoke on the drive to Superior. Each was occupied with his own thoughts: Lonnie planning how he was going to safely extricate himself from this job from hell, and Paul trying to figure out how he could put the operation back on a smooth path. Neither anticipated the scene that was waiting for them.

They pulled up in front of the little cabin where Lonnie had made the delivery the previous day. He was puzzled when he recognized Norman's Subaru parked along the side of the building. Then the seeds of suspicion began to germinate in his mind. The young man had followed him, but how could that be possible? He had been on the lookout for any sign of a tail for the whole trip. He walked over to the vehicle. It wasn't locked, and the keys were still in the ignition.

"Whose car is it?" Paul asked.

"Norman's, but I have no idea how it got here."

"He obviously must have followed you. At least, it explains why we were told to come here. You need to check your truck for bugs. If he was using a radio signal to track you, chances are you would never see him."

Inside, Norman's naked body was hanging from a rafter in the main room. His mouth and nostrils had been taped shut, and he had been cut open from rib cage to crotch. His intestines slopped out onto the cabin floor into a pool of dried blood. A note was nailed to his bare chest.

Both men were speechless. Paul had to run outside and throw up. Lonnie angrily tore off the note and went outside to read it.

'You were sloppy again. This will not be tolerated any longer. Our friend here followed you all the way from Wickenberg. You will receive no gold payment for this mistake as well, and. we suggest you do not visit your little squaw in Wickenberg anymore. You will not like what you find there. We also order you to dispose of this body before the police find it and start asking some embarrassing questions.'

"The bastards. So, this is the kind of people we're working for. I'm through running errands for them. They can transport their own dope from here on in. I'm done."

"Don't you understand? They won't let you out. If you stop obeying their orders, they will kill you, and make it as painful as possible. It's as simple as that."

"Maybe. We'll see about that. They'd have to find me first. I've been thinking of getting out of this part of the country anyway. As far as this goes, we should let them clean up their own mess."

"You would be lucky to get out of town alive," Paul replied. "They have people down here checking up on all of us. This whole operation is too important to them to let one little courier screw it up. Just forget about running, and follow orders if you want to stay alive. Now, let's get Norman out of here and into the ground somewhere and ditch the car where it won't be found for a few days."

Paul didn't have the stomach to look at the body, much less deal with getting it down. Lonnie cut the rope, dropping the remains into an old tarp from his truck. He wrapped and tied it securely. He left the chore of cleaning up the blood and guts from the cabin floor to Paul, who drove the Subaru into the El Portal Hotel parking lot in Superior. Lonnie dumped the body in his truck box and drove to Superior where he stopped at a hardware store to purchase some shovels and a pick before going to the hotel to pick up Paul. They then took Highway 60 for half a dozen miles northeast of town into the hills, where they cut north on a dirt road up a narrow valley. The road deteriorated into a poorly-marked trail as they drove deeper into the hills. Finally Lonnie stopped the truck at a point where the trail was blocked by a large boulder.

"This is about as far as we are going unless you want to pack our boy deeper into the canyon," Lonnie observed. "We should be able to plant him on the other side of that rock without too much trouble."

Paul was obviously shaken by the whole episode, as Lonnie began taking special pleasure in agitating him further.

"I'll get the tools while you drag Norman out on the ground," he said, knowing there was no way his partner was going to summon enough nerve to perform the task.

They were only able to dig down about a foot and a half in the rocky soil before they hit bedrock. Rather than look for another site, they stretched the body out in the narrow trench and covered it with dirt and rocks. Brush was piled over the grave as a partial cover.

"The varmints around here will get to this pretty quick," Lonnie observed. "There shouldn't be much left but bones in a few days."

"Are we going to say a few words over the grave?" Paul asked.

"Sure. How about 'good riddance to a useless human being'."

"You didn't have much use for your stepson, did you?"

"Naw. First off, he wasn't her son; he was her lover. And secondly, he was a bit of a creep as far as I was concerned. However, there's gonna be a bunch of old broads missing him in Sun City. He spent most of his time servicing them and making a pretty good living at it."

They packed the tools back in the truck, managed to turn it around on the narrow trail and headed south. By the time they got back on the highway, it was midnight. Each man was lost in his own thoughts as they headed for Sun City. The event of disposing of a human being was a sobering experience. A question had been bothering Lonnie ever since Paul had lured him into the job. The more dangerous it was becoming, Lonnie couldn't figure why Paul had taken on the project in the first place. He certainly didn't need the money even if he did have a high maintenance wife to look after.

"Who are these people, and how did you ever get involved with them?"

Paul hesitated. He wasn't sure how much to tell his companion, but he knew it had to be done in such a fashion as to discourage Lonnie from thinking any further about pulling out.

"I don't know who they are. I have tried to find out, but all contact is made from untraceable phones. The only man I have talked to has a deep Mid-Eastern accent and calls himself 'The Arab'. Somehow he amassed information on a few of my former activities, which could bring some serious charges against me and probable jail time. Back then, I figured it was safer to go along with the job, which he emphasized had minimal risk. When I finally found out what was really going on, he threatened to kill both myself and Misty in a most painful manner, and that is exactly what will happen to you if you harbor any idea of quitting."

Lonnie was hyped in spite of Paul's warning. His thoughts were directed at figuring out a way to cash in on the next drop and then disappearing. There was no question in his mind he was getting out, but he realized now he had to shut up about it around Paul. The man was too scared and would rat him out in a heartbeat. "These guys can't be everywhere," he thought. "I just have to figure out a foolproof means of getting away." A number of ideas came to him, but all were rejected as being too risky. Then, he had it. Duplicate packages was the answer. All the packages he had couriered to date had been wrapped in the same manner, boxes in brown paper with duct tape holding them together. The number of packages had ranged between two and six. He just needed six fakes of roughly the same weight, size, shape and appearance. He smiled. "I'll fill them with dog shit and leave them at the delivery location. That should get my point across."

Lonnie dropped Paul off at his house and quickly drove away. They had said little more to each other on the final leg of the journey. When he had received the original order to go with Lonnie to the cabin, Paul had also been told to call as soon as he returned to Sun City and give the location of the burial and a description of Lonnie's reaction to the discovery of the body.

"Do you think he will try anything stupid? We are getting very tired of him screwing up and are thinking we may have to terminate him as well. You recruited and vouched for him, although we had our doubts, so it's up to you to make sure he does his job properly."

"I don't know. I'm working on him, but his actions can't be predicted. He wants out, but I warned him of the danger of that kind of thinking," Paul replied.

"Just remember, he is your responsibility. You recruited him and assured us he would be reliable. This has not been the case so far. It's up to you to see that there are no more problems, especially on the next delivery. It will be larger than usual and is presently scheduled for about two weeks from now. The message for the date, time and locations will come through the normal channel, but it is imperative you keep a tight rein on this man. We will tolerate nothing less than a perfect performance. Do you understand?"

The threat was very disturbing to Paul. He knew he had no control over Lonnie's actions and that a perfect performance was probably out of the question. The man thought emotionally, not rationally, hence was totally unpredictable.

In Paul's mind, all he could do was to continue to impress on him the danger of not following orders. The only other option he saw was to take over the deliveries himself, but he concluded, "I am too old and crippled to get physically involved."

16

Rafael was getting antsy sitting around the house all day and night. He missed his friends and gathering at the cantina to drink beer. He loved his family, but being cooped up in the house with only Miranda and the girls for company was driving him nuts. The abject fear he had felt was slowly giving away to anger and a desire for revenge. He had thought of calling his dad or one of his friends to come over, but there was still that trace of apprehension over what might happen.

His dilemma was solved when Miranda's brother Luis arrived with a bottle of pain pills. Luis kept a supply of prescription tablets obtained from his Mexican supplier on hand as part of his small but lucrative business dealing in illegal drugs. Miranda was out shopping when he arrived, so Rafael invited him in. They were seated in the living room, having a beer when Miranda returned.

Rafael motioned her to a chair. "I need to tell you something that has been bothering me since I got home. I lied to you before. I did not lose my hand in a chainsaw accident."

Miranda got up quickly, put up her hand, and told him to stop. She walked over and whispered in his ear.

"I think some people have put listening bugs in our home and are hearing everything we say."

"How do you know that?" He asked.

"Shhh! Come outside. We can't talk any more in here. We will sit in Luis' car and I will tell you."

When the three of them were seated in the car with the windows closed, she explained how she had gotten the call from this man, Dusty Sherant, who was trying to locate Fred. She was afraid to talk to him at first but had called him back and arranged to meet him at her mother's house. She had relayed to him the story Rafael had told her.

"He knew all about your hand. He told me it had been found in the sand at a golf course in Sun City. He also said that it had not been sawed through by a chainsaw. It looked like it had been cut off by a doctor. He said the police are trying to find out whose hand it is. He agreed not to tell the police what I told him but said it was up to us to let them know. He thought they would be able to protect us. I don't know how safe we are because, after he left Mama's, he was beaten by two men who told him to stay out of their business. He said the only way they would know he was involved would be if one of us had told someone, or if they had listening bugs in our home, Mama's home, my car, or your truck. He arranged for me and Mama to have new cell phones, which cannot be listened to by them. They are to be used only when we are outdoors."

Rafael was speechless for a moment then said, "If I knew all this I would not have talked to Luis. I think this Sherant is right; they must have bugs in our house. Why didn't you tell me what was going on before?"

"You told me not to talk to anyone. I knew you would be angry, but I had to tell Mama. I just don't know what to do now. I have been so afraid of what will happen since you got back."

Rafael settled back then told Miranda and Luis the story of what really happened.

She hugged him and said, "Now, I know why you were so afraid, but we must do something. We can't live with this fear all our lives."

"I can't go to the police. They warned me about that. I now think these people have many ways of finding out what we do or who we talk to. I agree that I have to do something, but I don't know what."

"Why don't you ask this man, Sherant? He sounds like he knows what he's doing. Maybe he'll have some ideas that will help," Luis offered. "If he took that kind of a beating, I'm sure he would like to get back at the men who did this to him. I know I would."

Miranda turned to her brother. "Did Rafael tell you anything about what happened while you were in the house before I got home?"

"I started to tell him the story, but hadn't got very far," Rafael answered. He stopped for a moment then continued, "If Sherant is right, they were probably listening to everything we said. If they were, we are in danger. I don't know what they will do, but they warned me they would do something bad to my family."

"In that case, maybe you should go to the police, tell them everything and get some kind of protection for us. I'll phone Mr. Sherant now and get his opinion on what we should do."

Dusty picked up the message off his cell phone early that evening.

"This is Miranda Teija. Please call me tomorrow at noon, when I will be away from the house. I will have the new phone turned on and wait for your call."

Dusty didn't have to wait for noon to make the call. His cell rang at eleven thirty.

"This is Miranda." She was hysterical and could hardly get her words out between sobs. "Something terrible has happened. Our daughter has been taken. Two men in a truck grabbed her on the way home from school. I was going to pick her up, but she got let out early for lunch and started to walk home with her sister. I don't know what to do. She is only six. I'm afraid of what they will do to her."

"Slow down," Dusty advised. "Have you called the police? Did anyone see it happen?"

"Juanita, our oldest was with Maria. They didn't touch Juanita. They just stopped their truck, one man jumped out, grabbed Maria, threw her in the back seat and they drove off. Raphael is frantic, but doesn't want me to call the police. I want you to tell me what to do."

"Miranda, listen to me carefully. I want you to call the local police and tell them what you have told me, with a description of the truck. Say that it might be a black Hummer, but you're not sure. You don't need to say anything about Rafael's condition or the hand. Let them treat this strictly as a kidnapping. Do it right now and call me back."

When she had hung up, Dusty went next door to tell Kellie what had happened. She and Jeremy were sitting down to lunch when he came in.

"You're just in time for soup." Jeremy announced. "Pull up a chair."

Not knowing how much Kellie had told her husband, Dusty simply said to her, "Rafael's daughter has been kidnapped."

"Who is Rafael?" Jeremy asked.

"He's a friend of Dusty. He met him while trying to find Uncle Fred," she replied.

Just then Dusty's cell rang.

"I'll take this outside and let you finish your lunch."

It was Miranda.

"I called them. They are on their way over. I don't know what else to do. Why would they take my little girl?"

"Miranda! Easy! Take a deep breath and listen to me. I was expecting something to happen, but I thought when they roughed me up outside your mother's house that would be it. I didn't expect this. What happened in the last few days that would make them want to hurt you? Did you and Rafael talk about this in the house or in your vehicles? Did you mention it to anyone else?"

"No, but Rafael was telling my brother Luis about what happened before I got home to warn him. He was telling him what really happened, not the story he told me."

"Where were they when they were talking?"

"In our house, in the living room."

"Didn't you tell Rafael that your house was probably bugged after I met with you and your mother?"

"No, I was afraid he would get mad at me for calling you. He was really serious when he warned me about talking to anyone. I only told him after he started to tell Luis about it. What am I going to do? I am afraid they will hurt Maria."

"Okay! I need to talk to Rafael and hear the whole story from him. Right now, the police are looking for your daughter. That is good. I don't know how successful they are at finding people, but I don't think these men will hurt Maria, or they would lose their control over you. They will probably contact you somehow and warn you. Should you go to the police and tell them everything? I don't know. If these people found out, you would probably not see Maria again."

Dusty could hear Miranda softly sobbing, and wondered if he had been too blunt with her. She was barely under control. He was afraid if he was too rough, he might tip her over the edge. Throughout his life, many had remarked on his general lack of sensitivity.

"I will do all I can to help you," he went on, "but Rafael and I have to meet if I am to have any chance of helping him, and he has to level with me and tell me the whole story, every detail, no matter how insignificant it seems."

Miranda agreed to talk to Rafael and convince him to set up a meeting.

When she called back the second time, she told him that Rafael would see him at his father's home Sunday evening. She gave him the address and told him they would also tell the whole story to Rafael's father, Arturo, who at present knew nothing about what had happened.

17

Dan had set the mixed doubles tennis match for Saturday afternoon at two. Anna had assured her brother that Dusty was recovered sufficiently to play. Since Anna would be his partner, Dusty felt a new tennis wardrobe would be in order, to impress her that he wasn't totally lacking in a sense of fashion. Friday afternoon was spent touring the sporting good stores for attire that would look neat without being too dorky. Since Dusty hated shopping for anything, he considered this bordering on the limits of what a normal man would do to attract a young lady.

Kellie's only comment when she saw him in his new outfit was, "You sure must like this girl to wear clean clothes on a date."

Anna looked beautiful all in pink. The short tennis skirt accented her long, shapely, tanned legs.

The first set was close. Dan and his wife were talented experienced players and dictated most of the play. Anna and Dusty were victorious, simply

because Dusty managed fewer bad shots than Dolly.
The second set teamed Dusty with Dan. They lost a
tie break to Anna's hard, well-placed ground
strokes. The third set, with Dusty and Dolly teamed
up, was a love six humiliating disaster.

After the match they returned to the Seaborne
home, where they convened on the patio with
drinks. Dan asked Dusty if he knew about the
formal Christmas dinner and dance that evening.
Dusty replied that he had heard something about it
from Kellie, but hadn't paid much attention to what
she had said. He turned to Anna and asked, "Are
you going to it?"

"No," she replied. "I was going to invite you as
my date, but discovered I couldn't get off work.
There was nothing I could do about it, so I didn't
mention it."

'Well, that's good, and it's bad," he replied.

"How's that?" Dan asked.

"It is a very sad thing that I won't have the
company of this beautiful lady, but good in respect I
dislike formal dances and most other events of that
kind. I purposely neglected to bring along any
clothes even remotely formal."

Later that afternoon, as Dusty was stretched out
half asleep on the lounge by the caseta, Kellie
appeared dressed for the evening. She wore a form-
fitting black dress cut just high enough and just low
enough to appeal to any man with a pulse. Her long
blonde hair and golden tan were accentuated by the
sun's dying rays.

"Wow! You look great. You didn't have to get
dressed up just for me. Jeans and a wet t-shirt would
have been enough."

"Go easy, will you? I'm really pissed off. As
you know, since I told you a week ago, the big

holiday dinner and dance is tonight. We have had these expensive tickets for over a month. Now, Jeremy phones me from Mexico and tells me he won't be home until next week. So, I came out to tell you to get dressed up. You're taking me to the party."

"Jeez, Kellie, you know how I feel about these uptight events. You are probably the most beautiful woman I know, and I can think of lots of fellows that would love to escort you."

"Nice try, but flattery isn't going to get you out of this one."

"I have no formal clothes. I didn't even bring a suit or a tie, and I'm sure they are not going to let me in with jeans and an old sweatshirt."

"That won't work either. I've laid out one of Jeremy's outfits. Since you two are close to the same size, it should fit. Now, any more excuses?"

"So, you're asking me to get cleaned up, dressed in somebody else's ill-fitting clothes, take the most beautiful woman in Sun City out for dinner and dancing, bring her home and I don't get to go to bed with her. You realize this is the ultimate insult."

"Well, think of it this way. You get a free meal, and I have to put up with your sarcasm and bitching all night. Life is just full of these little disappointments."

"Okay, I've run out of excuses. As long as I can get enough to drink, I can probably survive it."

"That's what we'll both need to get through it," she replied.

The Seguaro Room at the Activity Center was splashed with gaudy Christmas decorations. Each table was adorned with poinsettias, balloons and red and green holiday treats. A five-piece local band was belting out ditties Dusty vaguely remembered from his high school days. Half a dozen older couples were stumbling around the floor, presumably to the music. Dolly had organized a group table, with the seating arrangement designated by festive little name tags. In all, the Seabornes, the Corollis, the Trames and the Princes were allotted their spaces with little holiday treats at each setting. Only Jeremy was missing from the assemblage.

"Who invited him?" Lonnie questioned loudly as Dusty walked in with Kellie.

Dusty looked at him, waited for a minute to cool down, and replied, "It obviously wasn't you."

Kellie squeezed his arm and whispered in his ear, "Walk soft, will you. We have to get through this without a fight breaking out."

"You've really mellowed, Kellie. Fifteen years ago, you would have thrown the first punch."

The dinner, of which the food quality barely matched a Denny's special, went without incident. After the assortment of Costco bakery goodies made the rounds, the drinks began to flow.

"Dance with me," Kellie said. "We need to establish some ground rules."

As they moved out onto the floor, Dusty realized, that in their years of friendship, he had never danced with her. Holding her in his arms as they moved around the floor was a delight.

"I didn't know you knew how to do this," she remarked.

Stifling a smart aleck reply, he was quiet until the song was finished.

"What are our ground rules?" He asked.

She thought for a minute then replied, "I know you too well to think it's going to do any good, but try not and let Lonnie get under your skin. I've seen him like this before. I think he gets primed up with the pleasure of spoiling someone's good time. You're his target for the night, and he will keep at it until you lose your temper. I don't care if you punch him out, but wait until the end of the evening when most of the folks have gone home. And, watch out for his wife. Mildred will come onto you like a dog in heat. She can be big trouble and has the reputation of trying to get every man she meets into her bed. Also, please play down your relationship with Misty. I know that Paul says he isn't affected by her sleeping around, but I know that down deep, he is. I've seen the pained look on his face."

"That's a lot to remember, but okay mother, I'll be a good boy."

They danced back to the table and took their seats, although Dusty would have been content to spend the rest of the evening on the dance floor with Kellie in his arms.

The evening progressed with the drinking and dancing, and more drinking. At one point, Lonnie made a remark that Dusty considered way over the line.

"Where's your scarface girlfriend tonight, afraid to be seen in public?"

Both Dusty and Dan started to get up and move toward the little man, but were restrained by their partners. Instead, Dusty looked him straight in the eye and asked, "Lonnie, were you born an asshole, or is it something you've perfected over the years through practice?"

The remark brought out smiles around the table and a peal of laughter from Mildred. Lonnie's face turned crimson. He clenched his fists, pushed his chair back, but surprisingly, he didn't get up.

Dusty danced with Misty, holding her just close enough to enjoy it, but not enough to make Paul uncomfortable.

"You are playing it cool tonight. I appreciate you not embarrassing my husband by paying extra attention to me." She squeezed his hand as he led her back to the table.

Then Mildred took him by the arm and led him onto the floor. She pressed her body tight against him as they moved away from the table. Dusty was surprised at the strength and firmness of her little girl's body. As they moved to the music, she rubbed herself against him leaving little doubt as to her intentions.

"Lonnie is trying to get under your skin for that skuffle you two had on the tennis court. I think you are really getting into his head, especially after that remark tonight, but be careful, he carries a grudge and will eventually try to get even."

"I figured that out, but as far as I'm concerned it's over. Why does he act like that?" he asked.

"It's a long sordid story, but if you're interested, come over to the house some evening when he's away, slip into my bed, I'll tell you all about it."

"Sounds inviting," Dusty replied, "but I don't need that kind of trouble right now."

"Oh, it won't cause you trouble, and I can certainly make it worth your while."

By then, to Dusty's relief, the music ended, and he escorted Mildred back to her seat.

A few more dances with Kellie put him in a better mood. They had been drinking steadily, making the mixtures stronger as the evening progressed. As the clock moved toward midnight, Dusty felt the need for fresh air. He was sure he was going to pass out from all the alcohol, the heat in the room and the smell of the sweating bodies. He didn't want it to happen in front of everyone. He staggered out of the building into the parking lot and leaned against the wall by a cluster of bushes. His head was spinning and he felt like he was going to throw up, an act which he immediately performed on Jeremy's shoes and over much of his suit. He walked around taking deep breaths, trying to clear his head. It wasn't working. He found the Lexus, leaned against the door, and shut his eyes. He would have liked to crash in the car, but the door was locked, and Kellie had the keys. Out of the corner of his eye, he saw a form approaching. It was Mildred.

"Where did you go?" She asked. "I've been looking for you all over the building. I've got a special treat for you."

As she moved in close, she pulled her dress up over her head and tossed it on the hood of the car. Her naked body glowed in the moonlight. She moved in closer and began to unbuckle Dusty's pants. She stopped when they heard a voice behind them.

"Get the hell out of here and go back to your husband. You're drunk."

Kellie picked up Mildred's dress and threw it at her. She unlocked the door, grabbed Dusty by the arm, and pushed him into the passenger seat.

"It's time for you to go home and sleep it off," she said.

By the time they pulled onto the driveway, Dusty was totally out of it. Kellie couldn't wake him up. She shook him, slapped him, and even kicked him out of frustration, but nothing worked. She was tempted to leave him in the car and just go inside and go to bed, but her softer side prevailed, and besides, he was wearing her husband's vomit-covered clothes. She dragged him into the caseta, stretched him out on the bed, and loosened his clothing. Then, with a smile, she stripped him out of her husband clothes and covered his naked body with a quilt.

"Now to put together a story of what happened and how he ended up naked in his own bed that will blow his mind. Of course, it will have to include Mildred. Hopefully, I can make it as embarrassing for him as possible."

18

Dusty was jarred into a semi-conscious state by the sunlight streaming in his open door. His first reaction was that he was dead, and the two figures standing inside the doorway were angels waiting to escort him through the Pearly Gates, but then his rational side kicked in and suggested that probably would not be the direction he would be going. The spell was broken when Kellie said, "You've got a visitor. So, go get some clothes on. Anna is here. I thought I should warn her what to expect before we opened the door. On the other hand, I thought she should see you at your worst. I also told her about last night."

"Maybe you can tell me about it as well. I don't remember getting back here, undressing, or much else."

"It wasn't pretty, not one of your better performances," Kellie replied.

"It makes me kind of glad I had to work last night," Anna retorted.

"Well, I must have been sober enough to get undressed."

"Not quite," Kellie replied. "You had a little help in that venture. I was going to tell you Mildred came back with you, but my better judgment discarded that idea. Also, you threw up all over Jeremy's suit and shoes."

'I guess that means you won't take me to any more nice places."

Just as Dusty was about to add to his reply, his cell phone rang. It was on its eighth ring by the time they found it buried in the bedding.

"This is Miranda. We got a call early this morning from the people that took Maria. They warned us not to tell anyone what happened to Rafael if we want to see her again. The police listened in and tried to find out where the call came from. All they could tell was it was from Phoenix. And, Rafael's arm is bad. He has a fever, and blood and green stuff is coming out of the bandage. We don't know what to do. We are going over to Rafael father's house now. You will meet us there, yes?"

"I will be there, but are you sure Rafael still wants to do this? Is he willing to take this chance with your daughter's safety in danger?"

"Yes," she replied. "He is mad and tired of being pushed around."

"Okay, I will come. Hold on for a minute."

Dusty set the phone down and explained the situation to Kellie and Anna.

"Will you two go with me?"

They both agreed.

Back on the phone, Dusty asked, "Are you making this call away from the house on your safe cell phone?"

"Yes, we are in the mall."

"I want to bring two ladies with me; one is a nurse to look at Rafael's wound. The other lady is Fred's friend, Kellie, whom he has met. Ask him if that is okay with him."

"Rafael says it is okay. His arm is hurting and he wants treatment, but he is afraid to go to the hospital."

At three, they drove Kellie's Lexus to Anna's home to pick up her medical bag and supplies, after which they proceeded to the home of Rafael's father in El Mirage.

The Teija home was a two-story stucco, set back on a large lot among a similar group of prestigious houses. A recent-year Cadillac and a green Miata sat in the driveway. The landscaping was professionally done with a profusion of citrus trees and numerous varieties of cacti artfully arranged. An elderly gentleman, tastefully dressed in a tan, silk suit, greeted them at the door. His full head of white hair was neatly styled.

"You must be Mr. Sherant. I am Arturo Teija. Welcome to my home." His deep, vibrant voice was warm, yet commanding.

The entrance opened into a long foyer, which led to a sun room at the rear of the house, where seating had been arranged around a large table. In the background was an Olympic-size pool flanked by a cabana/bathhouse, which ran the full length of the pool. Seated at the table was: Miranda, who smiled at Dusty as they walked in, Rafael, who acknowledged Kellie from their previous meeting at the swap meet and Luis, Miranda's brother. After the introductions, a young woman entered the room carrying a tray with pitchers of lemonade and Mexican beer. Arturo introduced his step-daughter, Elsina. As she set out glasses and poured the drinks,

Dusty couldn't take his eyes off this beautiful
Hispanic girl. Her raven black hair was tied back in
a ponytail that fell over her suntanned shoulders as
she leaned over to hand out the drinks. Yellow
shorts and halter further accented the bronze tone of
her skin. Her figure and facial features were
flawless, and when she smiled, she lit up the room.
When Dusty finally averted his gaze, he saw Kellie
form a silent 'no' with her lips then switch her look
toward Anna. Dusty smiled and said, "We think it is
important that Anna have a look at Rafael's wound
while he tells us the full story of what happened."
    Anna began to carefully unwrap the bandages.
"This could be messy. If anyone doesn't want
to watch, I will let you know when I'm finished."
    "We have all seen it. It is the act of very cruel
and sadistic men. It saddens me that anyone could
do this to my son and then take my granddaughter.
We must find her and the people who have done
this and see that they receive the punishment they
deserve."
    There was no doubt the arm was seriously
infected. A portion of the stitched area had opened
and was oozing pus. Dried blood had formed a crust
around the surface of the wound and had flaked out
onto the bandage. Anna inspected it for a few
minutes then announced, "This amputation was
done by a professional surgeon. It was done well,
but it is seriously infected and should be treated in a
hospital."
    "No!" Rafael cried. "They warned me not to go
to hospital. I'm afraid if I don't do what they say,
they will hurt Maria."
    "He's probably right, Anna," Dusty said.
"These people are totally ruthless and are capable of
anything."

"I will do what I can," she replied, "but I'll need to see him again when I have some stronger antibiotics."

"They told me to see doctor in Nogales if there was problem. I have his name and number," Rafael said as he struggled to pull a torn piece of paper from his wallet and hand it to Anna, who, in turn, handed it to Arturo.

"Maybe you should go see this doctor," Kellie said to Rafael. "At least, he's a possible link to this bunch. Find out as much as you can about him. Maybe, we can get the Mexican police to lean on this guy to lead us back to the thugs that are holding your daughter."

"It's a good idea. If he's a qualified doctor, he will be able to treat you better than I can," Anna agreed.

"I will take my son to Nogales, and I will ask this doctor questions," Arturo announced.

After Elsina had refilled their glasses and treated him with a special smile, Dusty said to Rafael, "I need to hear the whole story, right from the start. Try and remember everything that happened. Even the smallest detail may turn out to be important."

"Mr. Sherant, I don't understand why you are so concerned with our welfare. You are putting yourself in extreme danger. As you said, these people are ruthless," Arturo inquired.

"At first, it was curiosity. I wondered why Miranda sounded so scared and wouldn't talk to me when I called to ask about Fred Prince, but when I was beaten by those two thugs, it got personal."

"So, it is vengeance you are after. Revenge is a dangerous road to travel."

"That's pretty much it, except I don't like

bullies hurting innocent people."

Rafael started slowly then really got into his story.

"Whoa, wait a minute. Who was this little man?" Dusty asked.

"I don't know his name. Fred knows him, says he bring gold dust home every time he goes to his claims. We were both going to look for the mine site, as we had good idea where it was. We were in Tucson deciding what to do when we saw his truck heading north out of town. I wanted to follow him, but Fred wanted to go home. He said he was too tired to go chasing around the desert, so I went alone."

"I think that's Lonnie," Kellie explained. "Fred told me he brings gold home every couple of weeks. Rafael, can you tell us what he looked like?"

"I don't see him up close. He is small, shorter than me and, how you say, wiry. He drove blue truck."

"That was Lonnie Trame. There is no doubt."

"Tell me about the packages. What did they look like; how were they wrapped, and how heavy were they?" Dusty asked.

"There were only two boxes, wrapped in brown paper and tape. I don't know what was in them. I was going to open one, but got scared in that cave and just wanted to get out. They grabbed me as I was leaving."

"So, they might have contained gold."

"No, too light, they not contain gold."

Before they left, Arturo took Dusty aside, "I had this house checked over for hidden transmitters before you came. There were six, and one in my car. This is normal, as my business competitors have done this before. I think I should have this company go over Rafael's house, cars, and phones."

"If you do, those people will get suspicious and know we are on to their system. It would be better to leave the bugs in place, but emphasize to everyone they don't talk about any of this unless they are in a safe area."

"Yes, I will tell them. I will take my son to the doctor in Nogales and call you when we return."

The three didn't talk much on the way back to Sun City. Finally, Anna voiced the question that had been in her mind.

"What do you think was in those packages?"

"Dope, probably cocaine or heroin," Kelly answered.

"That's got to be it," Dusty agreed. "I need to have a talk with Lonnie and see if I can scare him into telling me exactly what is going on, although I suspect he's just a small link in the chain and really has no idea what he's involved in."

After dropping Anna at home, Kellie pulled up beside the caseta. She turned to Dusty and said, "Anna is getting very interested in you. I warned her what you're like, but she doesn't seem to care. I know you, and that you have become unable to form any kind of meaningful relationship with a woman. I thought you and Lucie were perfectly suited to each other, but it appears you have managed to avoid commitment again. I saw how you looked at Elsina this afternoon. Please don't hurt Anna. She is too good a person and is very vulnerable. You can't treat her like just another plaything. If you feel she won't be part of your future, please don't encourage her."

"I hear you. I don't know how I feel about her. I really like her, but I just don't know. I'll admit I'm reticent about forming a meaningful relationship

GUY ALLEN

with any female. All my life, since I began noticing girls, I have had this problem. I guess that is why I treasure our friendship; there is nothing at stake. We can say whatever we want to each other."

"Okay, I get it, but while I'm dumping on you, there's another thing that's bugging me. You have to cut way down on your drinking. I care too much about you to see you end up like your father."

"Kellie, I know you are right, and I do appreciate your concern, but I am who I am. I need incentive to change, and so far, since Elena, I haven't found it."

19

Lonnie had been expecting a visit from the cops ever since he saw the news report in the Republic. The Wickenberg police had discovered the bodies of a young native woman and a small child in a cabin on the outskirts of town. Their throats had been cut, and their bodies undetected until the odor was noticeable from the outside. The police were trying to locate the father of the child. There were no other suspects mentioned. Neighbors in the vicinity were being questioned.

Lonnie's anger was overwhelming. The news prompted him to remember all of Paul's advice to him about being careful and not angering their employers, which he was now ready to totally abandoned. He vowed revenge, but he didn't know who they were or where he could find them. Paul was useless; he was too scared to tell him anything, even if he knew. Ellerie was just another woman, but she had been good to him, a hell of a lot better than his bitch of a wife, and he was beginning to care about Marshela, her daughter. He'd had enough, but he knew it was just a matter of time until someone remembered his truck parked there at various times over the past few months.

As if on cue, two Surprise police officers arrived at his house Monday morning.

"We would like to speak with Lonnie Trame and Norman Lawrence."

Mildred answered the door and ushered them into the house.

"My son, Norman is not here, but Lonnie is out back. I'll go and get him."

Lonnie found the two officers seated in his living room leafing through a report.

"Mr. Trame, we're investigating the murder of a young woman, Ellerie Sanchez and her, as yet, unnamed infant in Wickenberg sometime in the past two weeks. Neighbors reported seeing a truck registered to you in her driveway on a number of occasions. Would you care to comment?"

Lonnie thought for a moment then decided for one of the few times in his life, he would tell the truth.

"I visited Ellerie. The little girl was her daughter, Marshela. The last time I saw her was a week ago yesterday. She was alive and well at that time."

"What was your relationship with her?"

"I helped her pay her bills and she provided me with sexual favors. It was a casual thing. We were friends. I certainly didn't kill her."

"Do you have any idea who might have done this to her?"

Lonnie knew at that point he could have blown the whole thing wide open, but it probably would have resulted in his own death. That was not an option.

"I don't know. She confided she was a bit afraid of Marshela's father returning, but I have no idea other than that."

The police seemed satisfied with his answers. He was relieved he didn't have to go into more detail and create a fabric of lies. Any attempts he might make in identifying the real killers would undoubtedly lead to his involvement in their other activities.

"We also had reports of Mr. Lawrence's red Subaru parked along a side road near the cabin. It is registered to this address as well."

The news was not a surprise to Lonnie, and it answered the question in his mind as to how Norman had been able to follow him.

"My son was up there. I suspected my husband of being unfaithful, and I sent him to follow Lonnie and see where he went. Obviously, I was right, but he hasn't returned since then."

"Have you heard from him?"

"The last time he called was a week ago last Saturday. He said he was somewhere near Apache Junction."

The police left with a request to contact them if Norman phoned or showed up, or if Lonnie thought of anything else that might help their investigation.

"What the hell was that all about?" Lonnie shouted.

"Just like I said. I wanted to know who you were screwing."

"Why would you care? We don't give a damn about each other, and you can stop this crap about Norman being your son. I've known about you two sleeping together for some time."

Lonnie had made a point of not revealing that

Norman was dead either to the police or to his wife. They would probably find out soon enough, hopefully after he was long gone from Sun City.

His next visitor was a complete surprise to Lonnie. Dusty Sherant was the last person he expected, or wanted to see.

"What the hell do you want?" Lonnie asked as he opened the door.

"There's something we need to discuss."

"I can't think of anything I want to talk to you about."

"How about your visits to the desert in the middle of the night?"

Lonnie waited a beat before answering. "Come in," he said as he held the door open.

"Those trips are my business. What do you have to do with it?"

"I think you're in big trouble, not that I give a damn, but it does affect a friend of mine. I know you've picked up packages flown in from somewhere, and delivered them somewhere else. I also know that you were followed north of Tucson one time, and that the person who followed you had his hand cut off as a result. It was his hand that ended up on the golf course. I don't know what was in the packages, but I suspect illegal narcotics of some kind, probably cocaine. I'm taking a risk in telling you this, but the people you work for have kidnapped a little girl, and I want to find them before they hurt her. You cooperate with me, or I will get you so deep in shit with the police, you will never dig your way out."

Lonnie sat looking at him. For the first time since he had been recruited for the job, his anger was enriched by an element of fear. He started slowly, composing his story.

"I don't know who took the child, but they are probably the same people I work for. They make contact by phone or ads in the paper. This happens about twice a month. That's all I know."

Dusty sensed he wasn't lying, but was sure he was not telling the whole story. He also knew he wasn't going to get anything more out of this little man.

In parting, he said, "Think about what I told you. If you are protecting this bunch, consider how much your life really matters to them."

Lonnie had definitely thought about that a number of times.

When Dusty left, Lonnie immediately called Paul.

Dusty walked back to his truck, which he had parked down the street. He hadn't expected to learn anything from Lonnie, and was surprised the little man admitted as much as he did. He knew he was taking a chance, using himself as bait to lure the kidnappers into coming after him. He also knew he had put a scare into Lonnie, and was hoping he would make a stupid mistake as a result. He sat and waited for something to happen. He didn't have to wait long. The garage doors on Lonnie's house went up and his truck backed out onto the road. Dusty followed him at a distance. He wasn't worried about being spotted. He was quite sure Lonnie wouldn't recognize his vehicle. The little man headed west into the affluent part of the city and eventually parked in front of a large expensive house that was immediately familiar to Dusty. It was Misty's home. Dusty pulled around the corner, where he had an unobstructed view of the house.

"Who is he going to see, Misty, or Paul?" Dusty wondered.

As Lonnie walked up to the front door, Dusty could see Misty get up from her lounge on the deck and peer over the railing to identify their visitor. She made no move to go to the door and welcome him. It was Paul that opened the door and hustled Lonnie into the house. Misty stood at the railing, apparently deep in thought. After a few minutes, she went into the house.

It was obvious to Dusty that Lonnie's visit was to Paul. He pondered what role the older man could be playing in this apparent smuggling operation. There was little more to be learned hanging around any longer, so he drove back to the caseta.

Kellie was sitting on the patio sunbathing when he drove up. Her brief bikini did little to hide the gentle curves of her well-tanned body.

"You're getting more beautiful as you grow older," Dusty remarked.

"Thanks, if I believed you weren't lying just for the free rent, I'd be flattered."

"Oh, I realize I will eventually have to pay in some manner. Anyway, this is what I have done."

He went on to describe his conversation with Lonnie and the resulting trip to the Corolli residence.

"Dusty, are you out of your mind. You've just set yourself up to lose your life. They're going to come after you. I don't find it too hard to believe that Paul is tied into this somehow. I had Dad check out his background when he started rounding up investors for Mexali. He used to be tied in with some questionable characters in the Unions in Detroit and Chicago. I just don't understand him getting hooked up with a small timer like Lonnie."

"What about these investors? Do you know who they are?"

"Supposedly they are friends and old co-workers of Paul. He recruited them originally without Jeremy's knowledge, but as soon as Jeremy starting looking for start-up money, Paul offered his group's contributions. I've asked Jeremy for their identities, but he's kind of evaded the question and strongly requested I not pester Paul for their names. Since Mexari is a private unregistered corporation, the information is not available to the public. I think he keeps all the Company records in his office downtown in Phoenix."

"It's probably not important. I can't see how it would be tied into this drug mess."

"Dusty, what are you going to do to protect yourself?"

"I want to put motion sensors around here, in the caseta, and in my truck and tie them to my cell phone. I might get one of those fancy bullet-proof jackets, but short of buying a vicious dog as a companion, I guess I will just have to be extra careful. I want to flush these guys out as quickly as possible, and the only way I can see to do it, is to use myself as bait. We have to find Maria. Hopefully, she is still alive."

Lonnie had been seriously disturbed by Dusty's visit, but as far as he was concerned, it was not his problem to solve. He immediately got on the phone to Paul to relate the conversation.

"You better get over here right away. We have to figure out some way to deal with this man. He has definitely become a danger."

When they were seated in Paul's study, Lonnie said, "Can't we just tell your people. They would know how to take care of him. Let them sort it out." Thinking of Ellerie, he said, "They're pretty good at killing people."

"I don't know," Paul replied. "I don't really want to do that. It will probably look to them like we've screwed up again. That would not be good. They made it plain they would not accept any more mishaps. Do you think you can put him out of the way? You two aren't the best of friends, anyway."

"I'll have to think about that. I can do it if I find the right opportunity."

"Well, don't wait too long. He could be a serious problem."

As Lonnie drove home, he smiled to himself. If there were any doubts in his mind about getting out of this mess, they had been neatly resolved. Much as he hated Dusty Sherant, he was not going to commit murder. One more delivery and he was gone.

20

Misty was curious as to why Lonnie Trame would show up on her doorstep. Obviously, it wasn't to see her. Since their brief affair a few years ago, they had nothing but contempt for each other. Her curiosity was too much. She slipped quietly into the house after he and Paul had shut themselves in the den. Listening with her ear to the door, she heard most of what was said and was shocked that they were discussing murdering her friend.

"What was going on?" She asked herself. "What had Paul gotten himself mixed up in?" She knew very little about his business activities, but she had always assumed they were legitimate.

She knew she had to warn Dusty as soon as possible, but right now she had her date with Anna.

She had described to Anna her ongoing affair with Janet at lunch a few weeks ago. Anna had been very interested and asked all kinds of questions about how two women carried on a physical love affair. Misty had, against her better judgment, offered to show her. They had met and gone to bed together the following week, but Misty had found her partner too inhibited to actively participate. She had decided they needed more sessions to break down Anna's barriers and help her find pleasure. The girl had a beautiful body, but was ashamed of it. Misty rightly deduced this was a result of the ugly scar on her face. She sought to give Anna more confidence so that she could enjoy sex whether it was with a man or a woman.

As they lay side by side, Misty felt the girl was much more relaxed and radiating a greater sense of confidence.

"Would you like to meet again?" She asked.

"I don't know. I enjoyed it, but I just don't know. I am developing feelings for a friend of ours here in Sun City, but I can't tell if he feels anything for me."

"Is it Dusty?" Misty asked.

"Yes."

"Be careful, Anna. He is not a good candidate for a serious relationship."

"Kellie has told me the same thing, but I feel we could have a good love. You've been with him. Kellie told me you two slept together. Do you have feelings for him?"

"He's a friend. I enjoy being with him. I like to go to bed with him. We have fun together, but that's it."

"So, you're not in love with him?"

"I'm not in love with anyone. I don't live to fall in love."

"What about your relationship with this other lady that you have had for years?"

"She has strong feelings and is very possessive. She has warned me not to get involved with another woman. That is why I am a bit uneasy about us getting together. I don't know what she would do if she found out. She once said in a fit of anger that she would kill me if I was cheating on her. Since she was drunk at the time, I didn't think much about it. I just go along with her fantasy as payment for all she has done for me through the years, helping me and my daughter survive when things got tough. I owe her a lot."

"I didn't know you had a daughter. Where is she?"

"Lara lives in Seattle, but please don't mention her to anyone. Paul doesn't know she exists."

As Misty was driving home, she was deep in thought when her cell phone rang. She pulled over and answered it.

"Hello darling. How's my sweet lady?"

"Fred Prince! Where the hell are you? I was beginning to think you had died on me."

"No, not dead yet, but getting closer each day. I've been staying down here, south of Tucson. I found this great little lady that believes all my bullshit and wants to take care of me. How are you? Have you found any new loves in your life?"

"Yes, in fact, it's an old friend of yours, Dusty Sherant."

"Dusty! What's he doing down here. Last I heard he was up somewhere in the frozen north, looking after an oil well. I sure would like to get together with him. It's been too long. That boy was like a son to me."

"Well, he's looking for you. Jeremy and Kellie asked him to come down here and help them find you."

"That's probably Kellie's doing. I don't think Jeremy is too anxious to have me around. Anyway, give me Dusty's cell number and tell him I'll call him. One of these days I'm coming up to take you on a wild holiday up in Vegas."

When she hung up, even though it was getting late, she decided it was important enough to drive over and see Dusty today. He was just getting ready for bed when she knocked on the caseta door.

"You must have been reading my mind," he said as she walked in. "I was thinking I needed someone to help me warm the bed."

Misty slipped off her dress and came into his arms.

"That wasn't my main purpose for coming over, but it does sound like a good idea. Fred called me this evening," she said as she slipped out of the rest of her clothing.

"Great," Dusty replied, as he drew her naked body close to his. "How can I reach him? Did he give you a phone number?"

"No, he said he'd phone you. I gave him your number."

For the next twenty minutes there was no talk.

Later, Misty said, "We're beginning to do this like an old married couple."

"You mean that it only happens once in a blue moon?"

"No, it's like it's not wild and passionate. It's more calm and relaxed like we're becoming more conscious of each other's likes and dislikes."

"It sounds like you're getting bored with it."

"No, it's just that I'm not used to this type of a relationship. It's just so nice to be totally at ease with someone."

"So, you figure we might stretch it out a while longer?"

"Absolutely," she replied.

"The other thing I wanted to tell you is that Lonnie plans to kill you."

"Whoa, where did that come from?"

Misty proceeded to tell about the conversation she had overheard and the concern she had for Paul's involvement. Dusty, in turn told her about following Lonnie to her house after meeting with him. He pointedly omitted telling her anything about the subject they discussed, even though he knew it was going to come up.

"Why did you go to see him? I thought you two were enemies?"

"Misty, I can't tell you what this is about because I don't know all of it myself, and anything I do tell you would probably put your life in danger. Let me just say that Lonnie is mixed up in something illegal with some very bad people. I don't know how Paul is involved, but from what you've told me tonight, it sounds like he's in just as deep. I think it would be a good idea for your safety if you got out of here for a while. Go someplace where it would be difficult to find you."

"You really think it's that bad?"

"Yes. My life is in danger right now, not so much from Lonnie, but from the people he works for, and the same would go for you if they thought you had any idea what is going on. I'll watch out for Lonnie. Although I have an extreme dislike for the man, he doesn't strike me as a killer, but I could be wrong."

"Okay. I can go visit my daughter in Seattle. I think that would be safe. Lara has an apartment with a spare bedroom. Paul doesn't know she exists. I've always told him I go to see my sister in LA. Since Christmas is coming up, it should be a good cover."

"That would work. Go out and buy a new cell

phone and use it only it for private conversations."

"Why? Do you think my phone is bugged?"

"I wouldn't be surprised if your phone, your car, and the house all have transmitters."

"In that case, if this is my last night, I guess I'd better stay here with you, where it's safe."

Misty left early the next morning for home to pack her bags and drive to Seattle. She promised Dusty she'd keep in touch.

21

The ad read, 'Aurumographer wanted. Call 122-531-0140'. As expected, it was brief and to the point. Lonnie had been waiting all week, scanning every issue of the Arizona Republic for his next assignment, and there it was, a week before Christmas. The drop was to be at 3:10 AM on Dec. 25 at location #1, and the pickup was set for location #4. Lonnie dug the code book out of his desk and checked the phony phone number against the number codes. This was great. The drop was set for the Paradise Lake site, with the pick up at that old abandoned warehouse on Grand Avenue. At least he didn't have to make that long tiring drive to Tucson on Christmas morning.

"It figures that these bastards want me to work on Christmas day with no pay," he thought. "Well, this time they're going to get the surprise."

He had a week to perfect his plans, which he had gone over many times in his head. Although he had never opened one, he was pretty sure the packages contained dope, probably high-purity cocaine. Selling it shouldn't be a problem if he made the right contacts a long way from Sun City. In fact, it wasn't that important a concern to Lonnie. He just wanted to taste a suitable form of revenge. He probably had enough money stashed away to last him the rest of his life. Maybe he would just take the stuff down to skid row in one of the big cities, distribute it to the losers, and watch them overdose.

His next step was to visit the local animal shelter and offer to clean out some of the cages. He explained his strange request to the shocked manager by telling him that dog crap helped his cacti grow, especially the Seguaros. He came on so sincere, they bought the story, and talked of packaging their product for commercial landscapers. He diligently shoveled up his supply and even filled a barrel for his hosts. His only regret was that he wouldn't be there to observe their efforts in trying to market the product to local stores. The largest number of packages he had ever delivered was six. So, next in his garage, he put together six packages of this canine product in the same manner as his delivery packages were boxed and wrapped.

As delivery day approached, he made his final arrangements to disappear with his booty. He withdrew enough cash to cover anticipated living expenses for the next six to eight months. He paid his outstanding bills by cheque, but was somewhat dismayed when the sequence of cheque numbers from each of his accounts did not appear on the online statements. Although he had kept no records, he assumed he had written these cheques, but they had not been cashed. He then cut up all his credit cards to avoid the temptation of creating a paper trail of card purchases tracking his movement. On Christmas Eve, he packed his truck with those essential and treasured items he wanted to keep.

"Let Mildred have the rest of it," he thought. "Maybe she can sell the house for enough to go somewhere far away out of my life and start over."

Just after one-thirty, he drove out to Paradise Lake and parked next to the open area that had been marked out in the code book. A bright moon in a cloudless sky lit up the landscape as the small single-engine aircraft came in low over the dry wash and dropped the packages. This time there were four. Lonnie had made no attempt to determine if he was being followed. He didn't care. Everything would look normal. He drove over beside the landing spot and made the pick-up. He drove away from the Lake and over to Grand Ave and the warehouse where he made the delivery. If anyone was keeping an eye on him, they would have no cause for concern until they opened the packages. He smiled as he thought of their reaction and only wished he could be present unnoticed to see it. At the warehouse, he parked by the back door and carefully selected four of his specially prepared parcels. As he had expected, the door was unlocked and a dim lamp cast just enough light to guide him. He left his delivery on an old workbench and locked the door as he went out. With a full tank of gas, he drove to Highway 10 and headed west.

Although he had made most of his preparations while Mildred was out of the house, she was aware that something was going on. He had been acting strangely all week. She had suggested they celebrate Christmas Eve with dinner out or a movie, but Lonnie flatly refused. Then, when he took off in the middle of the night, she was convinced that he probably wasn't coming back for a few days. She decided the time was ripe to put her plan into action.

She had been practicing writing his signature all week until she had it so it could be scribbled off easily, and, to her eyes, it was an exact replica. She had taken two blank cheques for each account from his cheque books earlier in the week. In return for more sexual favors, she had Jerome access the accounts for current balances. She was a bit surprised to see how the totals had been recently reduced, but she took it for another sign that Lonnie was planning a prolonged absence. When Lonnie had been gone for a couple of days, she decided it was time. First of all, she needed a believable fake identity. On her internet searches, she learned the interesting fact that she could establish herself as a Mexican national living in the United States with a Matricula Consular Identification Card. She could also buy a fake Mexican Birth Certificate and Driver's License off the street in Los Angeles if she knew where to go. This was perfect. Her sister lived in LA with a boyfriend who had been in and out of jail for the past ten years. Hopefully, he could make the contacts she needed to get these documents. She called Louisa, who encouraged her to make the trip. Louisa and her boyfriend agreed to get her set up. He would use his network to put her in touch with someone who could supply the documents.

Mildred dyed her hair black and applied a dark tanning solution and heavy makeup to her skin. A side trip to the Goodwill outlet supplied her with a couple of sexy Hispanic outfits. Then she went to the local photographer and had a passport photo taken. She paid cash for everything, but made her first mistake when she decided to drive her own car to Los Angeles. She was all set. She left Sun City the next day around noon and drove to Blyth, just across the California border, where she stayed for the night. Here she made her second mistake, using her Mildred Trame Visa to pay for her motel room. The next day she was in LA, and that evening her sister took her to see a man in the McArthur Park area who agreed to have the documents for her in a couple of days for two hundred dollars. She paid the man half the money as a deposit and hoped for the best. Two days later, as promised, she became Juanita Rojas, a dark-haired beauty, born in Tijuana on her own actual birth date. This was the third mistake. The newly created Juanita made out the six cheques with Lonnie's signature to herself. The amounts were enough to make the venture worthwhile, but not so much that Lonnie would be notified by the banks. She then used her forged documents to open accounts in six different banks as Juanita, deposited the cheques, and waited for them to clear. She was getting more excited with every step and couldn't believe how smoothly the whole plan was unfolding. It took two weeks for all the cheques to clear. Juanita was a rich woman. Now she believed she needed to pull the money out and become Mildred again and make deposits in her own accounts. When she revealed her plan, Louisa's boyfriend strongly advised her against it.

"If your husband puts the cops on this, they will have no trouble chasing you down, especially since you didn't take all the precautions in hiding your identity coming out here. You close out those new accounts now, and the cops will have no trouble identifying and finding you. Leave the money in the Juanita accounts for at least a year until you can be sure it's safe. You can still make small withdrawals as Juanita, but don't provide any information so that they can track you, and don't withdraw any money from Sun City branches of these banks. It would be a good idea to keep this new identity and let Mildred cease to exist. Use a General Delivery post office address for mail, but never pick it up."

Mildred could see the value in his advice. She withdrew enough money from one account to cover her expenses and drove back to Sun City.

She half expected to find Lonnie had returned home with a whole bunch of questions as to where she had been, but there was no sign that he had come back. When she checked phone messages, she found a dozen calls from Paul Corolli during the first week to Lonnie, frantically asking where he was. There was nothing from Lonnie, but since she hadn't made any effort to contact him while she was away, she wasn't surprised. She tried his cell phone a few times before giving up. Although, she sort of expected his return at any time, she never saw him again.

At the end of the month, when the mortgage and other major bills came due, she began to be concerned. She had not anticipated these eventualities and was running out of money. If she paid everything off, she would have to live on her Visa for a while until she could make another trip to Los Angeles. Since she didn't have a Visa in Juanita's name, this wasn't an option. She phoned Paul and asked him and other acquaintances if anyone had any idea of where Lonnie had gone. No one had. Strangely, Paul was more concerned than she was as to his whereabouts. Since she wasn't aware of any close friendship between the two, she became suspicious of his reaction.

Finally, after exhausting all other avenues, she contacted the Sun City police and filled out a missing person report. She paid the outstanding bills with her dwindling reserves of cash and waited.

22

During the second week in January, Arturo
Teija and Rafael traveled to Nogales, Mexico to
visit the Doctor Garcia, whose name was written on
the slip of paper given to Rafael. His office was
located in his home on a popular side street and it
was obvious from the clientele in the waiting room
that his practice mainly served American tourists,
who made the journey south to escape the high cost
of U. S. healthcare. The doctor was a short heavy-
set man with swarthy skin and a bushy black
mustache. His English was adequate for the tourists,
but Arturo decided to converse in Spanish for
clarity.

If Rafael's wound became infected or was
causing trouble, he had been instructed, not to go to
his own doctor or a local hospital but to visit Dr.
Garcia to receive any necessary treatment. The arm
was continuing to heal from Anna's work on it, so
when Dr. Garcia unwrapped the wound, he could
see no need for further action other than

rebandaging. Satisfied with his son's progress, Arturo questioned the doctor as to why he had been referenced in this case. Doctor Garcia rummaged through his file cabinet for a few minutes and eventually emerged with a letter, which he passed to Arturo.

"This physician, Ernest Lucarno, in Chicago referred your son's case to me. He indicated that he had performed the surgery, but due to his distance from the patient's home, he requested that I deal with any problems that might arise."

"Have you had contact with this doctor before?" Arturo asked.

"No. I had never heard of him until this letter came, and there has been no other communication between us. In fact, I had forgotten about it until you called and made this appointment. There is an address and phone number on the letter if you wish to contact him. I will give you a copy of it."

Arturo was convinced the man was telling the truth and saw no need to question him further. He received the copy of the letter and thanked the doctor for his time.

When they had returned to El Mirage the next day, Arturo called Dusty and relayed the results of his visit.

"I think we need to find out more about this Dr. Lucarno," Dusty observed.

"I agree, but we may be putting my granddaughter in greater danger if we contact him directly. Do you have any suggestions for making inquiries without alerting these people? While we were away, they phoned here and warned us against making any efforts to locate her. Elsina took the call and demanded to speak with Maria. They let her talk very briefly. She told my daughter that she wasn't being hurt."

"That's good news just to know that she s alive, but we can't stop trying to find her and bring her home," Dusty replied. "We must be more discreet. I suggest you have the police put a tap on your phone in case they call again."

Arturo didn't reply to the suggestion. He thought briefly about it, but he had his own reasons for not wanting the local police listening in on his conversations.

Dusty went on, "We can check this doctor out through the AMA without him knowing about it. They should be able to look up in their records and tell us if he's been blacklisted, license suspended, or anything like that."

"That is an excellent idea. I will contact them and let you know what they report."

Dusty was bringing Kellie up to date, when Arturo phoned back.

"This is very disturbing. The Medical Association has no record of a Dr. Ernest Lucarno ever being registered in the State of Illinois. However, the young lady I spoke with mentioned they had received a number of inquiries about a supposed doctor with this name in the past, and they had been unable to find out anything about him."

"How about the address and phone number on this letter?"

"I called the City offices up there and those of the telephone company as well. The phone number is a phony, and the address is that of a vacant lot. This appears to be a dead end."

"Not necessarily," Dusty observed. "I would be interested in the sources of the other complaints about this phantom doctor. I also expect the Chicago police have a file on this person. If he has been involved in illegal activities before, they are probably aware of him."

"How would you get that information? I can't see the police opening up their files to us without some sort of a court order."

"They might, if we could get someone with some clout on our side to make the requests."

"How would you do that?"

"Let me get back to you after I make a call."

That evening, Dusty phoned Lucie Hansen in Saskatoon. Remembering their last conversation, he wasn't too sure what to expect.

"My Gawd, you're still alive," she replied after picking up on the fifth ring.

"Yes, but the way things are going, that could change any day now. The prospects for enjoying an old age are getting dimmer."

"Dusty, what the hell have you got yourself into this time?"

Dusty proceeded to tell her the whole story, leaving out only the episodes involving Misty.

"Lucie, I am at a loss as to what to do next. I need your advice. We have to find a way to rescue this little girl soon without getting her and all of the rest of us killed. These people seem to know everything we are doing. We have found a number of bugs, and I know there are more, but if we pull them, they will know. We don't know how to resolve this quickly and rescue Maria."

Lucie was silent for a few minutes then answered slowly, "As usual, you have done a few things that were smart and a bunch of stuff that was incredibly stupid. I understand using yourself as bait, but as time go on, if nothing happens, that becomes increasingly more dangerous. I do have a friend down there, who might be able to help. A few

years ago, when I was with the Mounties, I had
contact with a deputy from the Maricopa County
police. We were extraditing a druggie to the U S.
The agent's name was John Hebrano, and he came
up here to escort this fellow back for trial. I got to
know John a bit. We compared the crime situation
and police tactics in both our districts. He seemed
like a good guy. At that time he was getting up in
years and is probably retired by now. I'll see if he is
still down there. If I can find him, I'll put him in
touch with you. The other thing is that I will use my
contacts in the RCMP to check out this Dr. Locarno
with the Chicago police. Other than that, I don't
know how else I can help unless I fly down, and I
can't do that for at least a month."

"Lucie, you're beautiful. Thank you."

"You be careful. These do not sound like small
timers you're messing with. Besides, I don't want
you dead until I decide if I ever want to see you
again."

Lucie phoned back the next afternoon.

"I checked out your Dr. Locarno with Chicago.
They've heard of him and have had a number of
complaints, but they've never been able to locate
him. They figured he's a legitimate physician,
working for the mob under an alias, and they were
never able to put the two together. It seems he has
performed some very painful services for the bad
guys. The good news is that I located John Hebrano.
He's retired, living in Scottsdale and has no
affection for the Sun City administration. I guess
the City screwed him around on his pension. His
lawyer tried to fight their lawyers and lost. He told
me that he's getting bored playing golf every day
and needs some excitement in his life. He would be
glad to help. Here is his phone number. He's

expecting to hear from you."

"Lucie, Lucie, Lucie, why did I ever let you go?"

"I figured that out when you left. I know we didn't part on the best of terms. I just put it down to me being a scheming, marriage-hungry bitch, and you an insensitive, womanizing commitaphobic, and we will probably deserve each other some day, when we're too old to care."

"Yes, that sounds about right."

"Dusty, keep in touch and let me know what happens. Your action down there sounds a lot more interesting than what I'm doing up here."

"So, why don't you drop everything and come down here for the excitement?"

"Uh uh! I'm just bored, not stupid."

Dusty was beginning to feel that in spite of his efforts and the chances he was taking, he was getting no closer to finding Maria. He phoned Arturo Teija to relay Lucie's message about Locarno. After ten rings and no answer, he hung up. Two minutes later, Arturo phoned him back on a cell phone.

"I quit using my home phone after our last conversation. It's the only way I can explain these people knowing what goes on in this house. Your news is about what I expected. Also, I forgot to tell you that Dr. Garcia received payment of $1,000 with that letter from this Locarno. I phoned Garcia to see if the payment was made by cheque, as I thought we might be able to trace it through the bank, but he informed me it was in the form of ten, one hundred dollar bills stuffed in the envelope. I would like for us to meet, possibly tomorrow, if you can come for dinner around six. I wish to discuss what further steps we might be able to take to rescue my granddaughter. It has been two weeks now, and as far as I can see, the police have made no progress."

"I will be there at six," Dusty replied.

An hour later, while Dusty was working out at the Rec. Center, his phone rang again. He got outdoors in time to answer on the seventh ring.

"What took you so long, and who are you in bed with?"

"Dammit, Fred, where the hell have you been? I've been looking for you ever since I got here. So far, I've managed to get myself into a mess just trying to find you."

"Listen boy, as long as I've known you, you've never had any problem getting into messes without my help. What's happening?"

"Kellie and Jeremy have been so worried about you that they phoned me in the middle of the night and hassled me to come down and search for you. In the course of doing that, I got involved with Rafael and all his problems."

"I haven't talked to Rafael in over a month since we parted company in Tucson. What happened to him? Is he alright?"

After Dusty related the entire sequence of events, Fred was quiet for a few minutes then said, "I warned him not to track Lonnie when we spotted his truck in Tucson. I had a bad feeling about it then. We have to get together and talk. There's something going on over there in Sun City that isn't making a lot of sense, and what you just told me makes it even more confusing. You need to get down here as soon as you can get away. There is something fishy about this company Jeremy has put together."

"He told me you weren't too impressed with

his mining claims, both here in Arizona and down south. Is that what you mean?"

"That's part of it but ... we need to talk face to face."

After getting directions to his place south of Tucson, Dusty agreed to drive down on Saturday.

23

When Mildred saw the police car pull up in front of her house and the two officers get out and walk to the entrance, she almost had a fit.

"What had she done wrong? Where did she screw up?" She frantically asked herself as she went to answer the door. It was the same two policemen who had come to see Lonnie about his girlfriend's death before Christmas. She let them in, led them to the living room, and offered them a coffee or soft drink, which they refused.

"Is your husband home? We'd like to talk to him as well as to you."

Mildred informed them that Lonnie had left suddenly on Christmas Eve and hadn't as yet returned. She didn't know where he had gone or when to expect him.

"We have some bad news for you. We found the remains of the man who called himself Norman Lawrence up east of Apache Junction in the Superstition Mountains. When we were here before you told us he had been away for a week or so. You also told us that he was your son. We identified him from his fingerprints, or what was left of them. The identity came up as Lawrence Norman and a bunch of other aliases. He had accumulated an impressive criminal record since his youth. Of the few things we did learn, one was that he was not your son. Now, we would like some straight answers, starting with the whereabouts of Mr. Trame."

"Okay! Lawrence was my boyfriend, not my son. We kept the charade up for Lonnie's sake, but he told me before he left that he had known about it for a long time and really didn't care. As far as where he is, I was telling you the truth. I have no idea. He didn't tell me where he was going and when, or if he was planning to come back. I really don't care if I ever see him again."

"Do you know Juanita Rojas?"

The question caught her off guard and her momentary change of expression was noticed immediately. She realized it but recovered quickly.

"I've heard my husband mention the name," she replied. "Why do you ask?"

"Your husband made out a number of cheques for substantial amounts to this woman. We think he may be on the run with her. He's definitely wanted for questioning regarding Norman's murder. We request you not leave Sun City until we get this cleared up, and get in touch with us immediately if you hear from him or find out where he is."

After the police had left, Mildred, worried that they had tapped her phone, went out in the back yard, called her sister on her cell and told her the story.

"I don't know what to do. I need a chunk of that money, but I'm afraid the cops will be on top of me if I try to make a withdrawal."

"I don't know, Mildred. Give me a minute to put it to Guillermo."

When Guillermo came on the phone, he listened patiently while she went through the whole story again.

"They obviously don't know that you are Juanita, and they probably haven't got a fix on that bank account. You could hustle out here fast and get some cash before they find the accounts, but that would also involve some risk since they told you not to leave town. Other than that, you could write a cheque to someone you trust, and get them to cash it right away and give you the money. Just don't make it out to Louisa, her being your sister, or me. They could trace it back to you in a minute."

When Mildred hung up, she was more confused than before. She could think of no one she could trust to the extent of writing a cheque that big and trusting them to hand over the money.

Friday afternoon Dusty drove over to the Teija mansion as Arturo had suggested. He was intrigued by the fact the old man had been unclear as to the purpose of the meeting other than to invite him for dinner. He considered they had covered all aspects of the kidnapping, and it had been agreed there was little that could be done unless the kidnappers made a move, or the police were able to track them down. He called ahead and Arturo requested he park on a side street and enter the property through the back gate. This heightened the sense of mystery.

The gate opened into an expanse of yard landscaped with a wide assortment of cacti, succulents, and other desert-loving plants. In the middle was a large swimming pool surrounded by tables and umbrella-covered deck chairs. Along one side, a cabana extended for the full length of the pool. Arturo was seated at a table busily leafing through a file folder. He was dressed to fit in with the ambiance. He looked as if he had just stepped off his fifty-foot yacht, or was sitting for a gig as a male fashion model. The man was a class act and didn't show the slightest disdain for Dusty's attire of blue jeans and his cleanest t-shirt.

"Welcome to my home again Mr. Sherant. I am pleased you could make it. Would you care for a drink before dinner? In this heat, I prefer a margarita."

Dusty agreed that would be an excellent choice and settled into a chair on the opposite side of the table.

"No doubt you have asked yourself why I requested your presence when we met so recently. The fact is, I am troubled over a series of recent events. Since we last talked, the kidnappers have contacted me again, and issued a serious warning to me to quit my investigations and cease making contact with you. They reported in detail our conversations at the last meeting and the results of my trip to Nogales. I assume from what they said that they had planted listening devices here. As you suggested, I had a team of professionals come in and search for these devices in the house, the car and my phone; they found nothing. So, I asked myself how these people could get this information, and the only answer I can come up with is that someone in the group that was here that day is reporting to them."

"That makes sense, but it doesn't explain them knowing the details of your trip to Nogales. Do you have any idea who might be spying on us?"

"I was about to ask you the same question. Would you consider either of the two ladies that accompanied you as suspects? I don't know either of them, so I have to take your word for their reliability."

Dusty thought for a minute before he answered, "My simple answer would be no. I have known Kellie for many years and totally trust her. I have only known Anna for a short time, but the only reason she was here was to treat Rafael's injury."

"I see. I have no reason to suspect my daughter, or Rafael and Miranda. However, Miranda's brother concerns me. Luis has been in trouble in the past and has been charged a few times for dealing in drugs. I need to have some of my friends check him out and see where he goes and who he talks to."

Elsina bringing the tray of drinks to the table interrupted their conversation. She was dressed in a simple form-fitting white dress, which accented her tan and the lovely curves of her body. She held Dusty's gaze as she set the glasses on the table.

"I will serve dinner in just a few minutes," she said as she returned to the house.

"You find my adoptive daughter attractive."

"Very much so," Dusty replied.

"It is so very sad. The girl has had such a tough life. Her father was a friend of mine. He was with the Government down in Mexico City. I had occasion to do business through him for export licenses. Eight years ago he was kidnapped by one of the families in the drug trade. They threatened to kill him unless his wife, who was well known and respected in the Country, would smuggle their products across the border. She had no other alternative if she wanted to see her husband alive again. This went on for two years until she was

SUN CITY

caught and imprisoned here in Arizona. The authorities used some very harsh methods in an attempt to get her to identify her employers, but she held out, hoping it would save her husband. I tried to intercede for her with the authorities, but they refused to listen. Unfortunately, her silence was to no avail. He was assassinated and his body dumped in the street. When she heard of this, she appealed to me to get her daughter out of the country. Through other contacts down south, I was able to bring Elsina here. Her mother eventually died in prison, but she passed on knowing the girl was safe. After her death, I adopted Elsina."

As he was finishing his story, there were tears in his eyes. At that moment his daughter reappeared with the main course.

"Elsina has prepared her specialty, a Mexican-style pasta dish for us tonight. This young lady is an excellent cook. I know you will enjoy it."

Not being a fan of Mexican food, Dusty was tentative in tasting what he expected to be a very spicy dish. It was, however, mild and delicious. His compliments to the cook brought a smile to her face, which lit up the night.

Halfway through the meal, Arturo's cell phone rang. He walked to the far side of the pool to answer it. After he had hung up, he announced to Dusty and Elsina that it was an important call, and he had to leave immediately. He apologized and urged Dusty to finish his meal.

When he was gone, Elsina confided, "I think he is going to see his girlfriend. Every time she phones, he rushes away. She leads him around like a puppy."

Dusty was in no hurry to leave the company of this beautiful young woman. They sat by the pool and explored each other's lives. Elsina told her story in a fashion similar to Arturo's. Her tale differed with the inclusions of her personal feelings and emotions while she was enduring her parents' ordeal. Throughout her story, Dusty could detect a sadness and bitterness that she felt something more could have been done to spare her mother the torment of being locked up, and her premature death.

"Arturo has been so very kind. I owe him my life."

She went on to tell Dusty of earning her degree in Business Management from the University of Phoenix and her job managing the office of an import company downtown.

After an hour of getting to know each other, she asked, "Would you like to go for a swim? The water is so refreshing this time of the evening after such a warm day."

"That would be great," he replied, "but I failed to bring a suit."

"That's okay. I seldom wear one."

She walked to the edge of the pool: slipped out of her shorts and halter, dove in, and swam with smooth, easy strokes to the far end. The pool lights accentuated the gentle curve of her breasts as she stood up in the shallow water.

"Come on in. The water is just the right temperature tonight."

Dusty quickly got rid of his clothes and joined her in the shallow end. She swam slowly toward him, stood up and put her arms around his neck. He pulled her close and kissed her, at first gently and then with passion. He picked her up and started to carry her to a lounge when he spotted a flash of light out of the corner of his eye. This was followed by a thrashing sound in the bushes outside the back gate. Dusty set her down at the edge of the pool and rushed to the gate in time to see the black Hummer pulling away from the curb.

"What was it?" Elsina asked.

"Somebody has been watching us. I don't know how long they've been there, but I recognized their vehicle. It's the same bunch that beat me up outside Miranda's mother's house. I'm sure they are the ones that took Maria."

By now, Elsina had toweled off and gotten dressed. The mood of the evening was lost.

24

Dusty was looking forward to getting together with Fred Prince. After all, that was supposedly the reason for the trip. Fred and Dusty's father, Shelly, had been close friends. When Dusty's mother took off to make her presence felt in the world, which was most of the time, Shelly was left to raise his wild little boy. He was emotionally unable to undertake the task, and it fell upon his best friend to mentor his son. Fred had also been delegated to guide his nephew Jeremy through the pitfalls of adolescent life. As a result, Dusty and Jeremy had become inseparable throughout the high school and college years.

Dusty followed Fred's directions, taking 1-10 east from Sun City then along a bunch of secondary roads bypassing Tucson and ending up west of Highway 19 on the edge of the Sierra Mountains. Fred had told him to forget about using the GPS because he didn't really have an address the device would be able to find. At the end of a graveled road was a small adobe cabin with a flagpole sporting 'Old Glory' and the Canadian Maple Leaf above it. It had to be Fred's place. No one else he knew would openly piss off the neighbors by flying both flags, especially in that order.

As he pulled into the yard, an old dog attempted to get up and check him out, but stumbled and fell. The recognition came slowly to Dusty. Brownie had been a pup the last time he had seen the dog. "It has to be at least ten years," Dusty thought.

As he bent down to pet the old dog, the front door opened and a middle-aged lady stepped out. She walked over and put out her hand. She was Dusty's height with a compact muscular body. The copper cast of her skin, which was smooth and wrinkle-free belied her mixed heritage. Her natural open smile was warm and inviting. Dusty guessed her age as anywhere between forty-five and seventy.

"You must be Dusty. The old man's been telling me all about you ever since you spoke on the phone. By now, I'll bet I know you better than most of your girlfriends. My name's Lucinda and my penance in life is to put up with this crotchety old bugger. He's waiting inside for you. I can't seem to separate him from the air conditioning."

Dusty went inside to a twenty-degree drop in temperature. Fred Prince was stretched out in a recliner, but got up slowly, walked over, and put his arms around him. There were tears starting to moisten his eyes. He quickly wiped them away then stood back and looked searchingly at his younger friend.

"Daryl, you're looking older. I sense you are not living that clean, healthful life we hear so much about."

"No, I haven't tried that one yet, and I'm sure you haven't. And, by the way, I don't go by Daryl anymore. I told you about that a long time ago."

"I know. I was just trying to get a rise out of you. I remember you changed it to piss your mother off."

"Yeah, and it worked. I haven't heard from her in years."

Fred barely showed the signs of an octogenarian. He stood tall, over six feet, with a minimum of fat on his large frame. His full head of snow-white hair capped an interesting road map of a face. His one sign of a misspent life was the pinkish alcohol tinge to his nose. He walked with a full limpless stride, and his movements were more smooth than jerky. The normal ravages of old age had been kind to him.

'Well, I will tell you one thing," Dusty went on, "your lifestyle of alcohol consumption and bedding younger women has worked. You're looking great for an old fart."

"That calls for a drink. It's early here, but it must be Happy Hour somewhere in the world. Lucinda, would you dig us out a couple of beers and come and join us?"

A few minutes later, she came in with three chilled bottles of Corona.

"Let's hope this is the first of many," Dusty observed. "I've missed your stories and observations on life."

"You've met my lovely Lucinda. She is the joy of my life. She took this old fellow in out of the goodness of her heart. There is not a kinder woman on this planet."

"Well, I'm telling you, Fred, you had better be

good to her or I will come down here and steal her away. She's far too hot for you, old man."

Lucinda smiled and looked at Fred. "That sounds like a plan," she said, "maybe I should go and pack a few things right now."

The quick flash of concern on Fred's face told Dusty that he might have hit a nerve and to back off. He quickly changed the subject.

"What do you think of what happened to your friend Rafael?"

"I don't know. I haven't talked to him in quite a while. I tried to phone a couple of times, but there was no answer or recording machine. How did you come to know him?"

Dusty proceeded to tell Fred his story of being summoned to look for him, how he'd finally contacted Miranda, and the punishment Rafael had received. He went on to describe the beating he had taken and the kidnapping of Maria.

Fred's face grew graver as the story unfolded, but he said nothing until Dusty had finished.

"You do have a knack for getting involved in the damnedest of situations. I warned Rafael not to take off after Lonnie Trame that day last year, but he wouldn't listen. He was too intent on finding Trame's mine. I had suspicions then that there was no mine, but I had no idea where he was getting the gold he brought back. Obviously, it was payment for some sort of illegal work."

"I think he was transporting drugs, but from where to where, I don't know. I took a chance and went to see Lonnie and told him my suspicions in order to see if I could flush out these bandits that have Rafael's little girl. It freaked him out, and he immediately went to see Misty's husband, who appears to be tied up in it as well."

175

"That doesn't surprise me," Fred replied. "Corolli has always been a bit of a hood, ever since his early days in Chicago. I doubt if he's changed, but he's not bright or brave enough to be running an operation like you suggest. Does Misty know anything about this?"

"Yes. She warned me that Lonnie was going to kill me. She had listened in to a conversation between him and her husband. For her safety, I didn't go into details about the whole thing, but I told her it would be a good idea to go away for a while. I think she did, as I haven't heard from her since. She thought she'd go visit her daughter in Seattle."

"So, who else knows this whole story you have spun for me?"

Dusty thought for a minute then replied, "Kellie, and Rafael's father, Arturo know all of it. Rafael is aware of the part that relates to him. Anna Seaborne learned a bit when she offered to treat Rafael's arm. I can't think of anybody else other than, maybe Elsina, Arturo's daughter."

"What about Jeremy?"

"I haven't talked to Jeremy about it. I figure it is up to Kellie, but she seems reticent to do it. I don't know why. Maybe it's because she thinks he's got enough to worry about with this Mexari business and managing the Amyot operations up in Canada. He spends a lot of time away. I don't see him very often."

"So, was it Jeremy who asked you to come down and look for me?"

"He phoned me, but I gather it was mostly Kellie's idea."

"I can believe it. I got the feeling he wasn't sorry to see me leave. I guess I was asking too many questions. Has he told you much about this Mexari deal?"

"No. I've asked him about it and offered to have a look at the properties. He showed me some silver ore, which looked pretty good, but it was mostly high-grade galena, which supposedly has a good silver content with the lead. It's funny; I thought most of the rich stuff from that part of the country was native silver. When I started to question him about it, he informed me I was mistaken. Since then he has clammed up about it all. Kellie tells me the same thing. If she can't squeeze the information out of him, no one can. I have the feeling he is pursuing this to show the world, especially Martin Angleton, that he can be a success without the influence of his wife's money and connections. I'm just afraid he's headed for a major screw-up. He had a knack for getting himself into situations when he was younger that he couldn't get out of."

"How well I remember that," Fred replied. "It was either me, or sometimes you, getting his messes sorted out with a minimum of damage. Remember the girl that claimed he had knocked her up and demanded he marry her, until we located at least half a dozen other fellows who had slept with her."

"Yeah!" Dusty replied. "That one was messy."

Fred leaned back and closed his eyes for a few moments.

"You know, you are both right about that Chihuahua silver ore. Some of it is argentiferous galena, but the good stuff is pure silver."

"I know. I looked it up later, but I didn't tell him. I figured his ego didn't need a boost at that point," Dusty admitted.

"So, you come down here to my love nest with

these two major problems to disturb my sleep, disrupt my sex life, and hasten the ravages of old age."

"Gee, if I thought I could have that strong an effect, I would have come earlier."

"Fred, obviously Dusty needs help. You need to get off your ass and get involved in this. From what I'm hearing, Rafael's little girl is in extreme danger, and it would appear that Jeremy could use some guidance. I can't see how you can help Rafael, but you two need to find out exactly what Jeremy is into before it is too late."

"She's right, Fred. I need your sage advice and help. I'm at a loss as to where to go from here. I can't just walk away from Rafael's problem. I want a piece of those bastards that beat on me. The police have done nothing, so I've kind of put myself out there as bait."

"I don't see what else you can do. I'll drive up and see Rafael and Miranda and maybe get some ideas. As far as Jeremy is concerned, we need to get the legal descriptions of his Mexican claims as well as those here in Arizona. Also, we need a list of Company directors and management, as well as the shareholders. That would be helpful in determining who all is involved in this thing. I have some bad feelings as to whom he is doing business with, especially since Corolli lined up a bunch of his friends as investors."

"And, how do we do that short of breaking into his office files?" Dusty asked.

"That is exactly what we have to do. We need to get into his files before we can check all this out. That has to be where all the information is located, either in his files or on a computer. I don't know if Kellie will help you. If you explain to her that we're trying to keep Jeremy out of trouble, and we need to rely on her computer skills, she might go along with it."

The afternoon sun was sinking into the horizon as they finalized their plans. Dusty, hopefully with Kellie's help, would access the files. He would prospect the Arizona claims once he had their locations pinned down. Fred would do the same in Mexico in conjunction with some of his friends south of the border; although he was confident he was on the right ground when he was there before. Dusty would enlist Arturo's help in identifying the Mexican principals, and they would ask Kellie to get her father to background the investors and shareholders. They had a nightcap to celebrate finally resolving a course of action.

Dusty stayed overnight with Fred and Lucinda and left the next morning for Sun City.

25

The police report was brief and only occupied a small corner of the back page of the Republic. An Arizona State officer had discovered an abandoned truck, registered to a Lonnie Trame of Sun City, hidden behind a souvenir shop in Quartzite. In his report, Officer Terrant described finding two neatly packaged boxes of dog excrement in the back, and gobs of the same material smeared all over the cab.

"That truck would probably still be hidden if it wasn't for the smell. We presently have no idea exactly how long it was parked there, as most of the local vendors had closed up shop for the holidays. Mr. Trame's whereabouts are not known, however Mrs. Trame has advised the police her husband left home on Christmas Eve. A missing person report has been filed. I guess that's the kind of Christmas gift you give to people you don't like."

Mildred had missed the article when she skimmed through the morning paper, but a call from Paul Carolli, who pointed it out to her, caused her to dig the paper out of the trash. Carolli was frantic.

"Where is Lonnie? Did he tell you where he was going or when he was coming back?"

"No, and no. I don't think he's coming back. He took most of his clothes and cleaned out his bank accounts. Does that sound to you like a man that's planning to return home?"

"I need to talk to him. If you hear from him, tell him to call me immediately. It's urgent."

"What's the big deal, Paul? Why the panic?"

"I can't talk about it," he replied, and hung up.

Paul Carolli was way beyond worried. The Arab had called and driven his blood pressure off the scale. The Arab was angry, and Paul knew they would take it out on him if he didn't produce Lonnie. His fear of this man had no bounds. He had observed what he was capable of. What made it worse was that he had no idea where to start looking for Lonnie. Mildred was his last hope. To cap it all, he would have to make the deliveries unless he could find someone else to take Lonnie's place. After two blood pressure pills, some acid reducers, and fifteen minutes of deep breathing, he relaxed and started to think rationally. Who could he find that was crooked or stupid enough to take on the job. Lonnie had been a poor choice, but he had been the only one suitable. Unfortunately, he developed into too much of a loose cannon. Norman could have been trained, but he was deemed totally unreliable. Anyway, now he was dead. The only candidate he could think of was Mildred. The woman made him uneasy, but maybe, with Lonnie gone, she was desperate enough for money to take it on.

Lonnie smiled to himself as he sat in his motel

room looking out over the Sacramento River. He was pleased that his employers had found the truck before the police. He had turned their tracking bug back on when he arrived in Quartzite, and it apparently worked. He would have loved to have seen the look on their faces when they opened his packages. However, he was certain they got the message. The article in the Republic said it all as far as he was concerned. He could see their anger as they spread all that dog crap in his truck. The whole thing had gone like clockwork. After he deposited his packages in the warehouse, he drove to Quartzite with the remaining parcels, parked his truck out of sight and caught a series of buses taking him to Sacramento. He figured it was safer than staying in LA or going to Vegas. He had paid for everything in cash. Now his only problem was to get rid of the cocaine. He had enough money of his own to live on for quite a while without taking any chances, but he couldn't bring himself to dump half a million dollars worth of dope into the ocean.

After four days and nights in his room, leaving only for meals, he was beginning to get cabin fever. It was time to get out and have some fun or at least do a bit of exploring. He had rented a storage locker for most of his money and the dope, so that was not a problem, but getting around was a concern. He would have liked to buy a car, but that would have left a paper trail, which was not an option at this stage. There were too many people out there just itching to know where he was hiding.

On the afternoon of the fifth day, he finally ventured out with the idea of going for a walk. He strolled down Garden Highway watching boats go up and down the river. It was a cool but calm afternoon, and even at a leisurely pace, his wandering took him over a mile from the motel. A sign showing a scantily-clad lady advertising the Crawdad's River Cantina caught Lonnie's eye. All of a sudden the walk had made him thirsty for a long, cool beer. He walked the gangplank to the floating patio, which overlooked the river. There were many empty tables prompting Lonnie to take one in the corner with a wide view of the surroundings scenery. He settled in and waited for the waitress to come over for his drink order.

As the sun moved lower, the patio started to fill. A country-band had assembled and was tuning their instruments as half a dozen young people took the table next to his and started to chatter to each other. It was soon obvious that they were local college kids kicking back after classes. Lonnie was about to move to a quieter section away from the noise of the band and the chatterers when he noticed one of the girls sitting off by herself with an open book in her lap paying little attention to her companions. She was beautiful. Although she was dressed in a bulky sweatshirt and loose-fitting jeans, Lonnie could tell she had a little girl's body, similar to Mildred's, but accented with curves in all the right places. Her auburn hair fell about her shoulders and often over her face as she moved her head. She was continually brushing it back. Lonnie was fascinated by her and didn't realize he was staring until she looked up. A wisp of a smile flitted across her face, causing Lonnie to look away quickly. When he chanced to look back, she was staring at him with a puzzled look. The talk at the table was getting louder with excitement about a party set to start as soon as they left the Cantina. After an hour, the group got tired of the band grinding away and got up to leave. They encouraged the girl to join them, but she appeared determined to stay with her book and declined. She put her feet up on an empty chair and proceeded to underline passages and make notes as she continued to read. Lonnie found he was definitely interested in her and longed to make contact. This had never been a problem for him before tonight. It was a strange feeling to be deserted by his nerve, as he began to list in his mind all the reasons this young lady would reject his advances. After all, he was old enough to be her father. He had no problem handling rejection. In the past he had either reacted with anger, mouthing some sort of cutting remark, or with apathy by just walking away. Why was it bothering him now? Why couldn't he just get up, walk over, introduce himself and see what happened? He knew in his heart he wasn't going to do it. It didn't make sense; she was just another female. Accepting the futility of the whole idea, Lonnie finished his drink and was about to leave when he noticed the girl's glass was almost empty. On a whim, he called the waitress over and ordered a refill.

"Would you get another round for the young lady at the next table and put it on my bill?"

When it was placed before her, she looked up and said to the girl, "This must be for someone else. I didn't order it."

The waitress nodded at Lonnie. "This gentleman ordered it for you."

She looked at Lonnie for a moment then closed her books. She put them in her pack, picked up the drink and walked toward Lonnie's table.

He couldn't tell if she was going to thank him or throw it in his face.

"I thought I should come over and thank you

and enjoy the drink in your company."

She pulled out the chair across from him, sat down, set her drink on the table and extended her hand.

"Hi. My name's Cara."

"I'm Lonnie, Lonnie Trame. It's a real pleasure to meet you, Cara."

"I noticed you were looking at me, and I didn't know whether to be freaked out or flattered. You did look kind of lonely sitting here by yourself."

"I trust you're not freaked out, as you say, or you probably wouldn't be sitting here, and you're right, I was feeling a bit lonely. Thank you for your concern."

Lonnie was picking his words slowly, trying desperately to win this young lady's confidence. As the evening progressed the effort became easier, and he began to feel more relaxed with her. He sensed she was becoming more receptive to his attention, and it bolstered his ego to think that at his age he still was able to turn the charm on when he needed it.

The remainder of the evening was spent by each of them telling lies and made-up stories about themselves. By closing time Lonnie was completely smitten with this young, nubile college girl, and Cara was suitably impressed by the potential in this retired mining executive. Lonnie walked her to her car, and they made plans to meet again the following evening.

26

Dusty called Kellie on his way back to Sun
City. He had expected Jeremy to answer but was
relieved when she picked up the phone. All the way
back from Fred's he had thought about what they
planned to do, and he really didn't feel good about
going behind his best friend's back. He rationalized
it as being for Jeremy's benefit, but that didn't seem
to lessen the guilt. After all, he thought, you can
justify anything you do if you try hard enough.

"Dusty, where have you been? Did you forget
you were supposed to play tennis with Anna
yesterday? She was kind of hurt that you stood her
up. Jeremy filled in for you."

"I did forget. I'm sorry. I'll call and try and
make it up to her. The last thing I want to do is hurt
her feelings."

"Wow, that's a switch. Are you starting to
mellow in your old age? She is starting to get under
your skin, isn't she?"

"I guess so, and go easy on that 'old' stuff. You

aren't that much younger."

"Thanks. At least I don't have to worry about you mooning over me."

"Okay, if that's the way you feel, I'll take the ring back and scrap my proposal to you. Is Jeremy home now?"

"Yes. He's getting packed to fly up to Amyot again. Dad phoned last night and ordered him to go up there and settle an environmental problem at the mine. The natives claim that drainage from the mine is poisoning their fish. It's a bogus claim. We've got all kinds of filters and monitors working, and the drainage is damned up so it doesn't get into the creek, but the ones in the band that don't work there are looking for all kinds of ways to cause trouble. Jeremy is flying up to Saskatoon tonight and into the mine tomorrow."

"Tell him to find out if that bunch of environmentalists that used to haunt the area has come back. They can stir the locals up pretty fast and could be the cause of your trouble."

"Dad says the mine manager identified a bunch of them from Ottawa."

"Anyway, we need to talk. I spent yesterday with Fred and Lucinda. He is very concerned about this Mexari setup and Jeremy's involvement in it. He wants to get to the bottom of it."

"I know. They got into it before Fred left. In fact, I think that is why he went. Jeremy won't open up to anyone about it. Dad and I have both tried to find out, but he continues to stonewall us."

"Fred and I have decided to take more direct action. If things go like they have in the past with Jeremy, disaster will have struck before we hear anything about it. I need to talk to you about what we plan to do."

"Okay. I get it. I have to drive Jeremy to the airport, but I should be back about ten."

"Good. I'll see you then. Just don't bring the subject up with him yet."

It was closer to eleven when Kellie knocked on the caseta door.

"What's the deal? You sounded all mysterious over the phone."

They moved out on the patio where it wasn't quite so stuffy, and Dusty could be reasonably sure their conversation wasn't being monitored.

"Fred thinks that Jeremy may be into something way over his head this time, and I agree."

"Dad has the same feeling. He thinks Jeremy is trying to prove something and that it is not going well, and he doesn't want to admit it. I've tried questioning him, but he gets so defensive I stopped."

'Fred and I have decided to go behind his back to sort it out. I don't feel good about it, but I think it's what we have to do, and we need your help."

"What do you want me to do?"

"We need to access the Mexari records. We need descriptions of the mining properties, maps, and any reports on them. In addition, we want a list of the directors, officers, and shareholders of the Company."

"That's a pretty tall order," she observed. "I'm not really sure where you'll find it. I've looked around the house for anything to tell me what's going on, but he has no files in his desk, and there's nothing on the computer. He's got a Company office downtown. I think he keeps all that stuff there."

"So, how do we get into his office?"

"Dusty, you're not thinking of breaking in, are you? That's over the top even for you, but I guess when you and Fred get together anything is possible. I suppose you want me to go along with this?"

"That sort of spells it out. Have you got any better ideas?"

She thought for a moment, and then that gleam came into her eye. The old Kellie, who would try anything, was back.

"Sure. What the hell. Let's do it. Things have been going downhill between us ever since he got into this. We have no life together, and he doesn't even want to spend time with me anymore. Maybe, if we do this, it will fix our marriage, or destroy it completely. I can't stay with him if it doesn't get better."

She started to cry. Dusty put his arm around her, and she leaned into his shoulder as the sobs wracked her body. It was a strange feeling for him to see this beautiful, tough woman, whom he had known for so many years, experiencing such sadness. He sat there quietly while she let it all out.

Finally she said, "Jeremy keeps a set of keys here in his desk drawer plus the card to get him into the building. I've only been there once, when he first rented the place. It's a tall building on North Central. We went there after hours, and he had to use the card to open the front door, but I would guess those doors are unlocked during the day. There's a sign-in desk at the front with a security guard."

"That shouldn't be any problem. You sign in as his wife. If they ask any questions, you show your ID and the keys. Jeremy won't check the log unless he suspects something. Do you have a digital camera? I don't want to have to photocopy all that stuff if he doesn't have it on computer. I was hoping I could just burn it into a couple of flash drives."

They decided to go for it the next afternoon. When they got to the building, they were able to bypass the security desk by being lost in a large bunch of people returning from lunch. Dusty and Kelly walked in along the edge of the group away from the desk. The mass of workers were all wearing their identity badges, but the guard appeared to be paying little attention to them. The building register showed Mexari Resources on the fourteenth floor with an insurance company, an import group, and a couple of stock brokers. Jeremy's office was between Darnell & Co. Insurance and East Arizona Imports. They squeezed into the crowded elevator and were whisked to their destination. Kellie fumbled with the keys until she found the right one, and opened the door into a small, sparse, neatly arranged office, which didn't appear to get a lot of use. There was a simple wooden desk with a matching chair, a three-drawer metal filing cabinet, and a small table, which held the computer and a printer.

"Jeez, is this ever dreary. He doesn't even have a picture of me on his desk."

"You can redecorate it later. Right now we need to find those documents, maps, and get out of here."

The filing cabinet wasn't locked, and it was obvious why, there was nothing in it.

Kellie fired up the computer and was immediately stopped by the need for a password. She looked at Dusty questioningly: He just shook his head.

"Have you got any ideas?"

"I was going to ask you the same thing," he replied.

For the next hour they tried every possible word or word and number combination that they thought Jeremy would use. Then Kellie had an inspiration.

"He is always talking about how he wished he could move back to Calgary and return to his old teaching job at SAIT. Let's try that."

It worked, and they were immediately launched into the mysterious world of Mexari. Kellie punched a few more keys and the whole Directory of Files appeared. They were in luck. All the files they wanted were on the hard drive in separate folders. Dusty plugged in his 8GB flash drive and copied everything. Since he had brought two drives, he made an extra copy. They didn't take time to look at any of the material but packed everything up quickly, made sure that they hadn't left any evidence of being there, and got out.

"I don't know how much trouble you just got me into if he finds out I broke in there."

"Just tell him I beat you up and forced you to do it."

"Right, and he's going to believe that."

"Don't worry about it, Kellie, I'll take the blame. He doesn't have to know you were here."

Back at the caseta Dusty transferred everything over to his laptop. He hooked his machine up with Kellie's printer and made some copies; a list of shareholders for Kellie's father, names and addresses of all the directors and contractors in Mexico for Arturo, maps and reports covering the Mexican properties for Fred, and all the stuff on the Arizona claims that he was going to check out. A cursory look at all these documents as they were printing gave him the uneasy feeling that their suspicions might be justified. Dusty phoned Fred, who agreed to meet him in Tucson the next afternoon.

The next morning as Dusty was getting ready to leave for Tucson, his phone rang. The caller identified himself as John Hebrano.

"Lucie Hansen, from up in Canada called me and asked me to look after you. She explained as much as she knew about your situation and kind of got my interest. That lady is real concerned about you. I'm free just about any time if you want to get together."

"What are you doing this afternoon?"

"No plans. Why?"

"I'm driving to Tucson to meet an old friend who is helping me sort out this mess. I can bring you up to speed on the ride down there. Besides, I think you might enjoy meeting Fred."

Dusty picked John up in Scottsdale and told him the whole story.

When he finished, John said, " Lucie Hansen was right. You do have yourself in a mess. I think the most important immediate task is to locate that little girl. From what you are telling me, it would make sense that they would keep her alive as a gambling chip in case things start getting too hot for them. I would like to concentrate my efforts on that while you are sorting out your friend's company situation. I wouldn't hold out much hope for the local police finding the little girl after this length of time."

As he pulled into the parking lot at Biosphere Two, where he was to meet Fred, Lucinda was leaning against the driver's side, while the old man was napping in the cab.

"I've seen more signs of life in him since you came around than I've seen in a month," she said.

Dusty introduced John to her and to Fred after she woke him up. He encouraged John to tell them a bit about his background on the Sun City force.

"So, you know Lucie. The dumbest thing this boy ever did, and he has done some dandies, is not hooking up permanent with that gal. Although, I figure she's just too smart to get tied down with him."

In desperation, Dusty steered the conversation to the problem at hand. He felt a lot more confident with John Hebrano on his side.

27

Mildred was at home still trying to figure out how she could get a chunk of her money from the bank without alerting the police to her other identity. Funds were getting low and the bills kept coming in. She thought about making a cheque out to Guillermo, but he had convinced her it could still be traced back to her through Louisa. She had considered using Jerome but immediately saw the risk in that action. As she pondered her possible solutions, Paul Carolli rang the doorbell. When she let him in, she was surprised to see his agitated state and how much he had aged since she had last seen him. He was a walking ghost of his former self.

He started right in as soon as she opened the door.

"Mildred, I have a proposition for you that can make you a lot of money. It's your chance of a lifetime. Since Lonnie disappeared, I need someone to take over the work he was doing for us. You know yourself he made a lot of money. There is a certain amount of risk and danger involved, but it's easy work, and the payoffs make it worthwhile."

"Slow down! Slow down! Come on in and sit and we'll talk. I always wondered how Lonnie got his money. I asked him over and over, but he would never tell me anything. He said that as far as I was concerned, the gold came from his gold mine, but I never really believed it."

"He was paid well for the small amount of work he had to do. I don't know why he would leave such a good deal."

"What about his gold mine?"

"There was no gold mine. He was told to use it as a cover story."

"So, now you want me to have a phony gold mine and do something illegal to get paid a bunch of money. What would I have to do?"

"I can't really explain it all unless you commit to take it on."

"You have to be kidding. Why the hell would I agree to something if I don't know what it is? You must think I'm as stupid as him."

Paul thought for a minute then said, "No, I don't think you are stupid. If I did, I wouldn't be making this offer. I can tell you this much. It involves picking up some packages at a prearranged spot and delivering them to another location."

"That's it, doing delivery work? Why don't you just hire UPS? What's in the packages that makes this such a big deal, dope, guns, hot money?"

"You don't need to know. Your only concern is the where and when of the pick-ups and drops."

"What kind of bucks are we talking about?"

"Probably about five thousand for each delivery."

"So, five grand for a night's work and possibly

thirty years in the slammer. Maybe it's not such a good deal, but okay, I'll do it on one condition. I will write you a cheque for a large amount of money under another name. The cheque is totally legal, and the funds are in the bank to cover it. You are to cash this cheque at your bank and give me the money. These are my conditions, and they are not negotiable. The same secrecy goes for my deal as for yours. You don't have to know anything more about it, so don't ask. I am going to write you a cheque for a hundred thousand dollars. You bring me the money before you want me to go to work, and I will take on your next delivery."

Paul certainly didn't like it and was tempted to cancel out, but he was desperate. At least it solved his immediate problem and got him off the hook of playing delivery boy. He took the cheque down to the Wells Fargo branch, where he was known and had his account and collected the cash, which he delivered to Mildred the evening of the same day.

After she had carefully counted the bills to be sure he hadn't skimmed her, she said, "Explain to me what I have to do."

Paul outlined the next evening's pick-up, which was to take place in a field just north of Sun City. The drop point was a mailbox in the Sun City Post Office. The key for the box would be with the packages. After passing on all kinds of warnings about being late or talking to anyone, Paul returned home. The potential for screw-ups was still there, and he really didn't feel that good about dealing with Mildred. "Who the hell is Juanita Rojas?" He wondered.

There were three phone calls recorded on the answering machine when he got home. There were no messages. The call display was blocked, but Paul had no doubt in his mind as to who it was.

Mildred had been entertaining Dan Seaborne most of the evening. He had finally taken her up on her offer and hadn't been disappointed. At midnight she crawled out of bed, pulled on her old jeans and gardening shirt, and headed out on Grand Avenue. She left Dan with a smile on his face. Traffic was light and by one-thirty she was at the pick-up spot ten miles southeast of Wickenberg. She pulled into a dry river bed at the end of a rough gravel road, settled back and waited. Paul had told her that the plane would come in low, drop the packages attached to small parachutes and take off. Consequently, she was surprised when the small aircraft landed on the road behind her. No one got out. She turned the car around, drove up beside the cockpit and walked over to the pilot's door. The door opened wide enough for six packages to be handed out.

"What are you doing here?" Mildred asked. "I was told you were going to drop the stuff."

Her question was met with silence. She backed away from the aircraft as the pilot revved the motor and turned around to take off. She had been instructed to take the parcels immediately to the drop point, but curiosity had won out. She needed to know what they contained. She drove home, took one parcel into the garage and opened it. Tentatively, she tasted the white powder. She was not a user and had no idea what cocaine tasted like, but she had seen them do this on TV. The bitter taste and the numbing effect on her mouth were immediate. The whole mystery of Lonnie's financial success was now clear. He was running dope for Corolli and whomever he was hooked up with. Mildred smiled. "Now I can use him to get all my money out of those accounts."

She put the package back together, grabbed the key that was taped to one of the parcels and took the whole lot to the drop point.

28

John Hebrano had no love for the town administrators who had screwed up his pension and robbed him of the retirement he had so carefully planned. He did, however, have a number of friends still working on the Force, some of whom owed him favors. He made a few calls and in a roundabout way got an update on the investigation of Maria's abduction, which had come up empty so far but was ongoing. It was more or less what he had expected. He did get clearance for Dusty to look at some mug shots of local hoodlums on the chance that he could identify his attackers. They got one hit, a Carlos Atriba. Carlos had numerous charges of assault and a few convictions in cases where the victims had enough courage to testify. A profile study of Carlos suggested his mental capabilities fell far short of taking on a planning or supervising role.

"According to his sheet, the guy's a thug. You want some muscle and meanness for a job, you call Carlos," John observed. "If we can track him down and lean on him, maybe he can lead us to Maria."

John's friend dug out the rest of the file on Carlos, and John and Dusty spent an hour making notes on all the aliases, addresses, companions, and places he normally frequented. It was an extensive list.

"This one is interesting," Dusty observed. "He has been picked up for domestic violence three times in the last five years. The lady involved is a Miss Loretta Squan in each case, and the addresses in El Mirage are identical. I think we should pay Miss Squan a visit."

"Well, that's better than anything I've got. Let's find her and see if she can point us to Carlos."

The address in El Mirage was a squalid little frame house clothed in yellow stucco that had weathered to a rainbow of colors. There were large chunks, which had broken off and were lying in the weeds. A scrawny dog was chained to the clothesline, which ran across the yard. The mongrel was determined they were not going to enter its domain. It barked incessantly and bared its teeth as they approached. They managed to creep along the fence just out of its reach and knock on the back door. A squat, chubby woman of indeterminate racial heritage and age answered. She was packing a diapered baby under one fleshy arm with two other infants hiding behind her.

"Whadda you want?"

"We are looking for a friend of yours, Carlos Atriba. Can you tell us where we may find him? It is important that we talk to him."

"I haven't seen that sonabitch for long time. I don't ever want him comin round again."

"Do you know any of his friends or where he might hang out?"

"No!"

Without another word, she slammed the door and left them standing on the small porch.

"What do you think?" Dusty asked.

"She's lying. Somebody has to be paying the rent on this dump, and I'm willing to bet it's not her. I'll go with you and get my car. Since I've got nothing better to do for the rest of the day, I think I'll come back and hang around down the street and see who shows up."

That evening John phoned just as Dusty was finishing his workout at the Rec. Center.

"Carlos appeared about ten minutes ago and went into the house. I'm going to keep on him and see if he goes anywhere tonight. Keep your phone on."

Half an hour later another call came through. "Dusty, he took off about fifteen minutes ago heading in the direction of Sun City. He was moving fast, and unfortunately I lost him in traffic. I'll keep looking for his car and call you if I get anything."

Dusty was getting into his truck when his phone rang again. Expecting an update from John, he was surprised to hear Kellie's voice. He could sense her anxiety as she gave him the message, "Dusty, something is going on outside. The motion sensor light came on and I thought it was you, but when I went to the window there was no sign of your truck. Where are you? I can't tell for sure, but it looks like someone is moving around in the caseta."

"It's not me. I'm still over at the Center. I think my bait is working, and I've got some bad company. Lock your doors and windows and turn off the sensors. I will be there in a few minutes and

John Hebrano is not far. Keep an eye on the yard in case he leaves and keep your phone on."

When Dusty got in the truck he phoned John and described the situation.

"I think I know where our friend Carlos was heading. Meet me at the caseta, but park down the street. This could be our chance to get him and make him talk."

Dusty stopped his truck around the corner and walked quickly and quietly. The property was in darkness. No light was visible from either the house or the caseta. He crept into the patio and attempted to peer into his room, but the curtains had been pulled shut since he had left. He picked up a couple of pebbles, stood by the door, and tossed them lightly against the window. He heard movement inside. The door started to open out and a leg appeared. At that moment Dusty charged the door and put his shoulder into it, catching the man in mid-stride as he attempted to get out. The man yelled with pain as he stumbled out through the doorway. As he fell forward, Dusty kicked him hard in the groin and delivered a knee to his chin. The man went down. It was Carlos, and he was doubled over in pain.

John came running down the street, and Kellie emerged from the house at the same instant. Carlos started to come around and tried to get up until Dusty kicked him in the jaw. His head snapped back and he was still.

"Go easy," John said. "Don't kill him; we still have to get him to talk."

"I know. I'm cool. That was payback. The anger kind of boiled up for the moment. We need some rope and duct tape to keep this guy under control for a while. We have to get him to tell us where they took Maria, and I don't care what we have to do to make him talk. Do either of you have a gun?"

"I left mine back at home," John replied. "I didn't expect this kind of action when I left this morning."

"I don't have a regular gun," Kellie said, "but I have this stun gun Jeremy bought for me a couple of years ago when there were reports of prowlers in the neighborhood. I figured it was kind of useless because you had to be close enough to the person to touch them with it, and I really didn't want to get that close. However, it's supposed to be very painful but won't kill."

Kellie went into the garage and returned with tape and a coil of rope, and the stun gun. Dusty and John proceeded to secure their prisoner.

"That should do it. Let's prop him up, bring him around and see what he has to say."

They dragged the big man over to the caseta wall and sat him up as he started to regain consciousness.

Dusty got down facing Carlos up close, face to face.

"You remember me, don't you Carlos? We had a little meeting on the street in El Mirage. I owe you for a lot of pain, and it's only because these people are here that I don't continue to pay you back right now, but I will if you don't tell me what I want to know."

Carlos spit in his face, and Dusty hit him hard along the side of his head. Carlos' head banged against the wall. He looked at Dusty with pure hatred in his eyes.

"I'm glad you did that," Dusty said. "It makes what I'm going to do to you a lot easier. I am really going to enjoy this."

He paused then asked, "Where is the little girl? Where is she hidden?"

When he received no answer, he slowly raised the stun gun and put it against Carlos' taped arm. They could see the fear come into his eyes. The two-second shot to his arm brought a scream of pain from the big man. He squirmed around, trying to get free.

"I think I'd better do this," John said. "You're a bit too emotionally involved and concerned with payback to do this right."

Dusty agreed and handed the weapon to him.

John turned his attention to Carlos, who was fully conscious and continuing his struggle to get free.

"You may think because I have the gun that it will go easier on you. I suggest you think again. I have a lot of experience with this type of weapon and have learned where to aim to cause the most pain. My friend shot you in the arm, and sure that hurt, but imagine getting hit in the crotch or the ear. My favorite is to hold the weapon up to your eye and fire. I've heard it is extremely painful and might even cause you to go blind. I've often wondered how much damage it can do short of killing a man. You're a big fellow. You should be able to handle it. I'm going to experiment and see how much pain you can stand."

By now he had Carlos' full attention and his sneer was quickly being replaced by fear.

"No!" he cried as John put the weapon up to his knee and fired. His scream of pain filled the air.

"Where is the girl?"

His face was now a mask of terror, but he said nothing and tried to back away as John brought the weapon to his genitals.

"One more chance to tell us where you have taken the girl."

Carlos continued to shake as drool started to form at the corners of his mouth.

"Do it," Dusty urged.

"Let's wait a minute. Dummy here is thinking it over."

A couple of minutes passed and the big man started to calm down until John brought the gun back to the spot between his legs.

"I can't tell you," he screamed. "He'll kill me."

"Who will kill you?"

"The Arab."

"Well, we will make so much hurt for you that you will wish you were dead if you don't tell us where she is."

"Who is the Arab?" Dusty asked.

"I don't know. He only calls us when he wants a job done. We've never seen him, but he has made it clear what happens to anyone who crosses him. He will kill me."

The blood-curdling scream produced by the next shot caused lights to come on in nearby houses, however, no one showed the courage to come out and see what was going on.

"Let's get this over with," Kellie urged. "I'd rather not get into a hassle with the neighbors over the noise. Someone is going to be calling the cops."

John put the stun gun up against Carlos' left eye, and the big man broke. They could barely hear him as he mumbled the address. It was so low John made him repeat it. Kellie wrote it down and handed it to Dusty.

"I am going to call the Surprise police to come and pick him up," John announced. "I'll tell them what it's all about, but they don't need to know this address he gave us just yet. Kellie, would you stay and keep an eye on him until they get here. Tell them what happened and give them the address then. Dusty and I will go there now. I'm afraid if their buddy doesn't return right away they will get spooked and move the girl. You keep the stun on him, and don't hesitate to fire if he tries anything."

"I can do that, but you two are crazy to go there without guns," she replied.

"We don't have time. We have to hope there isn't too many, and we can take them by surprise. They won't expect their buddy to talk. It's probably the only hope we have of getting her out of there safely. That is, assuming this bozo gave us the right address, which I think he was scared enough to do."

They took John' car and headed for the place in El Mirage. It was only a couple of blocks from Carlos' home.

"Will the stun gun really cause someone to go blind or kill them?" Dusty asked.

"I have no idea," John replied, "but I figured I might be able to bluff him into telling us what we wanted to know."

29

Cara Duchene was thirty-two. She looked eighteen. At five foot two with a blonde ponytail and classic features: and well-formed breasts, legs and rear end, she could stop the conversation in any room she entered. Her beauty had been her ticket to survival and sometimes prosperity. She had always used men to ease her passage through life.

She had spent the last two years enrolled in the Nursing Program at the University of Washington, supported in a lavish style by a Microsoft executive. He provided an upscale apartment and a credit card with a generous limit until his wife caught on. Cara was barely able to max out the card before it was canceled.

After a summer of spending lavishly and living in resorts along the Coast, she had applied to Sacramento College and was accepted. Now the money was running out and she was actively looking for a new sugar daddy.

She had decided to go to Crawdad's with her

classmates on a whim. She had very little in
common with these kids, but nothing else was
happening that evening. She knew she had to be out
there if she was going to hook up with anybody.
She hadn't noticed this little man sitting in the
corner when she first arrived; however, she soon
became aware of his eyes almost continually on her.
She could see he was interested, and although he
certainly wasn't attractive, she thought he might be
worth a short-term fling, especially if he had a few
bucks to spend. When he bought her a drink, she
decided to make her move.

"Hi. I'm Cara," she announced as she sat down
at his table.

He stood, and in a very gentlemanly manner
shook her hand and introduced himself.

.

Lonnie spent the next day shopping for clothes
he felt would impress her when they met again that
evening. He had put together a background story on
how he was a retired mining executive who had
made his fortune buying and selling gold properties.
He practiced his spiel to make sure he didn't get
tripped up if she started asking questions. Cara, in
the meantime, focused on how she would go about
convincing this man to look after her for the
remainder of the school year.

She invited him to a party Saturday evening at
a classmate's house. Saturday morning Lonnie took
a taxi to his storage locker and pulled out a wad of
cash and some powder. He had never used the stuff,
but he suspected she might have tried it and hoped it
would speed up his trip into her bed. The party was
a success and a disappointment. Although at least
twenty years older than the kids at the party, his
endless supply of cocaine made him the most

popular. Unfortunately, Cara was not a user.

As she drove him back to his motel she remarked, "I've got a bit of a problem. My roommate has moved out of our apartment, and I am stuck with all the rent. I was hoping to hang on until I finish the term, but it looks like I'll be out at the end of the month as I can't afford it by myself." She had tossed out the bait and waited to see if he would take it.

Lonnie thought for a while then said as they pulled up in front of the motel, "Maybe I can help. I wasn't planning on staying in Sacramento, but since I met you I'd like to remain for a while, so we can get to know each other better. Perhaps you could take me in as your new roommate. I can pay the rent, and there are no strings attached. Think it over and let me know."

"I don't have to think it over," she said as she moved closer. "I'd love to have you move in." She put her arms around him and kissed him hard on the mouth.

They moved his meager belongings in her car over from the motel to her apartment the next day. Lonnie slept in the spare bedroom for a week then moved into Cara's bed and they became lovers.

To Cara, it was an opportunity and a challenge to find out more about this man whom she had allowed to move into her life. Her key to survival was a sixth sense she had developed over the years in evaluating potential lovers. She seldom became emotionally involved, which in this case was not a problem. It was a game, a game that she seldom lost.

One evening after a dinner which, which she had prepared and medicated, she stayed alert until Lonnie was sound asleep. A thorough search through his clothes and suitcases answered a lot of her questions. She had never believed the line he had given her, and now she was able to piece together a truer picture. Slipped into the lining of one of the cases, she found: his driver's license, ID card, VISA card, and a key, all wrapped in a plastic bundle. He was from Sun City, Arizona and had a wife named Mildred. The ID was complete with home address and phone number. She had no idea what this numbered key unlocked, but she had the feeling it was important and was determined to make a copy of it when the chance arose. She was surprised to find very little money or dope in his belongings.

They lived in harmony as Cara continued to pry useful information from him. She eventually came to a conclusion that he must have been a cocaine dealer in Arizona. This worried her that he may be on the run from the police, placing her in danger if he got picked up. She decided time was of the essence. She focused her efforts on finding his money and getting far away from him.

Two weeks later, when his cash started to run low, Lonnie borrowed her car and made a run to the storage locker. When he returned with the back seat loaded with groceries and an expensive necklace for her, Cara had a pretty good idea where he had been and the purpose of the key. Since she had set the trip odometer on her car to zero, when he had asked to use it, she could tell that his hiding place was close. Her plan was now clear, She had to get the key long enough to make a copy and then follow him the next time he made a run, and she had to make this happen as soon as possible.

Lonnie was totally unaware of the devious nature of his beautiful young lover. He was completely under her spell. Never in his life had he felt this way about a woman. Mildred hadn't even come close. The day that Cara asked to borrow a substantial sum of money, he agreed without question and planned another visit to the locker. When he asked again to borrow her car, she knew she had to act quickly. That afternoon she prepared a special meal with an expensive wine she had again doctored to put him out of commission for a while. When she was sure he had passed out, she dug into his hiding spot and retrieved the key. A quick trip to the hardware produced a duplicate, and she was able to return the original within the hour. Next she called one of her classmates and offered to pay him to drive over, park near her apartment, and wait until she came out. When Lonnie awoke he was a bit surprised he had fallen asleep, but shrugged it off as a result of too much wine. When she reminded him that he had promised to lend her the money, he dug out his key and prepared to go to the locker.

Cara waited until Lonnie pulled away from the curb then ran down to her friend's car and directed him to follow. The trip was short, taking them to a recently constructed storage facility about half a mile away. They watched as Lonnie punched in a code to open the gate then drive down to the end of a row of small lockers. Cara recorded the gate code and drew a quick picture of the locker location on the back of an envelope. She was tempted to wait for Lonnie to leave then go in and clean it out, but she was reticent to let her friend in on what she was doing. He drove her quick.ly back home, arriving just before Lonnie returned.

Now she had all the pieces to the puzzle and was anxious to put the final stages of her plan into effect. In order to allay any immediate suspicions in Lonnie's mind about her absence, she told him she had to visit her mother in Seattle for a few days. Her final step before she left was to phone the number in Sun City that was listed on his ID for his next of kin. Mildred answered the call.

"Mrs. Trame, you don't know me, but I am a friend of your husband, Lonnie. I don't know if you have had contact with him, but I thought you should know he is living in Sacramento."

"Who are you? How do you know this?" Mildred asked.

Cara chose her words carefully, sketching over her relationship with Lonnie. However, she did provide Mildred with his address.

"That should heat things up," she thought as she headed for the storage locker.

Lonnie didn't suspect anything was wrong until the middle of the following week, by which time Cara hadn't called as she had promised. By Friday he became real concerned and the seeds of suspicion were beginning to germinate. He was getting low on funds and decided to take a trip to the locker. The shock of her deception and losing everything he owned was too much to bear. He walked back to the apartment in a daze too overwhelmed to notice the door was slightly ajar. Three men were seated in the living room. Two of the men were dressed in rough work clothes. The third man, whom Lonnie recognized, was immaculate in an expensive made-to-measure suit. Lonnie stopped short at the doorway, turned, and started to run, when the well-dressed man stood up and pointed a gun at him.

"Stay where you are," the man said. "You have made a very serious mistake. We need to have a little talk."

"What are you doing here?" Lonnie asked the one man he recognized.

"We'll ask the questions and for your own sake, you had better come up with the right answers."

He motioned to the other two men, who got up, grabbed Lonnie and tied him to a chair.

The first man continued, "We were not impressed with the presents you left for us. Where are our packages?"

Lonnie was confused. Until the moment, he hadn't connected this man with the deliveries, but as he thought about it, the whole thing started to make sense. He knew Paul wasn't running the show, but until now he had no idea who was calling the shots. This had to be the man Paul called 'The Arab', although there was no trace of any accent. When he didn't answer immediately, one of the other men hit him hard across the side of the head. The pain telescoped down his body, and he slumped forward in the chair.

"My friend here enjoys causing pain, so if you want to make him sad, just tell us what we want to know."

Lonnie's problem was he didn't know where the cocaine had gone; he just knew who had taken it

Two more blows to the head loosened his tongue.

"I don't know where it is. This woman I was with stole it all and took off. I don't know where she went. She said she was going to Seattle to visit her mother, but I don't know if she was lying."

"Well Lonnie it looks like you are going with us to Seattle to find her.

30

John Hebrano parked his car down the street
from the address they had dragged out of Carlos
Atriba. They each grabbed a heavy wrench from the
trunk. The street was well-lit by a string of lights on
both sides. Their target was a modest, well-kept
bungalow in a cluster of similar houses. Each was
enclosed with a fenced yard. They walked
cautiously to the house next door and quietly
entered the yard to observe. Their target was a
single story building, but windows at ground level
suggested a basement room or two. Lights were on
at the ground floor, but curtains and blinds covered
any chance to look inside from the front. There was,
however, a small sliver of light escaping from a side
window. Dusty crossed through a hedge and crept
down the side of the building to peer through the
small opening.

"I can't see much," he whispered. "There's a
large woman sitting on the sofa looking toward the
front of the room, probably at the TV. She looks

Hispanic. There's no way to tell if anyone else is with her. We're going to feel pretty stupid if Carlos gave us a phony address and we go busting in there."

"I know, but we've got to do it. If it's a mistake, we'll sort it out later. Do you speak Spanish?"

"No."

"Okay. I'll take the front. You go around to the back and have the wrench ready. The only thing we've got going for us is the element of surprise. If there's anyone else there, maybe you can jump him before he comes at me."

"What are you going to do, break the door down?"

"No. We'll do this in a civilized manner. I'll ring the bell then force my way in when she comes to the door. I'll give you two minutes to get in position at the back. Get the door open any way you can, and check out those back rooms. I'll keep the lady occupied up front."

Three steps at the rear of the house led up to a small porch. Dusty moved quietly and opened the screen door. He put his ear to the wood door and listened. When he heard the doorbell, he tried to turn the doorknob, but the door was locked. He was going to have to bust it to get in.

When John rang the bell, there was a thirty-second delay while the woman hoisted herself off the sofa and lumbered over to the door. She opened it as much as the chain would allow a split second before John hit it with his shoulder.

"¿Qué quieres," she yelled as he pushed his way into the house.

"¿Dónde está la niña". The question took the woman by surprise and she backed away as John came toward her with the wrench in his hand. He grabbed her and pushed her back on the sofa. "La policía está en camino. Ellos van a querer ver sus papeles." A sudden look of terror overtook the woman as a pool of urine began to form beneath her, and she cringed back on the sofa.

John silently congratulated himself on his instinct. He had guessed right. She was an illegal that lived in fear of being sent back home.

"Allá abajo," she sobbed and pointed a meaty finger toward the basement door.

When Dusty heard the doorbell, he kicked the door hard beside the lock. It popped open immediately, and he entered the dark interior of a small kitchen. Down the hallway that joined the kitchen at the opposite wall, he could just make out John pushing the woman back into the front room. He waited an instant then heard the shout.

"¿Quién está ahi?"

The voice, followed by a man, came from a room to the right of the hall. Dusty had his weapon ready, and as soon as the man appeared, he rushed him and hit him across the back of the head with the wrench. The blow was strong enough to take the man down. He tried to crawl his way down the hall, but Dusty was on him. He recognized him as the same man who had driven the Hummer when he took the beating. He grabbed his shoulder, rolled him over and hit him with another blow across the face. Then he wrapped the man's ankles and wrists together with a roll of duct tape and dragged him into the front room.

John stood in front of the woman who continued to wail.

"She says the girl is downstairs. I'll keep an

eye on these two while you take a look."

One weak bulb hanging from a cord above the stairs was the only light casting its dim glow over the interior of the basement. At the bottom, Dusty called out for Maria. There was no answer, but he could hear a scraping sound from the corner of the room. He felt his way along the wall to a door, which opened into another small room. Maria was strapped to an old bed on a thin, threadbare mattress. Her dress was in tatters, her mouth was taped, and her tear-stained face was clear evidence of her ordeal.

Dusty gently pulled the tape away and cut through her bindings. When he picked her up, she clung to him and wouldn't let go.

"It's all right now," he said in a soft voice. "You're going home."

As he carried her upstairs, the tears flowed down her face. When they reached the top and she saw her two jailers, she wrapped her arms tightly around Dusty's neck almost choking him.

"We'd better call the police, but I need to get in touch with Rafael and Miranda before we do. I want to get her to her parents before the cops take over," Dusty said. "If I take the car and meet them halfway, can you deal with your buddies until I get back?"

"Sure," John replied. "It will be a pleasure pointing out to them how an old retired fart like me can still do a better job at finding people."

"Take it easy. We've been pushing a few boundaries tonight. Like you said to me, you're too emotionally involved."

Miranda answered the phone and was speechless when Dusty gave her the news. He told he would meet them at her mother's house in half an hour. They were all gathered on the front lawn when he drove up.

Three police cars were lined up in front of the kidnappers' house when Dusty returned. A uniformed officer stopped him at the door until he explained his part in the event. John was seated on a bench answering questions from two plain-clothed officers. The smirk on his face told Dusty things were going well. No one seemed to want to occupy the sofa. He learned the man and woman had been taken into custody and carted off to headquarters for questioning.

"They want to talk to Maria," John said. "They're real put off that you took her away. They also want to know why we didn't contact them before we came here. I don't think you should give them your answer to that last question."

Dusty turned to the two officers and said, "The little girl was in a state of shock, and I thought it would be better for her if she hooked up with her parents before you started hitting her with a bunch of questions. I told them you would be making contact, but right now they needed to get Maria to a doctor. She had a rough deal here and probably needs a bit of medical care."

The explanation of the events, and their actions seemed to satisfy the officers. John and Dusty grabbed a couple of beers out of the bandits' fridge for the trip back to Sun City.

"One thing I neglected to tell you back there. Carlos got away from Kellie. He beat her up and took off."

"How did they know to come here?"

"She managed to put in a 911 call and gave the address."

"Is she hurt badly?"

"We'll soon find out."

"So, the police don't know about Carlos. How come you didn't put them on to him?"

"I thought about it, but decided that we would probably enjoy finding him and settling the account ourselves."

31

When Mildred got the phone call from Cara
Duchene, she was surprised to learn that Lonnie
was still alive. She had written him off when Paul
had sketched out a story of how Lonnie had double-
crossed his employers, and what his fate would be if
they caught him. Mildred didn't care what happened
to her husband. Now she was concerned he might
reappear in her life and threaten to change her plans.
Although he made enough money for them to live
well, he had been a pain in the neck ever since they
met. She could understand why this woman would
want to take him down. Most people that knew
Lonnie felt that way. After the call Mildred set
about to determine how she could use the
information to her advantage. She knew that Paul
and his bosses wanted desperately to locate him,
and the police wanted to question him in connection
with Norman's death. Telling the police wasn't
going to do her any good. In fact, because of her
own money-switching activities, the less contact she

had with the cops the better. Paul, however, was another matter. With luck, his bosses would make Lonnie disappear permanently. She had used Paul to cash one cheque from her alter-ego. Now she had two bits of information that should be enough to get him to spring the rest of her money out of the accounts: she knew where Lonnie could be found, and she had discovered the nature of the content of the packages.

She felt she needed to hit him with this without warning, so she drove over to the Carolli mansion. Misty was surprised at her arrival but opened the door and led her into the living room.

Without a greeting, Mildred said, "I want to see your husband."

Misty looked questioningly at her for an instant then led her out to the sundeck where Paul was nursing a beer beside the pool.

"What are you doing here?" he asked. "I told you to call if you wanted to meet."

"Oh, I think this is important enough for you to forget your rules."

They both looked at Misty until she got the message and walked back into the house.

When he figured his wife was far enough away to be out of hearing distance, he asked, "What is so important that you have to take the chance and come over here?"

"I know where Lonnie is, or at least where he was this morning. I got a call from a woman that has been with him."

The news gave her Paul's complete attention.

"Where is he? What's the address? My people want to know."

"I'm sure they do," she replied, "but it's going to cost you."

"Don't screw around with this, Mildred. This is serious. These people don't make deals."

"I know. You told me that before, but you do. My friend, Juanita, is going to write you another cheque for a slightly larger amount, which you will take to the bank and cash. When you bring me the money, I will give you a piece of paper with my husband's address. You can send some goons around to beat it out of me, and it would probably work, but you're going to look like a bigger hero if your employers think you chased it down yourself."

Paul thought for a minute and realized what she said made sense. He needed something to get the Arab off his back.

"Okay, get me the cheque."

"It's right here," she replied, as she fished it out of her pocket.

Paul looked at the cheque and said, "I'll give you half the money this afternoon and the other half after you make this next delivery."

"Just make sure you do. And by the way, I opened one of those packages. If anything happens to me, there is an envelope hidden away with a sample of the powder, your name, and details about its delivery. So, tell your people to think twice about taking me out of the picture."

When she was sure Mildred was leaving, Misty had to quickly turn off the intercom and disappear upstairs. She had heard everything. She didn't completely understand what it was about, but it was too troubling to ignore. She had known something was going on from the time Lonnie had come over and talked of getting rid of Dusty. She had told him, and he had advised her to get out of Sun City for a while. He said her life was in danger as well. Then there were the strange phone calls Paul had been getting from that man with the accent. They had scared her. She knew she was in danger, but she didn't know how serious it was. She had to find out what was going on and would have liked to have Paul explain it to her, but she was afraid he was too deeply involved. Fred might be able to help her, but he wasn't here. She had to talk to Dusty again, and besides, this new information made her nervous to be spending much more time around her husband. She feared he was no longer the kind generous man she had married.

When she drove over to the caseta, Dusty was not home. She knocked on the door of the main house. A bruised and battered Kellie answered her knock.

"My Gawd, what happened to you?"

"Come on in," Kellie replied, "it's a long painful story."

"Do you know where Dusty is? I have to talk to him."

"He's here. We're just having coffee. Come and join us."

Dusty was surprised to see her. When she had left Sun City, he had assumed she would not return for a long time, if ever.

"When did you come back?" He asked.

"Just a few days ago. I was beginning to think I was blowing this hush-hush stuff with Paul out of proportion, and besides, my daughter was getting tired of me hanging around her apartment all day. Now, after this afternoon, I'm sorry I returned. This thing is worse than I thought. Dusty, I'm really scared this time. Can we talk about it here?"

"Sure. Kellie knows the whole story and the house has been debugged. She's trying to help me sort it out. What happened?"

Misty described the conversation she had overheard between her husband and Mildred Trame. "Do you think Paul or Mildred had any idea you were listening to them?" Kellie asked.

"I don't think so, but I can't be sure. I listened over the intercom but turned it off as soon as Mildred started to leave. What does it all mean?"

"First of all, it doesn't sound good for Lonnie. The fact that Paul was so interested in Lonnie's whereabouts tells me he was under pressure from his bosses to locate him. We don't know why Lonnie disappeared, but I'm willing to bet it had a lot to do with the work he was performing for them. It would be interesting to know what's behind these cheques Paul is cashing for her. Either she is blackmailing him, or it's in return for something she's doing. My guess is he's got her to take over the deliveries," Dusty replied.

Misty thought for a minute then said, "Something else that puzzled me was a remark Mildred made as she was leaving. I didn't get it all as I turned off the intercom before she finished, but she referred to knowing what the powder was in the packages."

"That's it!" Dusty exclaimed. "Lonnie was delivering packages for someone connected with Paul. Just after Maria was kidnapped, I confronted Lonnie with what I figured was going on and warned him that he was in real danger. I must have been close to the truth as he opened up enough to tell me how the contacts were made. I made the assumption the packages contained dope, and he neither confirmed nor denied it. I had the impression he didn't know what they contained and was too scared to find out. Now Paul has recruited Mildred to take over the deliveries, not counting on her opening a package to see what she was carrying."

"That sounds about right," Kellie remarked. "Possibly Mildred knew right from the start and was waiting to use the information for her own benefit."

"Why would she rat out Lonnie if they were working together?" Misty asked.

"I don't think she knew what Lonnie was doing until Paul offered her the job. She was probably pissed when he took off, leaving her with all the bills and expenses. I'm guessing he cleaned out the bank account when he split, and she's using this knowledge of his whereabouts to get back at him and get her hands on some cash," Kellie answered.

"Whatever it is, Misty, you're not safe if they have any idea you know what's going on. You have to go far away, where they can't find you, until this whole thing is cleared up. I have a friend in Canada that can help you get relocated for a while."

"I don't know, Dusty, won't Paul get suspicious if I take off again?"

"Probably, but there's not much he can do if he can't find you."

"Let me think about it. I'll call you tomorrow."

"Okay, but don't wait too long, and call me from a land line at the club. I have no doubt that all your phones and vehicles are bugged."

Misty didn't want to go home. She no longer felt safe with Paul in the house. She would have liked to stay with Dusty, but this afternoon she could sense a connection between him and Kellie that she had not been aware of before. Maybe they were just old friends, as they had indicated many times, but her antenna had sensed an underlying current running between them. Where to go? If she was going away for a while or even for good, she felt obliged to spend some time with Janet before she left.

Her friend was home when she called and invited her to come over right away.

"Why didn't you call me and tell me you were back?" Janet asked as she welcomed her into the house.

"I've only been back a few days, and there is so much going on. I just didn't have a chance, and now I have to go away again. I don't know when I'll be back this time."

"I'll bet you got in touch with that Seaborne girl."

"What do you mean by that?"

"You know what I'm talking about, you teaching her all about loving. Is she a good pupil? I'm very unhappy with you, Misty. I was under the impression we had an exclusive relationship, but no matter, let's get these clothes off and go to bed."

"I'm too stressed out to be able to pleasure you tonight. Can we not just visit for a while?"

"Sure, we can visit upstairs then see what develops."

"Janet, I just came over to tell you I'm leaving again, this time probably for quite a while. I'm not safe staying here."

"I suppose you're going with your little girlfriend." She spit the words out. "Why don't you tell me the truth? I'm getting sick of you lying to me."

"I am telling it true," Misty replied. "I wouldn't lie to you. We've been friends for too long for me to try and deceive you."

Janet was angry. She got up, walked quickly over to her friend, grasped her roughly by the arm and led her to the door.

"You are going to be sorry for abandoning me. This friendship is over. I warned you not to cheat on me. I don't want to see you again unless you're ready to apologize."

Misty was shocked at her reaction. She tried to respond, but the older woman slammed the door. She had no other option but return to her car and try to decide where to go. She tried to phone Anna, but was informed by Dolly that her sister-in-law was working the late afternoon shift and wouldn't be off until midnight. As a final resort, she phoned Dusty to accept his offer and ask if she could crash there for the night. Dusty replied that he was about to leave to visit Fred and she was welcome to come along for the ride. She jumped at the chance to distance herself from Paul and Janet and visit with an old friend.

32

Mildred was feeling pretty good as she drove home. She finally believed things were working out in her favor, and she was in control. She had gotten rid of Lonnie, probably for good. She had developed a secure way of getting her money, and she had Paul Carolli on the hook. He was scared. She could almost smell the fear when she left his home. She didn't know who was pulling his strings, and she didn't particularly care. All she wanted was to get the rest of her money out of those accounts and leave Sun City as Juanita Rojas. If that required making another delivery, it was a small price to pay for her freedom.

Paul delivered half the money later that afternoon.

"Your next delivery is scheduled for tomorrow evening," he announced after he had handed her the cash. "This one is a bit farther from home. The pickup is along the north side of Highway 86 two miles beyond the turnoff to the Sonoran Desert Museum. There's a white-painted stone marker beside the road. You can't miss it. Park by the stone and wait. It is scheduled for 3 AM. Be there and don't be late. Stay in your car at the pickup spot until the aircraft drops the parcels. After you've retrieved them, drive back to Mesa to the Swap Meet grounds. Wait until one half hour after they open then drive in and park in the first row next to an old red GMC half-ton truck. A black toolbox in the back will be unlocked. Put the packages in the box and lock it with the locks that came with the packages then get out of there. Have you got that?"

"Most of it. What I don't remember is on here," she said as she pulled a recorder from her purse.

"You recorded all this?" Paul asked with alarm.

"Certainly, I've recorded all our conversations, especially the one we had at your home. I hope you haven't said anything you may regret later," she replied with a smile.

Paul went home in a panic. He realized he would have to be more careful with her than he was with her husband. Along with most people that knew them, he had been deluded in considering Lonnie the brighter of the two. He was quickly changing his thinking. This little broad was dragging him through the mud and scaring the hell out of him.

Misty wasn't home. He was disappointed, as he needed to talk to her. He had been wondering since Mildred left how much his wife knew about what was going on. He hoped she was oblivious to it, but with all these visits from Lonnie and then Mildred, he was sure she was suspicious. For her own safety, he had to defuse her interest.

Dusty found Fred and Lucinda in a booth at the back of the bar. Dusty knew his friend had returned from checking out the Mexican silver properties of Mexari and was anxious to hear what he had found. The presence of Misty deferred both men from mentioning this topic that was uppermost in their minds. Dusty had forewarned him that she was coming with him, and she was in a fragile state as a result of the meeting between Paul and Mildred. Instead, Fred slipped Dusty a thick sealed envelope when they sat down.

"It's all in there," was his only comment.

After the ladies were introduced to each other, Lucinda commented, "Fred, if you left this beautiful young lady to be with me, you're even crazier than I thought, or did she finally realize how weird you are and kick you out?"

Misty smiled and said, "I think he just got cold feet hustling a married woman."

Dusty had decided he was not going to talk any more about the events in the Carolli house that morning, but Misty made a point of telling Fred what had happened.

"Dusty thinks I am in danger and I should get out of Sun City for a while. What do you think?"

Fred thought for a few minutes then met her gaze. "I've known this young fellow for a lot of years, and I've found that he is usually right in reading a situation. I don't know all the details of what is going on, but if Dusty believes you are in danger, I would go along with his concern. I am familiar enough about Paul's background to know he is probably not much of a threat on his own, but what is more important, he has had associations in the past with some very dangerous people. You do need to get away from all this."

It was past ten when the meeting broke up. Fred pulled Dusty aside as the women walked out ahead of them.

"Lucinda is a bit of a shaman with her people. I have witnessed and experienced strong evidence of her powers of prophecy. She told me she senses an ominous aura surrounding Misty. She feels this danger in her near future. She can't pin it down as to when, or where, or what form it may take, but to her it is real. Look after her, Dusty. We don't want to lose our girl."

It was a troubling revelation. In the brief period he had known Lucinda, Dusty was impressed by the sense of spiritual strength, which emanated from this woman. If she had forebodings about Misty's future, he felt they should be taken seriously. As they drove back to Sun City, he made no mention of it. Instead, he asked, "Have you made up your mind what you're going to do?"

"Yes, I'm going to accept your advice and take off. I don't even want to go home and pick up my clothes. I've got enough money to make it to Canada and hook up with your friend Lucie. I'll figure out what to do when I get there."

"Good. I'm going to give you the debit card on my Canadian account. If you don't leave a paper trail, Paul will have a tough time finding you. Do you want to stay with me tonight and leave in the morning?"

"I'd love to spend this last night with you, but I'm too anxious to get started. I want to take off as soon as we get back, stop and say goodbye to Anna when she gets off work at midnight then drive all night."

Misty waited outside the Seaborne home until her friend drove up just before one o'clock. Misty got out and met her at the front gate. Anna greeted her and invited her in for a drink.

"We'll have to make it coffee or tea. I'm going to be driving most of the night. Dolly said you were working the late shift, so I thought I'd stop and say goodbye before I pulled out."

Not wanting to burden her friend with her problems, Misty simply explained she was going to visit her daughter again. They talked until around two. When Anna started to yawn, Misty took it as a sign to be on her way.

When she got into her car, she was a bit surprised she hadn't locked it. Just as she put the key in the ignition she heard a sound from the back seat. As she turned to have a look everything went black.

33

Dusty was anxious to see what Fred had discovered. It was frustrating not being able to talk about it when they met, so he opened the package and dumped everything on the bed when he got back to the caseta. The reports and maps he had given Fred covered his sleeping space and spilled over onto the floor. At the top was a lengthy note in Fred's handwriting.

Dusty;

As you can see, all of the Mexari holdings are in the State of Chihuahua. Most of the properties are down in the southwestern corner of the State, along the western slope of the Sierra Madre Mountains. This is an area of silver production that dates back before the Spanish arrival. A lot of silver and gold has been taken from the mines in this area, and I'm sure there are still some pretty good tonnages left. Whether any of it is on Mexari land is the big question. There are four prospects: the

*Madres, the Alta Plata, the Antiqua Mina, and the
Nuevo Tesoro. I just about killed myself climbing up
and down those slopes. All of the prospects have old
workings: tunnels, shafts, and prospect pits. I didn't
go inside any of them, as they just didn't look safe. I
did find some silver ore on the dumps, which I am
having assayed. There is no evidence of any recent
work, which I found puzzling after having Lucinda
translate the geologists report. I saw some old
machinery, but I doubt if any of it was in working
condition.*

*I wanted to meet with this geologist, Guillermo
Asada, so we went to the address indicated in his
report in Chihuahua City. We found his office with
his name on the door, but he wasn't in. Lucinda
asked at other offices in the building, and the
general consensus was that no one had any memory
of that office being used.*

*Our next step was to try and locate the vendors
of these properties. We used the names and
addresses on the transfer documents from Jeremy's
office. In each case the previous owners were small
farmers in that area. We had prepared a series of
questions to ask about the properties and the nature
of their dealings with Mexari. With one exception,
these people refused to answer any of our questions.
They were afraid to even talk to us. One woman,
however, was angry. In spite of her husband's
attempts to keep her quiet, she told us of how three
men had come and demanded they sign a paper
giving up their mine. They were offered nothing for
it. They were warned that their lives would be in
danger if they didn't do what they were told. She
said the paper was in English, so they had no idea
what it said. I showed her our copy of the title
transfer. She said that it looked like the paper they*

were forced to sign.

Dusty, this whole thing stinks. I don't know if our boy is being used and doesn't know what is happening or if he is a part of it. After you've read this, looked at the rest of the documents, and thought about it, give me a call and we'll decide what to do next.

Fred

Dusty did think about it to the point he got very little sleep. The next morning, after making sure Jeremy was not home, he invited himself next door for breakfast and showed Kellie the letter.

She finished reading then read it through a second time. She was quiet for a few minutes. Finally she said, "I know Jeremy has been acting strange for the past few months, but I can't believe he would knowingly get involved in something like this. You've told me how wild he was when you were young, but since I've known him he's shied away from taking chances on anything. If he knows what's going on, it's so totally contrary to his nature."

"I know, but we have to find out. I want you there when Fred and I meet. We all have Jeremy's best interests at heart, and I think he is going to need some help to get out of this mess."

They put in a call to Fred's cell, but it was kicked into his voice mail, so they left a message proposing a meeting. Fifteen minutes later, he phoned back.

"I think we should wait until we have more pieces to this puzzle before we confront him with it. Dusty, you need to have a look at the Arizona claims, and I would like to hear from Angleton and your friend Arturo before we proceed. That additional information could change this whole scenario."

Kellie was anxious to get to the heart of the problem but could see the logic in Fred's advice.

"Jeremy is coming home tomorrow. I guess I should just play it cool until you two decide what you are going to do."

"Exactly, and maybe you could call your Dad and see how he's doing checking out the shareholder list."

34

Jorge Esposa hated his job. It was just a year
ago he had applied to the Sandpiper Golf and
Country Club for this position of assistant
groundskeeper, and things had steadily gone
downhill since. Antonio, his boss, treated him like a
slave. Since Jorge was Mexican and not Puerto
Rican like the rest of his coworkers, he got all the
rotten tasks no one else wanted. He wanted to quit
from day one, but there were no other jobs. Finally,
yesterday he had enough and told Antonio in which
part of his anatomy he might relocate his job.
'Groso' became angry and threatened to blackball
him from ever working again in Sun City. The
biggest tournament of the season was to start the
next day. All the important people from Sun City
would be there, and the grounds had to be in top
shape for the event. This would require all the crew
to work through the night. If Jorge knew what was
good for him, he had better show up. Since he

wasn't too sure if 'Groso' had enough clout to shut down his chances for another job, he agreed to stick for the run of the tournament.

A couple of hours after midnight, as he was raking a sand trap on the No. 4 hole, he noticed a set of lights moving slowly along the cart lane. He watched as a car approached the embankment on the other side of the lake. The lights were turned off, but there was enough moonlight for him to make out someone opening the driver's door. The figure did not get out but appeared to be attempting to drag something. Suddenly the door was slammed; the figure walked around to the back of the car and started to push it down the embankment. The vehicle quickly gained momentum and plunged into the lake. It floated slowly out to the center then sank. The figure watched until the car reached the water then took off on foot.

Jorge debated for a minute whether to ignore this and just go on with his task, but the suspicion that there might be someone trapped inside the car overcame his indecision. He ran over to the point of entry, stripped down to his shorts and jumped in. The water was cool but not uncomfortable. He swam out to where a few bubbles were still surfacing and dove down. The car was resting on the bottom in about fifteen feet of water. A quick look through the windshield revealed a young woman strapped into the passenger seat. Jorge tried to open the door, but it was locked and the window was closed to within an inch of the top, not enough room for him to reach in. He swam to the other side and tried the other door. It was also locked. He realized he would have to break a window if he was to have any chance of getting the woman out. He surfaced and swam quickly back to the shore. He searched frantically along the bank until he found a baseball-sized rock at the water edge. The return swim with the rock in one hand was slow. On bottom he struck the window with as much force as the water would permit. It took repeated blows to produce a crack, which opened up enough for Jorge to get his hand in to unlock the door. After another quick trip to the surface for air, he was able to go down and open the door against the pressure of the water. He unstrapped the woman and pulled her out and up to the surface. When they reached the shore, he stretched her out in the grass and attempted to find a pulse. He couldn't be sure, but he thought he detected some response. He tried some of that CPR he had seen on TV, placing his hands on her chest then pressing and releasing quickly. The only result he could detect was a bit of water being expelled through her mouth. Jorge believed the woman was alive and knew she needed medical help badly. The nearest phone was at the pro shop. He ran back to his cart, drove it over to where she lay on the grass, loaded her body into the back, and high-balled it to the clubhouse. A group of women were working in the restaurant getting it ready for the day's activities. They carried the woman in and laid her on a table while Jorge called 911.

The EMS arrived in half an hour, and spent another hour working on the unconscious lady. A few minutes after their appearance, the police arrived and took a statement from Jorge. They checked to see if the woman was carrying any identification, but there was none. They roped off the lake as a crime scene and ordered a tow truck.

"She's alive, but we can't bring her around. We are taking her to the hospital" the one paramedic told Jorge when he returned.

The police crime lab truck showed up as the paramedics were loading her into their van. The examination around the point of entry showed two sets of footprints in the area. One set was immediately identified as belonging to Jorge. The others, which were much fainter, were made by a smaller shoe, estimated by the technician to be either a size five or six.

"These tracks were made by a man with small feet or possibly by a woman."

When the tow truck arrived, the driver was forced to wait until the examination was completed. The truck managed to tear up a stretch of the fairway as it maneuvered to get a cable attached to the submerged car. When they finally got it on shore and emptied of water, the police were able to determine from the registration in the glove compartment that the vehicle belonged to a Misty Carolli of 8632 Mesquite Canyon Drive. One of the officers was dispatched to the address.

.

35

Mildred Trame no longer existed. Juanita Rojas was here to stay. She had purchased two cans of tanning spray. The afternoon before she was to make her delivery, she stripped down and sprayed her whole body a deep bronze. She died her hair black and sewed padding into the garments she was planning to keep in order to fill out her skinny frame. She felt the transformation was effective as she admired her new look in the mirror. The rest of the day was spent packing a few essentials. At dusk she drove out of Phoenix on Highway 10 to the junction with eighty-six. It was just after midnight when she spotted the white rock.

She pulled off the road, parked on a level spot and wondered what to do next. She was too hyped to take a nap or just sit in the car, so she decided to go for a walk along a path beside the shallow arroyo. It was a beautiful, cool desert night. The moon was almost full and was slowly coming up over the horizon, lighting her path. After an hour she perched on a rock and let the warm wind gently blow through her hair. The only sounds were the night birds and the occasional small animal scurrying along the desert floor. She felt at peace, eager to start her new life. As she walked back to the drop-off spot, she noticed a pair of headlights slowly approaching from the east. She got down low and crawled until she was hidden behind some bushes. The car pulled up behind hers and shut off its engine and lights. There was no activity around the vehicle for about twenty minutes then the passenger door opened, and a man got out and walked over to Mildred's driver side and peered in. When he was satisfied the vehicle was empty, he opened the trunk of his car, took out a long rod and a square box, returned and jimmied her door open.

"What the hell is he doing?" She wondered.

He finally emerged from her car and returned to his own with only the rod in his hand. He got in, the car turned around and drove away in the direction from which it had come.

Mildred puzzled over the event for a minute before it hit her, "He put a bomb in my car. That bastard Carolli set me up."

She was furious and sat in her hiding spot for an hour trying to figure some way to get back at him. Slowly it began to dawn on her that she now had to figure a way of getting home. She had no idea how to neutralize the bomb. In fact, she wanted to stay as far away from her car as possible in case it blew up on its own. Since it was registered to Mildred Trame, she had no further use for it anyway. It was pointless to try and hitch a ride in the middle of the night, and it was too far to even think of walking back to civilization. There hadn't been a car since Paul's friends had pulled away. Her only option was wait until morning and hope some passing motorist would give her a ride into Tucson.

The sun was moving up into the eastern sky when she awoke. She had burrowed a little depression into the sand and fallen asleep. She took off most of her clothes and shook the sand out of them before getting dressed and climbing out to the road. She looked at her car and thought, "It's just sitting there waiting to blow somebody up."

Most of the traffic on eighty-six was moving west, but the few cars that were heading east passed her by until an old couple picked her up and drove her to the Hertz agency in the city to rent a car as Juanita and make the trip home. She was still without a plan for extracting revenge from Paul but was beginning to entertain the idea that maybe her best bet was to quickly gather up her things and get out of Sun City. She regretted having to walk away from the hundred thousand he owed her, but the quarter million in ready cash hidden in the freezer was more than enough to ease her sadness. She filled a suitcase with her Juanita clothes, bundled the money into another bag and donned the black wig she would wear until her own hair grew out. She was just preparing to leave when the doorbell rang filling her with an instant rush of panic. She crept noiselessly to the door and looked out the peephole. She was relieved to see Dusty Sherant.

When she opened the door he said, "I'm looking for Mildred Trame. Do you know where I can find her?"

Mildred was overjoyed at the effectiveness of her disguise.

"Dusty, it's me, Mildred, except Mildred is no longer. You are looking at Senorita Juanita Rojas.

Are you here to finally accept Mildred's offer of some bedroom adventures? I'm sure Juanita can satisfy all your needs and desires."

"It's tempting," Dusty said with a smile, "but we need to talk over a few things."

"Okay. Come on in."

"I get the impression you are getting ready to leave," he said as he noticed the cases by the door.

"If you had been any later, I would have been gone when you knocked."

"You know, that's probably the best thing you can do the way things are going. You know Misty is in the hospital. Somebody tried to kill her last night."

"No. I didn't know. I wasn't here last night. What happened?"

"Somebody knocked her on the head, strapped her into her car and pushed it into the lake over on the Sandpiper course."

"It was that bastard husband of hers. He also tried to have me killed last night."

"Why? Did your delivery go bad?"

"How do you know about that?" She asked then thought for a minute and continued, "Misty told you, didn't she? She must have been listening when I went over to talk to Paul yesterday. That probably explains why he tried to kill her."

At that point Mildred decided to open up and tell Dusty the whole story, of course leaving out the part about Juanita and the money.

"I think one of us needs to put an anonymous call into the Tucson police and tell them about the bomb in the car, before some kids blow themselves up trying to steal it. If you want, I'll do it from a neutral phone."

"Yeah, I was thinking that before," she replied.

"So Paul is running this drug operation and getting rid of anyone that gets in his way."

"I don't think so. He is running scared of someone higher up the pole. I got the impression he is just the middle man and takes orders."

"There is one other thing," Dusty said as he pulled a newspaper from his pocket and handed it to her. "This was in the Republic this morning."

Mildred read the back page story.

Seattle police announced yesterday the discovery of two bodies, a man and a woman, floating in Lake Washington. They were bound together naked with a heavy chain and duct tape. The coroner reports they were probably alive when they were submerged. The woman has been identified as Miss Cara Duchene of this City. Tentative identification of the man awaits confirmation by next of kin, but he is believed to be Lonnie Trame of Sun City, Arizona. The case is being investigated as a double homicide by local law enforcement.

"Looks like I put the kiss of death on Lonnie when I told Paul where he was. I only knew that because this Duchene babe phoned me. I think Mr. Carolli has a lot to answer for, but I don't care. I'm out of here now."

"Go far away, Juanita. As far as I'm concerned, we never had this conversation, and, look after yourself."

After Dusty had gone, Juanita loaded the rental car, locked the house and threw the keys in the garbage bin. As she headed north, she thought, "Tonight it's Vegas, and after that, who knows."

36

Ever since he and Lucinda had returned from
Mexico, Fred Prince was constantly worried about
what kind of a mess his nephew had gotten himself
into this time. Everything he had learned about the
silver properties and how they were acquired gave
him considerable cause for concern. He needed to
talk it over with Dusty and Kellie on one hand, but
he also wanted to see what other information on
Mexari would emerge from the investigations by
Rafael's father and Martin Angleton. Hopefully,
Dusty's field work would discover the Arizona
prospects had value. Fred and Lucinda discussed it
into the night, and she had cautioned him to wait.
This was the same night that had Mildred hiding in
the arroyo waiting for the parcel drop. It also
brought unexpected excitement to Fred and
Lucinda's little love nest. As the first hints of pink
were painting the eastern horizon, Lucinda's sharp
hearing awoke her, picking up a racket from the

chicken coop and a warning from Brownie's deep throated growl. She had lived too long in the desert not to be alerted by unusual noises. She never lost sleep to the coyotes howling or the javelinas scurrying across the yard, but what she heard was not part of the rhythm of the night.

Lucinda slipped quietly out of bed being careful not to disturb Fred's sleep. She moved barefooted through the back door and lifted the double-barrel shotgun off the wall of the sunroom. Once outside she crept slowly to the side of the house. She paused as her eyes picked up the movement of a shadow in the dim light. It was heading toward the front door. She turned and reentered the house just as a man appeared in the doorway of the bedroom. He had a rifle in his hands and was raising it toward the bed where Fred was still sleeping. Without thinking, Lucinda fired both barrels at the figure.

The police had no cause to suspect anything but self-defense. The man had died instantly without uttering a sound. He had no identification on his body or in the beat-up old Toyota he had driven to their gate. Neither Fred nor Lucinda had ever seen the man before and could offer the police no help in establishing his identity. When the police and the Lab personnel had left with the body and Lucinda had cleaned up the mess, Fred phoned Dusty, but the call was routed into his voice mail. His next call to Kellie brought him the news of the attempt on Misty's life.

"Too much is happening too fast," he said. "This whole thing is getting out of hand. We need to get together."

"Dusty's at the hospital now. He called me an hour ago to tell me she's still in a coma, but alive. The doctors don't know if she's going to make it.

I'll have him call you when he returns."

When Dusty phoned, Fred started right in, "My boy, this has gone way past being interesting; it's downright scary. The day after I get back from down south, this bozo comes into the house to kill me. If it wasn't for Lucinda's magic ears, you'd be talking to a dead man. I can't give that woman up; she's keeping me alive. The attack has to be related to what we're doing, checking out the claims, but how would they know?"

"I've got a few ideas. Don't use Kellie's number for a while. I'll get back to you real soon. I think we have a problem at this end."

When he hung up, he called Kellie over.

"Your place has to be bugged, especially the phone. It's the only explanation. You need to get it all swept: the house, the phone, the car, everything. It's the only way they could have known about Fred's trip. I am going over to the Rec Center and phone him again from there."

He rang Fred's number from the pay phone in the lobby.

"Fred, who was this fellow that tried to kill you? Did the police I D him?"

"No. They have no idea. They're trying to match his prints."

"What did he look like before she blew him away?"

"He was big, my height with another forty pounds. His body took all the pellets, so his face was untouched. He looked Mexican, but Lucinda tells me she thought he had a lot of Apache blood. He had a pock-marked face with a big mustache and beard trying to cover it."

"I think I know who he is. I'm coming down to have a look. Where is the body?"

"Probably in the Tucson morgue, but I'll find out, let you know, and meet you there."

Dusty called John and arranged to pick him up on the way. As he started to climb into the truck, Kellie opened the passenger door and hoisted herself onto the seat.

"Where do you think you're going?" he asked.

"I'm going with you. I haven't seen Fred since he moved out, besides I want to check out his new chick."

They picked John up at his home in Scottsdale.

As soon as he got in, he said, "The fun with you just never quits. What are you getting us into this time?"

"I'd rather not tell you right now. I have an idea what we're going to see, but I don't want to saddle you and Kellie with any preconceived conclusions."

Kellie knew Dusty well enough not to expect him to answer any more questions.

Halfway to Tucson, Fred called and instructed them to meet him at the Pima County Medical Examiner's Office on East District Street. Kellie set the GPS for the address as they approached the City limits. Twenty minutes later they pulled up in front of the building and met Fred at the door. They were ushered into a freezer room by a young lady in a lab coat.

"This was built specially to handle the large number of migrant deaths in the summer. It's mostly empty at this time of year."

She moved to one of the occupied cells, opened it, and unzipped a white body bag on a steel gurney.

"It's him," John exclaimed.

"Yeah, it's the bastard that beat me up. I feel better already seeing him dead. What did you do to him; he's a mess?" He asked Fred.

"Lucinda gave him both barrels in the gut. It does tend to spread a person's body parts around."

"So, you folks can identify him," the attendant observed. "Let me know and I'll pass the information over to the police."

"His name is Carlos Atriba. He lived in El Mirage, and the next of kin is probably a Loretta Squan at this address," Dusty said as he wrote out the address and handed her the paper.

As they were walking out, Dusty turned to Fred and said, "Tell Lucinda she has made John and me unhappy. We were looking forward to taking this creep out ourselves."

"I'm sure she'll be sad to hear that."

As they drove back to Scottsdale to take John home, he made the comment, "Something has been bothering me about all these incidents, which have happened and all the people involved. I am beginning to feel there is a strong connection in all of it. You have been looking at little Maria's abduction, Rafael losing his hand, and the beating you took as part of this drug importing operation. On the other hand are the mysteries involving Mexari. I think they are closely connected. Tonight clinched it for me. Why else would Carlos go after Fred, whose only involvement has been to check out Mexari's Mexican holdings? The second item, which got me thinking about it in the first place, is Paul Carolli's involvement in everything we've looked at. It might be coincidence, but I learned early in my police work to put very little credibility in coincidence."

Dusty was quiet for a few miles, thinking about John's remarks.

"Fred has come to the same conclusions, but two things bother me," Dusty announced. "Firstly, it would mean Jeremy is part of a serious illegal operation. I think I know him well enough to discount him knowingly getting involved in importing drugs, or a mining scam. There would be no reason. He doesn't need the money."

"He may not be aware of the true nature of the operation. What do you think, Kellie?" John asked.

"I don't know. Two years ago I would have totally agreed with Dusty, but Jeremy has changed. I can't pin down exactly how this has happened. It's just a gut feeling. He used to be a laid-back, happy fun guy. That person has left."

"What was the other concern, Dusty?"

"Well, if this whole mess is all tied together, there has to be somebody very ruthless and powerful calling the shots. I don't believe Jeremy or Paul has this capability. Somebody else has set this up and is pulling the strings."

As they drove up in front of John's house, Kellie asked, "So, where do we go from here, and are you two sure you want to get involved any deeper? For me, there is no option; I have to know what my husband is into."

"A friend I care about is in the hospital in a coma, and I also need to know what's going on with Jeremy. What about you, John?"

"Hey, this is the most excitement I've had since I quit the force. There's no way you can keep me out of it."

"Okay. We need a plan. I have Mexari's Arizona properties to evaluate, and I need to get together with Arturo and see what he's found out about the Mexicans involved in the Company. Kellie, I kind of hate asking you to do this, but we need information on Jeremy's activities: where he goes, and who he sees. John, can you do an in-depth investigation of Corolli. I think he's the major link in this whole thing. Maybe one of these threads will lead us to the boss."

Dusty and Kellie spoke very little on their return to Sun City. At the house Kellie turned to him before she got out of the truck and said, "No matter what happens, I can't live this life with Jeremy any longer, but I'll keep it together until we get this sorted out. Just promise it won't turn you against me."

Dusty took her hand and put his arm around her as she leaned into him.

"We've known each other too long for that to ever happen."

37

It was almost midnight, but Dusty was too wired to sleep. He had all these loose threads waiting to be chased down. He decided to get up and drive over to the hospital to see if Misty had regained consciousness. When he walked into the room, her husband was standing by the bedside. The serious look of concern on his face as he gazed down at his unconscious wife raised a shadow of a doubt in Dusty's mind as to whether it was Paul who tried to kill her.

"I've been here all evening, and she hasn't even stirred. The doctors still don't know if she is going to come out of it."

Dusty could see the tears welling up in his eyes as he held her limp hand.

"Did you try to kill her, Paul?" He had hesitated to ask, but all of a sudden it seemed appropriate.

Corolli wasn't shocked by the question.

"Is that what everyone thinks, that I did this? Dusty, I love her. I could never hurt her. I don't know who is responsible. I intend to find out, but I don't know where to start. So much of the life she is living here is a mystery."

"I'm trying to believe you, but I have so many suspicions and unanswered questions about your involvement in Mexari and the illegal drugs."

"I know, and I want to tell you, but I have to be careful. My life is in danger."

After Paul had gone, Anna walked into the room.

"How's our patient doing?" she asked.

"Looks like no change," Dusty replied. "Are you coming on shift or getting ready to go home?"

"I'm done for the day. I came down here to see if Misty is showing any change and to get a ride home with Paul before he left. Dolly has my car tonight."

"I'll give you a ride. I was about to leave."

As they walked to Dusty's truck, Anna asked, "Did Paul tell you the doctor found indications that Misty had received a blow to the back of the head, probably before she went into the lake? What bothers me is that she came to say goodbye to me about this time that same evening. She was heading to Seattle to see her daughter. We parted at the front door and she walked to her car. The next thing I hear she's been pulled out of the lake and taken to Emergency. Someone must have been hiding in her car."

"Do you think it was Paul?" Dusty asked.

"I don't know, but I don't think so. I sensed he cares too much for her to do anything like that."

"I agree, but I know he is connected with a person or people who are certainly capable of it, the same ones that cut off Rafael's hand."

"Maybe, but it doesn't seem like their style. If it was those people, Misty would be dead. There is one other thing. I don't know how to explain it except it is a strong feeling that this attempt on her life is related to a whole different set of circumstances. Misty was afraid of a woman she has been having a sexual affair with. She hesitated to tell me, but one evening when she had too much to drink, it came out. This woman is extremely jealous and has threatened her if she ever became involved with another woman. Well, I was that other woman. I wanted to experiment and she offered to teach me. I think this woman might have found out. I don't know how dangerous she might be, but it is something to consider. We need Misty conscious to find out who she is."

"Don't you know her identity?"

"No, but I had the impression their relationship has been going on for a number of years, even before Misty and Paul moved to Sun City."

Dusty thought about it as they drove to Anna's home.

"Have you any idea how we can identify this woman or figure out where she lives?" Dusty asked.

"Not offhand. I have the impression she has a home in a very expensive neighborhood and has no husband. Other than that, it's a mystery."

"Well, maybe it's something I can look into when I get back next week. Hopefully, Misty will be awake and talking by then. I have to go and check out some mining claims."

"Are these claims the ones in Jeremy's company?"

"Yes. How do you know about them?"

"My brother explained to me about a year ago

that Jeremy was forming a mining company and had some land here in the state. In fact, he helped Jeremy form his company and found him some office space in Phoenix."

"Is he still involved in the Company?"

"No. He told me he lost interest once Jeremy had it up and running. Do you want some company to help you do this? I know a little bit about geology and mining, and I have the weekend off. I'd love to go out and tramp around the desert with you."

"Are you sure? It could be a tough couple of days, but it would be great to have you along. You think it over. If I don't hear from you before tomorrow morning, I'll come and get you about seven."

The TV weatherman predicted Saturday was going to be a scorcher. By the time he picked up Anna, the mercury had hit seventy and showed signs of going higher.

She was certainly dressed for the desert: ankle-height boots, khaki shorts, which accented her long tanned legs, a snug-fitting khaki shirt, and a pith helmet. In comparison, Dusty looked like a bum with his 'Dire Straits' t-shirt, torn jeans, sneakers and a ball hat.

"You look great," he said. "Are you sure you want to get that outfit dirty?"

"I had to do something to impress you. So far nothing else has worked," she smiled. "Dan is quite concerned about me out roaming the desert with you. I don't know why. He seems to be getting more protective of me. I guess because he raised me after our parents were killed, he feels all this responsibility."

"Why? Does he think I will hurt you?"

"No, it's not that. He thinks you are dangerous

to be around. I told him about your encounter with those thugs last month."

"Are you worried?"

"Not yet. Where are we going?"

"Jeremy's company, Mexari, has most of their mining properties near Wickenberg. Since it's the closest, I thought we could check those out first."

Dusty had read through all the maps and reports on Mexari's Arizona prospects and wasn't impressed. He had been initially turned off when he found the author of most of the material was Dr. Mervyn Chipman, P. Eng. Dusty had previous dealings with Chipman in British Columbia and found him to be incompetent, crooked and stupid.

"How he ever got certified to write qualifying reports in Arizona is a mystery," he thought. Except for some sketchy historical data, however, it was all he had to go on.

They took the Vulture Mine Road out of Wickenberg and traveled southwest for about fifteen minutes then turned off on a rough trail. He had loaded the UTM coordinates for the claim center into his GPS. After half an hour of a bone-jarring ride, the instrument indicated they had reached their destination, a flat, dry area spotted with occasional stands of mesquite and seguaro cacti. There wasn't much rock exposed at the surface, but all the loose material scattered around suggested there was very little soil cover.

"Are we looking for some pits or tunnels?" Anna asked.

"There are supposed to be two short tunnels on the south side of the claim. If we walk over to the other side of that low ridge, we should find them along the edge of a dry wash."

As they moved toward the ridge, they noticed a

trail of dust being raised by a vehicle about a quarter of a mile away. It was moving slowly toward the main road. Anna watched their progress through Dusty's binoculars. She followed the vehicle as it passed out of view.

"What do you think they're doing out here?" Anna wondered.

"Probably a couple of prospectors going to their claims."

"I don't think so," she observed. "The two of them were too dressed up. They could be land developers, although I can't see what they could find to develop out here."

"You'd be surprised. Northerners will buy anything so they can say they have a piece of land in Arizona."

They found the two tunnel entrances, which appeared essentially as Chipman had described them.

"According to his report, he sampled a vein which ran along the roof of the main tunnel and got some pretty good assays. I think I better go in and get some pieces off the same zone and have them assayed as well. Would you stay outside in case this is bad ground and I get in trouble?"

"Sure," Anna replied, "just don't take any unnecessary chances."

Dusty climbed over the pile of debris that had accumulated at the portal and slid down into the main part of the tunnel. The light was good for about ten feet then he needed his flashlight to find his way beyond. The passage ended at a sheer face a hundred and forty feet from the portal. A quartz vein varying in width from a seam to five inches was exposed for most of the length of the passageway. At no place could Dusty see any evidence of it having been sampled recently. He took a few chips along its length then crawled out.

"It's kind of what I suspected," he said. "Chipman's report looks like a bit of science fiction."

"What do you mean? Didn't you find the vein?"

"There's a small vein, but he never sampled it. Either he made up these results or had some rocks from a real mine somewhere else assayed."

"Why would he do that? It's not like it was real dangerous going in there."

"That's one of the things worrying me about all this. Consultants like Chipman will write anything the client wants. It doesn't matter if there is any truth in it as long as he gets paid. I would hate to think Jeremy is knowingly behind this, but I can't think of any other reason Chipman would be involved."

"Maybe you are jumping to conclusions. I think you should hold off until we have visited all the properties," Anna advised. "I was looking through the report while you were underground. He came to some promising conclusions about the gold values in the dump outside the other tunnel. Let's take some pans from the pile and see if we can find some colors."

Anna was continually surprising him with the extent of her understanding of what they were doing. There was good value in her suggestions.

"Where did you get all this knowledge?" He asked.

"I used to go with my brother when he visited mining operations in order to evaluate their company stock. He made a point of learning all about geology and mining even to the extent of taking a bunch of courses. Then he would explain it all to me."

"Why was he checking out mining properties?"

"He was a stockbroker and believed in completely evaluating any company before he would recommend their stock."

"So, Dan understands this business."

"Totally," she replied.

They both dry-panned surface material from the second dump.

"Dusty, this is weird. I got one pan with lots of colors and four pans with nothing, not a speck."

"You're doing better than I am. I took six pans with no sign of gold. Let me try a pan from your rich spot." When Dusty panned it down to the black sand, he saw a tail of the yellow metal. A second pan ten feet away was barren.

"Let's dig down below the rich spot and try one."

They went down six feet and pulled another pan without any sign of gold.

"What's going on, Dusty?"

"It's been salted, an old trick, but obviously it's still being used. Whoever did this probably took a shotgun, loaded it with shot containing gold dust and picked spots on the dump to fire at. Let's go. We're done here."

38

It was mid-afternoon by the time Dusty and Anna drove back toward Wickenberg. They stopped in town, picked up some coffee and sandwiches, and had a look at the map.

"The other claims in this area are to the northeast of town. We have about an hour drive, dependent on the road conditions. Since we haven't had much rain in the past few days, they should be okay."

"Do you think we'll have time to have a good look before it gets dark?" Anna asked.

"If we don't find anything better than on the last property, it shouldn't take too long."

This time they found the claim posts and were able to locate the one pit that had been described in Chipman's report. The claims area was a series of hills and washes with the usual accumulations of mesquite bushes. Unlike the previous area, there was considerable bedrock exposed at the surface. Dusty was hard pressed to locate the myriad of mineralized quartz veins, which Chipman had mentioned in his report.

"If this was in Canada, we would call it 'moose pasture'," Dusty exclaimed.

"Down here it's a 'gopher ranch'," Anna added.

The entrance to the tunnel was cut into the side of a hill. The pile of rock outside suggested it had a limited length. Evidence of caving could be seen just inside the portal.

"Are you going to try and go in there?" Anna asked.

"If I want to get any fresh samples of the vein, I pretty much have to, besides, according to Chipman's report, he sampled it."

" Right, like he sampled the other one. Dusty, I think this one is a bit dangerous. I doubt if you can get through there unless we clear away some rocks."

It took half an hour to make the hole large enough for him to slither through. When he was half way in, his feet were unable to reach the floor of the tunnel.

"Anna, I need that coil of rope from the truck. You may have to pull me out of here."

They wrapped and tied one end around a large rock. He looped the other end around his waist and shoulders and lowered his body slowly until his feet touched the floor. The tunnel was actually a small, irregular room. The flashlight beam picked up a white quartz vein about a foot wide along one side. It thinned down to less than an inch at the far wall. There was little evidence of rock weathering, and Dusty was able to sample fresh quartz along the entire length. Like the previous vein, this one showed no evidence of recent sampling. This was the easy part. Getting up and out through the tiny portal was the challenge. With Anna pulling, her feet braced against another rock, and Dusty frantically scrambling up the slippery slope, they were finally able to get him back to the surface.

"There is no way Chipman went down there to even have a look."

They examined the samples, and Anna observed, "There are a few flecks of gold in these pieces. Maybe this property has some merit."

"Maybe, but that vein is really small. Any potential tonnage is limited."

It was dusk when they arrived back in Wittenberg.

"The last prospect is north of Tucson. We can drive back to Sun City and go to Tucson early tomorrow, or we can drive there tonight," he said.

"Let's go tonight. It's a beautiful evening, and I don't want to go home."

"Are you game to share a motel?"

"I don't know. Am I at risk?"

"Only if you want to be."

They found a motel on the north side of Tucson a few minutes before midnight.

"Shall I reward you with a fine dinner for all your help?" Dusty asked.

"All I want is a burger and a bed in that order. I'm beat."

Dusty lay on his bed fully clothed waiting to see what kind of loveliness appeared from the bathroom. By the time Anna had showered and returned, he was fast asleep.

Their plans for any early start the next morning were scuttled as soon as Dusty turned the key in the ignition of the truck. There was no response; the motor wouldn't even turn over. Popping the hood revealed a few engine parts missing. Spark plug wires were gone, as was the battery, and the power steering hose was cut.

"Looks like we had some visitors last night," Anna observed. "Do you think it was a bunch of kids?"

"No. They would have just stolen the truck for a joyride. This was intentional, aimed at us. Someone must have been following or tracing a signal from a GPS tracker. They obviously don't want us out snooping around."

Anna found the tracker taped up behind the rear bumper.

"If I'm going to finish this job, I think I need a bit more help," Dusty said as he opened his cell phone.

"Do you want me to call Dan and see if he can come?" She asked.

"No. If you call your brother he is going to be more worried than he already is. I'm going to get Fred Prince up here. He is just a few miles away."

When Fred heard the story, he agreed to come.

"I'll bring a couple of rifles in case these people are still on your tail."

In the meantime Dusty called Triple A and had a tow truck come and haul the Landrover away for repairs.

After Dusty had introduced Anna to Fred and Lucinda, they spread out the map of the last Mexari property.

Fred studied the map for a few minutes then said, "These claims are north of here. It looks like the same area Rafael described to me where he followed Lonnie Trame last year and ran into those fellows who cut off his hand. It seems like a strange coincidence, but I'm beginning to think like your friend John and discount coincidences. I'm thinking there is a connection."

"I don't know," Dusty replied. "John seems to think all of these events are linked together. I haven't reached that point yet, but he may be right."

Using the property coordinates, the GPS guided them north on Highway 77 to Oracle then northeast on an ungraded trail. About two and a half miles of rough travel took them to the claims.

"We're heading toward the old Mammoth Mine," Fred observed. "This is almost exactly where Rafael was when he met up with the bad guys. He described a blind arroyo which had a cave entrance hidden by a mesquite thicket."

Dusty leafed through Chipman's sketchy report on Mexari's Mammoth prospect.

"There's nothing like that described in here. In fact, there isn't much of anything shown for this one, only a couple of shallow prospect pits. He claims the potential for this property is in its proximity to the old mine."

It took about half an hour of tramping around the desert for Lucinda to spot the faint side trail wandering into the hidden canyon. Peering close to the ground, she could just make out the outline of tire tracks. Bushes were piled along one rock wall.

"We've got company!"

Anna was standing back on the main trail pointing to a ridge less than a quarter of a mile behind them. They all ducked as three shots smacked into the wall near Dusty's head. He frantically forced his way through the bushes trying to find the cave entrance as well as get out of the line of fire

"Get in here," he yelled. "You're sitting ducks out there."

They scrambled for the cave. Dusty and Anna got in safely, but the next shot caught Fred in the shoulder as he was crawling through the brush. He spun around and screamed with the pain but managed to get past the opening.

"Now, they've got me angry," Lucinda said quietly.

She unslung her rifle and crawled on her belly until she was hidden by the mesquite. She had no view of the men on the ridge, but she could see the corner of their vehicle, which was parked behind a rock wall.

"This should give them something to think about."

The first shot ricocheted off the bumper and banged around the surrounding rocks. The results of the second shot could be heard throughout the valley as a tire blew. Shots from the ridge came in bursts as the snipers tried to pinpoint Lucinda. Her third shot exploded the vehicle as it punctured the gas tank sending a ball of flame into the cloudless sky. Then the only sound to be heard was the crackling of burning bushes.

"I think I might have spoiled their day," she said as she scrambled out into the open. "Let's go have a look."

Dusty walked slowly with her, keeping behind protective cover as much as possible with rifles ready for any new encounter, but there was none. They found two badly burned bodies beside what was left of the truck. They probed the bodies looking for identification without success.

"I guess we need to report this," Dusty said.

"I suppose. You know it's going to mean a whole bunch of questions and papers to fill out," she replied. "Why don't we wait until we get back to town? Right now, we need to take care of Fred, maybe take him to the hospital."

When they came back off the ridge, Anna was sitting with Fred outside the cave.

"I need my medical bag. It's back in the Jeep. Can it be driven in here? He's in a lot of pain, too much to walk to where we parked."

After she had dressed his wound, she reported, "He's fortunate. The bullet went right through and missed the bone. I've treated it and given him a dose for the pain. He's going to be sore for a while, but it should heal with no problems. You can probably skip the hospital and a doctor visit. They would be legally bound to report treating a gunshot wound to the local law enforcement. I think you probably don't want to open that can of worms."

"That sounds about right," Lucinda said. "Especially since they have the report on me shooting that fellow the other night, and besides, Fred hates going to see doctors."

It was a slow ride back to Tucson. Dusty tried to avoid as many as possible of the potholes and bumps that dotted the trail. At the motel Fred stretched out on the bed while Anna worked on his wound, which had opened from the rough ride. When Dusty called about his truck, he learned they wouldn't have it fixed until the middle of the following week. Lucinda drove him into the city to get a rental. By the time they returned, Fred was ready to go home.

"Are you going to report all this to the cops?" He asked.

"I guess I'll have to, but I can keep you two out of it. I'll say I did the shooting that blew them up. Lucinda, leave me the rifle you used in case they want to do a ballistics check, although I have no idea how they would find the slugs. You just take him home and look after him. I have a feeling this thing isn't even close to being over."

By the time Fred and Lucinda left, the sun was grazing the western horizon.

"Where do we go from here?" Anna asked just as her cell phone rang. It was Dan.

"Where are you? Are you all right? I thought you would be home by now."

"I'm fine. Why do you ask? You sound worried."

"I'm concerned when you're with Dusty Sherant. He seems to court danger."

"I'm fine, Dan. I'll be home tomorrow."

"That was strange," she said after hanging up. "He isn't normally so concerned about my welfare. He sounded really worked up, and it's beginning to get on my nerves. I almost told him about our adventure, but something stopped me. Maybe I thought that would really set him off."

"Well, I guess that decided our immediate future. We might as well stay here tonight, the room is paid for."

"Wow! That really sounds romantic."

Later that evening, they lay in each other's arms. The progress to that moment had been slow and careful. This was no wild, passionate embrace. Anna wanted to be loved, to be held and to make love with him. It was Dusty, who held back. He cared very much for this girl in his arms, maybe too much, and maybe that was the problem. He didn't want this to be a brief affair. She wasn't Misty, who never took these moments seriously. This was Anna, a lonely, sensitive girl, a girl who could be easily hurt.

They kissed and she pulled him closer.

"I want to make love," she said.

Dusty said nothing as he tried to quell his inner turmoil.

"Anna, I feel the same, but we can't, not yet. I care too much for you for us to come together tonight in this second-rate motel. We need to get to know each other better as friends first."

"I think I understand. Kellie told me a little bit about what happened with you and the girl up north. She cautioned me not to get too interested in you. She doesn't think you would be able to commit to a long-term relationship."

"She's probably right. She knows me too well. I was in love with Elena and had asked her to marry me; unaware she was sleeping with someone else and carrying his baby. I vowed then never to let my emotions rule me again. We need time, Anna. I hope you'll understand."

"I'll try, and I'm willing to wait. I want to see if we can work it out together."

39

A phone call to the repair shop Monday morning told Dusty his truck would not be ready for at least a week, as the mechanic had to order a few items to be shipped in. Parts for a Landrover that old were not common in Arizona.

"We'll take the rental on a leisurely drive back to Phoenix after I call the cops and report yesterday's action," Dusty said, as he tossed his backpack into the trunk. "I'll drop the car off there."

After making his call to the Tucson police, he reported, "It looks like we will have to postpone our trip home for a few hours. The cops want us to show them where all the action took place and describe what happened. I'd better make up a good story on the way out."

The police car followed them out to the claims and the two officers spent an hour examining the site. A meat wagon was summoned to collect what was left of the bodies for transport to the morgue. The officers were somewhat mystified by Dusty's account of why they had come out there in the first place and the subsequent proceedings. They seemed to accept the explanation after being shown the maps and report on the property. Dusty had taken Lucinda's role as his own in shooting out the gas tank. He even had the rifle to support his version of the events.

It was well past noon by the time they were on Highway 10, heading west.

"You lie very convincingly," Anna observed. "Is that something I will have to watch out for?"

"Not unless you join the police force or go to work for the Government."

They made one stop at the hospital to look in on Misty. Her condition was unchanged; although the nurse on duty told them there were signs she was beginning to regain consciousness.

As they pulled up in front of the Seaborne residence, the door opened and Dan walked quickly to the car and opened Anna's door.

"Are you okay? We were expecting you this morning. Has anything gone wrong?"

Anna was about to launch into a story of their adventure, but hesitated. She was confused. Her brother's level of concern was troubling, and she hesitated stoking the fire with revealing the danger they had faced.

"No, everything went well. It was interesting. We had a great time."

Dusty remained a spectator to this interchange. It was encouraging to observe Dan's apprehension for his sister's welfare, but some indefinable emotion was niggling at the back of his mind. He was confused as to the depth of this relationship between brother and sister.

Anna walked around to his side of the car and

gave him a strong lingering kiss through the open window. They said goodbye and she disappeared into the house with her brother.

Dusty needed to talk with Jeremy. All the evidence he had seen so far suggested there was much wrong with his Company. He wanted answers. None of it made sense. His friend wasn't stupid, far from it, so why would he be so eager to promote a company, which had very little evident potential value? And, how did he get hooked up with a crook like Mervyn Chipman?

When he got back to the caseta, only Kellie was home.

"I don't know where he is. He was supposed to be going back to Amyot to settle the mine strike, but Dad phoned me to find out why he never showed. Dad had to fly up and sort things out himself, and he was not happy about it. I'm beginning to get worried."

"Doesn't he answer his cell phone?"

"No. All my calls end up in voice mail. That doesn't bother me so much, as you know how lousy cell reception is in that country, but I would have expected him to phone me from a land line. It has been almost two weeks. Do you think we should contact the police?"

"Kellie, I believe the last thing you want to do right now is bring the police in. I'll ask John to track him down. There is something going on here that does not look good."

Dusty proceeded to launch into a detailed chronicle of their explorations in the desert and the resulting attack at the cave.

"Who were they?"

"Who knows? There wasn't enough left of either one for even a mother to recognize. Maybe the police can get a DNA identification."

"So, these hot Arizona properties he's been bragging about are as worthless as the ones Fred looked at in Mexico," Kellie observed.

"It appears that way."

"What are you going to do now?"

"I need to find Jeremy and talk to him. I'm hoping there is a simple logical explanation to all this. I do have one question for you. Was Dan Seaborne ever involved in Mexari? Something Anna said led me to believe he was working with Jeremy when the company was first being organized."

"They spent quite a bit of time together about a year ago, but I don't think they associate now, other than socially. I don't know for sure, but my take is that Dan is not involved. Dusty, all of this is really beginning to worry me big time. You're right. We have to find Jeremy. I'll call John and see if he will help us. He has been backgrounding Paul, but right now I think locating my husband is more important."

When Kellie had John on the phone, she motioned to Dusty to pick up the extension.

"He has some stuff to tell us about Paul, and he's agreed to try and find Jeremy."

When Dusty picked up, John started in.

"Paul Corolli's bio states he is a retired union executive from Chicago. He was evidently pretty good at it, negotiating some very lucrative contracts for the members. This is public knowledge. What aren't in the records are the methods he used to get these contracts. He was using union funds to manipulate the stock of small corporations, which employed his members. The share transactions were carried out through a major brokerage house headquartered in Detroit. When the Feds caught on to his scheme, they tried to acquire supporting evidence from the brokers. They denied any knowledge of Corolli or his accounts. The Government got a court order for the firm's records, but it was as the brokers claimed, as far as they were concerned, Corolli didn't exist. The Feds believed the information had been professionally erased, but they couldn't substantiate their suspicions. It would also appear Corolli is still actively tied in to the Union. The investors he lined up for Mexari to purchase the initial issue of common shares are all Union officers and members. The shares are recorded in the names of relatives, but it all leads back to the Union and Corolli."

"Are these Union people still buying stock?" Dusty asked.

"No. As far as I can tell they just put up the seed money, which totaled around three hundred thousand dollars at a buck a share. That stuff you downloaded shows the Company has a total of ten million shares issued, giving the Union only a small minority position."

"So, where is all Mexari's money coming from?"

"I guess we won't know that until you acquire the Company's financial records. It doesn't appear to be coming out of Chicago."

After John hung up, Dusty said, "Kellie, we have got to find your husband, and soon. This is way beyond being just a curiosity. I'm beginning to think Jeremy's life might be in danger if, in fact, he is still alive."

"I've had that thought as well, but I've run out of ideas where to look next. Are you sure we shouldn't get in touch with the police?"

"I'm not totally sure, but I have the feeling we could make the situation worse than it is. I would like to see if John is able to talk one of his buddies into instigating a covert investigation."

40

Jeremy Prince stretched out on the lounge beside the pool. He was totally relaxed and at peace with the world for the first time in months. It was a beautiful, sunny California day. He had a long cool drink and a gorgeous woman, practically naked, in the pool. He knew he was walking on the edge, but at this point he really didn't care. He was sick and tired of being careful, and besides, he felt confident it would all work out for the best. After all, it always had, no matter what mistakes he had made in the past; there was always someone around to straighten things out. He was a bit disturbed when José had told him about some old man, who he knew immediately was Uncle Fred, nosing around the claims down in Chihuahua. When he got distressed over the news, however, José had told him not to worry; it would be taken care of. Then word had come down from Sun City that Dusty had been out in the desert digging around on his claims. He didn't know what to do about that, but again, he was told to put it out of his mind, and the minute she climbed up out of the pool, he did.

She was so beautiful, the most exquisitely attractive woman he had ever seen, and she was his. Today, her deeply tanned body, exposed by the string bikini, took his breath away, as it did every time he looked at her. She walked with that practiced grace over and sat beside him, wrapped him in her arms and kissed him long and passionately.

"Do you want to help me out of this wet bathing suit?"

Jeremy's fingers trembled and fumbled as he tried to undo the tiny clasps.

"I see you are going to need more practice in taking my clothes off."

He smiled sheepishly as the last garment thread fell to the deck.

"Do you want to go inside or make love to me here?"

His answer was interrupted by the ring tone of his cell. He hesitated for a beat, trying to decide whether to answer, but he finally flipped it open, fearing it might be someone who would be angry if he didn't respond immediately.

"You need to be more careful. Someone broke into your office. We don't know who or when, but the thread we put across the doorway was broken. Time you got back to Sun City and looked after business. We're coming back tonight, so pack up and get out of there now."

Jeremy started to reply, but the caller had hung up.

"Who was it?" Elsina asked.

"Don't know, probably José or Javier. He didn't identify himself, just told me to get out of here and go back to Sun City."

"We had better go. They don't like it when someone doesn't do what they're told. I'll get us packed up, and we can leave this afternoon. I suppose it's time I got back to Arturo's and played my part."

"I don't want us to be separated any longer. These last two weeks were heaven. Why don't we go away, far away, where they can't find us, and we can be together."

"Jeremy, there is nowhere we can escape them. I know, I tried to hide when I left Mexico, and they knew where I was all the time. It's no use. We have to wait this out. As soon as they sell the Company, we will be free to go away and live our lives together."

With a strong feeling of despair, Jeremy drove out of La Quinta and back on Highway 10 to Sun City with Elsina curled up beside him. His paradise was slowly being lost, replaced by that gnawing dread of what the future would hold. By the time they crossed the Arizona border, she was asleep. Jeremy was lost in his dilemma. How was he going to handle Uncle Fred and Dusty? Dusty was too smart to be fooled by Chipman's report. Jeremy had staked the Arizona claims as window-dressing for the Company, fully aware of their limited potential, but somehow his backers had convinced Mervyn Chipman to write this glowing report of their value. Obviously, Chipman had been bought, but he was a registered professional engineer, and it would take another engineer to dispute his findings. As far as Fred was concerned, he was an old man and, even by his own admission, frequently confused. He couldn't understand why he worried. He had done nothing really illegal. His partners had raised all this money by marketing a company with practically no value. Promoters and brokers in Vancouver and Toronto did that all the time.

When they arrived on the outskirts of Phoenix, they drove to the storage lot to retrieve Jeremy's car so that Elsina could return the rental. It was difficult for Jeremy to say goodbye, and he hung on to her as long as he could.

He drove home slowly with the dread of facing his wife and all her questions. He had concocted what he considered a plausible story of getting seriously sick while driving north from Edmonton and checking into the Meadow Lake hospital. They had taken his cell phone and kept him sedated for over a week. He suspected Kellie wouldn't believe him and would check out everything he told her, but he was past the point of caring. All he could think of was Elsina and the time they would have together.

No one was home when he pulled up on the driveway. He went in, had a shower, put on clean clothes, and poured a strong drink. He settled in his favorite chair and waited for the showdown.

As soon as Jeremy was out of sight, Elsina pulled out her cell phone and put in a call to her lover. They arranged to meet at the little cabin near Sun Lakes. She could hardly wait to be in his arms, especially after having put up with Jeremy's fawning all over her for two weeks. He had arrived first and was standing in the doorway with a pitcher of margaritas waiting for her. He took her by the hand and led her to the bedroom. As he slowly undressed her, he said, "We have a lot of catching up to do and the whole weekend to do it."

41

John Hebrano picked up Jeremy's trail on a
fluke. John had his friend in the Department put out
a search for the Lexus. By mid-week it was reported
to be on a storage lot in the West Valley. The owner
of the lot told him the car had been there for ten
days, but was due to be picked up on the weekend.
With no other leads, John decided to stake it out to
see if and when someone came for it. His efforts
were rewarded on Friday afternoon when a white
Toyota pulled on to the lot and Jeremy emerged
from the driver's side, and a very attractive
Hispanic girl opened the passenger door. Jeremy
and the girl embraced passionately. Finally he
walked over to the lot office while the girl drove off
in the Toyota. John had taken a couple of good
shots with his cell phone camera, and since he had a
pretty good idea where Jeremy was headed, he
decided to follow the girl. Her identity and
destination fascinated him. He tracked her south,
through Chandler into the suburbs of Sun Lakes.

She pulled into the driveway of a modest little cottage set back from the frontage road. John drove as close as he could to the entrance without being spotted and parked behind a group of bushes. He was just in time to see the girl get out of the car and rush into the arms of a man standing in the doorway. He took pictures through the foliage, but he was too far away to capture a recognizable image of the man. Sensing the two were about to settle in for a while, he made a note of the address and the license plate number of the car and drove back to Sun City.

Dusty was pulling out of the driveway to return the rental car to Tucson and pick up his truck when John phoned.

"Did Jeremy arrive home yet?"

"He pulled in about an hour ago. I was going to drive over and get my truck before I talked to him. I think Kellie might have a few questions for him right now."

"Wait until we talk before you confront him. There is something going on you need to know. How about I join you on your drive over to Tucson."

John arrived at the caseta half an hour later. As they drove out of Sun City, John narrated his progress over the past few days.

"I think you had better pull into that rest stop coming up," he continued. "I have some interesting pictures for you, and I don't want you at the wheel when you look at them." The first picture was of the girl emerging from the Toyota; the second was of her and Jeremy embracing. It didn't take Dusty long to react.

"That's Elsina."

"You know her?"

"Yes, she's Arturo's adopted daughter. He took care of her when her father was killed and her mother was put in jail for running dope across the border. I don't see how she got hooked up with Jeremy, although they obviously have something hot going."

"Maybe not," John observed. "Have a look at these other pictures."

"Too bad you couldn't get closer. The man is not clear enough to get any kind of an idea what he looks like."

"I know. If I had gone in any further they would have spotted me."

"What do you make of all this, John?"

"I gave it some serious thought on the way over. I have the impression she's playing Jeremy. She was in a definite hurry to get away from him and drive over to Sun Lakes."

"Something has been bothering me ever since Kellie and I broke into Jeremy's office. It has been like a shadow creeping around the back of my mind, but seeing the two of them together triggered it. Jeremy's office is on the fourteenth floor of the Dial Tower on North Central. When we went up there I noticed the office next door belonged to East Arizona Imports. Now I get the connection. That is the company Elsina works for. When she told me, I was too busy trying to figure out how I was going to get her into bed to take much notice of it."

"That explains how they met, but why is she doing a number on him? What is her motive for cozying up to him? It is obviously not infatuation."

"John, I'm beginning to come around to your way of thinking. There is too much here that cannot be explained by coincidence. Jeremy's bogus mining company and this drug running operation have to be related or possibly all part of the same plan. I think we need to make that assumption in order to come up with any sense out of this mess. My immediate problem is how much do I tell Kellie about her husband's affair, and what do I say to Arturo about my suspicions regarding Elsina's activities."

"Until we get some more answers, I suggest you say nothing to either of them."

"The only way I can hope to get some answers is to talk with Jeremy and Paul Carolli. Paul is definitely tied into both sides of this problem. As you found out, he lined up the original investors in Mexari, and was running Lonnie's part in the drug smuggling. He might be the only one, other than those who are in charge, who knows the whole operation."

"Unless he is the big boss," John countered. "Why don't we both go talk to him."

"Yes. I'll set it up. My other concern is what Jeremy's role is in all of this. Why would he set up this company with worthless mining properties? He's a geologist by training. Surely he must be aware of their lack of value. Either he's on a massive ego trip to impress Elsina, or Kellie and her Dad and doesn't realize what is going on, or he is tied into the drug business by choice."

"The other possibility, Dusty, is that he believes these bogus engineering reports and is convinced his company has some potential. You do need to talk to him and find out where he fits in this picture."

It was late when they returned to Sun City. Dusty was too wired to think of sleep so he drove to the hospital. He wanted to look in on Misty, and he knew Anna would be off shift at midnight. He longed for her calming influence.

Paul was at his wife's bedside again when Dusty walked in.

"Any change?"

Paul looked up and smiled, "She's starting to come out of it. She's not really aware of anything, but the doctors are positive about her recovery."

"That's great, Paul. I need to talk to you about a few things that are going on around here. I've got some problems I need to sort out, and I think you might be able to help. Is this something you would be willing to do?"

"Yes, I think it might be time for me to unload some of this," he replied hesitantly. "Dan and Anna have organized a tennis match for Saturday afternoon. We were going to invite Jeremy, but he was away when I called. Kellie didn't know when he would be home. If you can join us, we can get together at my place afterward."

"That sounds good, although I was hoping to speak to you in private. And, by the way, Jeremy is home now."

Dusty waited around the hospital until midnight when Anna finished her shift.

"I kind of expected you to come by for me tonight. Did Paul tell you Misty is starting to show positive signs?"

'Yes. That is good news. I'm itching to talk to her and try and find out who did this. I don't think it was Paul. Either he is innocent or a good actor, but either way, I no longer suspect him."

"I don't think he is responsible for it either. He's been here every day. I believe he genuinely cares for her and couldn't cause her harm, but he is afraid of something. He's wound up pretty tight. Let's get out of here. I would like to go to the golf course and see the spot where her car went in. Do you think we can find it?"

"Sure, I went there the day after they pulled the car out. It's easy to find. The tow truck tore the fairway up quite a bit. Besides, it's a beautiful warm night for a walk, but why does it interest you?"

"Nothing special, I guess, just curiosity."

They drove to the course and parked on the roadway beside the green. It was a short stroll down to the lake.

"Evidently the car came off the road close to where we parked. Whoever was in the vehicle with her put it out of gear and let gravity take over."

They walked down to the water's edge where attempts to fix the fairway were not totally successful in masking the damage done by the truck.

"If it wasn't Paul, who would have done this? They were obviously trying to kill her, but why? I told you about the relationship she had with an older woman here in Sun City and how the woman had threatened her. Do you think it could have been the same woman? We should be trying to identify her."

"It could have been her if she was serious with her threat. I think you're right, but the big problem is, how do we locate her? We would have to wait for Misty to regain consciousness, or dig into her background, and with a lady like Misty, that could be a challenge," Dusty replied. "There is another possibility. Paul is involved in something, which is scaring him. You were right about him being on edge. It involves bringing drugs in from Mexico. I am afraid Misty might have found out about it and the people behind the operation tried to shut her up. I need to know what she knows in order to try and sort this out."

"Dusty, it's really not your problem. Why can't you just walk away from the whole thing? You settled the score with those thugs that beat you."

"I don't know. It's mostly for Jeremy's sake. He's been my friend for most of our lives, and he's mixed up in this. It's also for Misty. She is my friend, and I don't want to abandon her."

"Please be careful. I don't know what I'd do if anything happened to you."

"That's a tough request. Being careful is not really part of my nature, but for you, I'll try to stay alive."

"Thank you."

"Anyway, I was going to ask you about your brother's connection to Mexari. You told me Dan helped Jeremy organize the Company. Is he still involved in it?"

"No. I'm pretty sure he isn't. As far as I know he just helped Jeremy fill out the forms, register the Company, find an office, and stuff like that. I remembered he remarked at the time that Jeremy didn't have a clue as to what he was doing."

"So, how did your brother become so knowledgeable about corporate workings?"

"He operated as an independent stock broker and researcher for most of his working life. He had a following of clients who made their investments based on his recommendations. I think I told you before, after my parents were killed, I went to live with him in Detroit. Dolly and I used to tag along when he traveled all over the world to evaluate corporate assets. It was an exciting life."

"Why did he quit?"

"He didn't. He's still involved, but on a less intense schedule and travels only part of the time. I just sometimes regret my job prevents me from joining him."

Dusty was mildly surprised by this new information. He had always prided himself on being able to size up a person quickly. He had pictured Dan Seaborne as a mild-mannered, laid-back, pleasant gentleman. He had figured him for a retired accountant or middle-management executive, not a high-rolling stock broker.

The eastern horizon was streaked with pink when Dusty pulled up in front of her home.

"I'm off tomorrow. If you're not busy, we could maybe do something together."

"I'd like that," he replied. "I have nothing to do that can't wait. How about a swim over at the Rec. Center then lunch?"

"It's a deal," she said as she kissed him goodnight. "Let's not make it too early. I think we both need some sleep."

42

Dusty's much-needed sleep only lasted three hours before he was dragged from total unconsciousness by the incessant banging on his door. He opened it to find Kellie and Misty --- except it wasn't Misty. In his sleep-deprived state he must have been imagining what a younger Misty would have looked like.

"It's encouraging to see you are still alive and recognize the sound of someone frantically knocking on your door."

Kellie was saying something, but Dusty had tuned her out. His attention was totally focused on this beautiful young lady beside her.

"Dusty, this Lara, Misty's daughter. Can we come in? I think you need to hear what she has to say. We could go over to the big house, but Jeremy is roaming around over there, and I don't think any of this is his business."

"So, he finally made it home," Dusty observed. "What happened to him for all the time he couldn't be located?"

"He said he was sick and stuck in a hospital in Saskatoon."

"Okay, but why didn't he call and let you know?"

"He claims he lost his cell phone."

"That's not exactly the boondocks. They do have other phones up there."

"I know. Can we talk about it later? I want you to hear what Lara has to say."

They moved into the caseta and Dusty dug out an extra chair. He took his time in order to observe this attractive young lady more closely. It must have been his slow return to consciousness that caused him to momentarily mistake her for her mother. Lara was shorter and slimmer, and lacked Misty's eye-catching figure. Her auburn hair matched her mother's and was styled in the same manner. She had Misty's facial features but on a finer scale. Where her mother's actions were aggressive and open, Lara was a demure, private lady. She was beautiful but in her own manner.

"My mother phoned me a few days ago to tell me she was driving up to Seattle again and would be staying with me for a while. I thought this a bit unusual as she only escapes Arizona when the hot weather settles in. I asked her about it, but all she would tell me was that you suggested her life was in danger and that she should get out of Sun City. When I asked her for more details, she said she would explain it all when she arrived. She did say, however, if she didn't arrive within a week, I should contact you. So, here I am. Kellie tells me an attempt was made on her life, and she barely survived. I want to go see her right away, but Kellie suggested I should talk to you first."

Dusty thought for a minute then said, "We can go now as soon as I get dressed. She was conscious for a short while yesterday, and hopefully she will be awake today. Have you contacted your stepfather, Paul?"

"No, as far as I am aware, Paul Carolli doesn't know I exist. Mother has never told him about me and was quite adamant he not find out. It has something to do with his estate and heirs."

"This may be a good thing. He's not totally clear of suspicion."

Dusty phoned Anna before they left, apologizing for the change in plans.

"I called the hospital this morning when I got up and talked to the nurse on duty," Anna said. "Misty had been awake for a couple of hours. She's groggy, but coherent. I'll meet you over there. I'd like to hear what she has to say."

They all arrived at the hospital at the same time and went up together. Misty was conscious but showed the effects, both physically and mentally, of her ordeal. She had lost weight and appeared haggard and drawn. She was overjoyed to see them, especially her daughter. Paul was at her bedside when they walked in.

Dusty and Kellie had the same thought, "This will be awkward."

Misty was slow to pick up the thread until she saw the shock on her husband's face. Before she could say anything, Kellie motioned Paul out into hallway and explained about Lara. When they returned Paul took Misty and Lara's hands, sat down between them and said with tears in his eyes, "I wish you had told me about this beautiful daughter of yours, so I could have loved her as much as I love you. Kellie explained why you kept it from me. You didn't need to hide her existence from me. Lara, I'd like for you to stay with us a while before you return home. I want us to get to know each other. I'm going to leave and let you two spend some time together. I will be back this evening, and maybe I can talk the doctors into letting your mother out soon."

"I'll talk to her doctor and let you know what his plans are," Anna put in.

When he was gone, Dusty, Kellie and Anna went down to the cafeteria for coffee in order to give mother and daughter some time alone.

"I still say he has to be a hell of an actor, or he is totally innocent."

"He didn't try to kill her. I can tell. He cares too much for her," Kellie replied.

Anna nodded her head in agreement.

"What brings you to this conclusion, women's intuition?"

"Sure, why not. It works better than some of the ideas you come up with."

"Do you want to talk about Jeremy?"

"I guess so. I need some feedback from you two."

"If Anna is to be of any help, she needs to be brought up to speed."

"Well, Jeremy was gone for two weeks. He was supposed to be up north settling a workers' dispute at the mine. I didn't hear anything from him, nor had my father, who sent him up to do the job. After a week, the mine manager phoned Dad to tell him Jeremy hadn't arrived, and the worker situation was getting worse. Dad had to fly up himself and sort things out, which did not make him at all happy.

Finally, my husband shows up yesterday explaining that he was ill in the Saskatoon hospital for the whole time, and the reason he didn't call was he had lost his cell phone. He didn't think to use the hospital phone."

"That's it?" Anna asked.

"That's it."

"Do you believe him?"

"I should believe him. He's my husband."

"Kellie, you're evading the question."

"I don't know if I suspect him of lying or not. I just don't know."

"What about your father? Have you called him and told him what happened?" Anna asked.

"No. I guess this is my next step. I'll call him when I get home."

"Phoning him should have been your first step. You need to go outside with your cell and call him now. He deserves to have some answers after being forced to travel up to that God-forsaken country in the middle of winter," Dusty said.

While Kellie was making her call to Toronto, Dusty pulled Anna aside and told her what John had observed at the storage lot and the cabin at Sun Lakes.

"Anna, what do I do with all this? They are both close friends, and I don't want to be the cause of either getting hurt. As I see it, I have three options. I can talk to Jeremy, tell him what I know and find out if there is a logical explanation for his actions: I can tell Kellie the story I just told you, or I can do nothing."

"I see another alternative. You can call Kellie's father, tell him the story, and suggest he call the hospital up there to check it out. Then it's his problem."

"That is beautiful. I would have never thought of dumping this mess on him."

When Kellie returned, she plunked herself down in the chair and said, "Dad doesn't believe him at all. He thinks Jeremy is lying about even being up there. He's putting a call into the hospital to see if they have any record of Jeremy being admitted."

"What a brilliant idea," Dusty observed.

When the three returned to Misty's room, mother and daughter were in a hug with tears in their eyes. Misty seemed to have gotten noticeably better in the short time span they were away. Lara had opened the curtains allowing the light to stream in and brighten the room.

"Thank you for looking out for me." To Dusty, she said, "The doctors tell me you, Paul, and Anna have been in to visit every day. I guess I was completely out of it, and I don't remember much of what happened. The last thing I recall was getting into my car at your place, Anna. I sort of have a cloudy recollection of being driven somewhere then a terrible pain, after which I woke up in here. Paul told me someone had hit me and pushed my car, with me inside, into the lake."

"Do you have any idea who it was?" Dusty asked.

"No. I didn't see anyone. I don't know. You told me my life might be in danger; you probably have a better idea."

"I have an idea, Misty, but I can't put a name or face to it. It could be tied in with the illegal stuff Paul was involved in."

"You don't think Paul did it, do you?"

"We did at first, but I don't believe so now."

"The one thing I do sort of remember was a strange smell in the car. I've smelled it before, but I can't place when or where. It definitely wasn't my air freshener."

"Can you describe it?"

"Not really, only that it was kind of sweet, like maybe fresh-cut flowers."

"I need to find out where they towed the car. Maybe there is enough of an odor left so that we can identify it. I'll try and track it down later today."

"I think we need to let her get some sleep. This has already been a long first day for her," Anna observed.

Kellie turned her cell phone back on as soon as they walked out of the hospital. It immediately started to chime. The call was from her father.

"The Saskatoon hospital has no record of Jeremy ever being admitted, nor do any of his credit cards show purchases anywhere in Canada for the past month. I'm coming down in a couple of days and we'll straighten this out, and tell Dusty I have that information on the Mexari investors he asked for."

When she relayed the information to Dusty, he took her gently by the shoulders and said, "I knew this would be the case, but I just didn't want you to hear it from me before I had a chance to talk to Jeremy and find out what's going down. Will you promise to wait until we talk before you confront him with this?"

Kellie hesitated but then tearfully agreed.

"That was rough," Anna observed as they drove back to Sun City. "When are you planning to talk to him?"

"Tonight, if I can. I don't know how long I can depend on Kellie to keep her anger under control."

"Do you want me along for support?"

"No. This is something that has to happen between two old friends. I hope there is some reasonable explanation for all this, but the doubts are increasing rapidly. I have to know for sure how deeply he is involved and explain to him how he is apparently being used by Elsina for some ulterior purpose,"

"Did you say her name is Elsina?"

"Yes, Elsina Teija. You remember her from our visit to Arturo's when you treated Rafael's arm."

"Yes, she was that beautiful young woman who served the drinks. How is she tied up in this?"

That's another thing I want to find out. I am inclined to discuss her situation with Arturo, but I'm somewhat concerned he may be involved in some way. This whole thing is becoming one giant puzzle with the good guys against the bad guys, and I'm having trouble figuring who is who. I am also having a talk with Paul on Saturday after our tennis match. Hopefully, he can answer a few questions."

43

Dusty called Jeremy and arranged to meet on the patio. When Jeremy finally emerged from the house, Dusty suggested they go for a walk along the bike path.

"Thank you for giving me an excuse to get out of the house. I feel like Kellie is about ready to explode and dump all over me."

"After what you tried to pull with your fake hospital stay, I don't blame her."

"So, she told you. I figured she would. She always has confided more to you than she ever has with me."

"What is that supposed to mean?"

"C'mon. Don't give me that. She's been hot for you ever since you two worked together up north."

"I don't think so, otherwise why would she have married you?"

"I'm pretty sure that was her old man's idea. Little Kellie does whatever Daddy says."

"That may be partly true, but I've found she does whatever she wants no matter what anyone else thinks. However, that is not what I want to talk to you about."

"Okay. What's bugging you?"

"I spent a weekend prospecting all your claims here in Arizona. There are a few small, low-grade showings and some old shallow diggings, but I sure didn't find much to encourage me to want to do any work on them. Why did you stake them?"

"You may not think much of them, but I have an engineering report indicating these prospects have promise. It recommends further exploration."

"I know. I read Chipman's report. Jeremy, I've had dealings with Mervyn Chipman. He is a crook. You know enough geology to figure out there is nothing on that ground."

"How the hell did you get that report?"

"I downloaded it from your computer downtown."

"So, it was you who broke into my office. I should have figured that. They told me someone had been in there. Why did you do it?"

"I was concerned about why you have been acting strange about these so-called great prospects of yours and evading all my questions ever since I arrived."

"I suppose Fred was in on it. You two never give up. You've been poking your noses into my business ever since we were kids. I think it's time you let me live my life without your interference."

"You have been lucky we did. We bailed you out of a lot of messes."

"Yeah, but that was then, this is now."

They had been walking slowly along Oasis Avenue, where the wind was just strong enough to blow puffs of dust into their faces. When they came to a sidewalk bench, Jeremy sat down and motioned Dusty to join him.

"Okay. You deserve to get the straight deal. For a long time I've wanted my own show. I have been, and still am, sick of working for Angleton. He is a total pain in the ass. He sits in his plush Toronto office making piles of money, while I slave away trying to keep that damn mine operating, and he is totally unappreciative of any of my efforts. I decided it was time to do my own thing, so I formed Mexari, staked some open ground that had a few showings, and paid Chipman to write a glowing report recommending further work. You're right about Mervyn Chipman, he'll write whatever you want him to say. Anyway, on the basis of Chipman's report, Paul Carolli raised the seed money from his contacts in Chicago. I planned to use these funds to option some promising prospects with indicated reserves."

"Okay, that makes sense, but why didn't you?" Dusty asked.

"I'm getting to that. In the meantime I was introduced to two Mexican businessmen who held silver properties in Chihuahua County. They had a geologist's report that indicated recoverable tonnages of high-grade silver ore. They offered to put them into the Company for a control block of shares, and they assured me they could raise more money to develop the deposits. I tried to negotiate them out of control, but they wouldn't budge, so I agreed to their offer. I know it wasn't a good deal, but I figured it was better to have a piece of something with value than total control of nothing."

"Who are these guys?"

"José De La Pena and Javier Cruz. You have probably never heard of them, but they evidently are big time business men and well known down there."

"Oh, I've heard of them and their reputations. They stole those properties from the original farmers that owned them and threatened these poor folks if they didn't sign over titles."

"Who told you that story? I don't believe it."

"Fred talked to the farmers. They were too afraid to tell him much, but his lady Lucinda got the story out of one of the wives who was too angry to keep quiet. Besides, he couldn't locate this geologist that supposedly wrote the report. He got the strong impression the guy doesn't exist. Didn't you go down and check them out yourself?"

"Of course! I showed you some of the samples when you first arrived. So, you sent Fred down to look at those claims and stir up a bunch of trouble."

"Jeremy, you're paranoid. Fred went down on his own accord. He and I are just trying to help. Did Elsina introduce these two partners to you?"

"How do you know about Elsina?" He asked with obvious concern.

"I met her at Arturo's. He's her adoptive father, and Rafael, the fellow who had his hand chopped off is her brother, and while we're on that subject, I have something to show you."

Dusty dug his cell phone out of his pocket and clicked over to the pictures John had emailed to him. He showed the first group to Jeremy.

"Kellie asked my friend and me to try and locate you when she hadn't heard any news and knew you hadn't been to the mine. My friend located your Lexus at the storage lot and waited around until the two of you showed up in that white Toyota. What's going on with you and Elsina?"

Jeremy waited a couple of beats before replying. His face was a mask of anguish. "I love her, and she loves me. I think about her all the time and want to be with her as much as possible. We spent the two weeks together at Javier's villa in La Quinta. You obviously haven't shown these pictures to Kellie or told her about this, or she would have been all over me."

"No. That's up to you. All she knows is that you weren't up in Saskatchewan. Angleton checked with the Meadow Lake hospital and ran your credit card records."

"That bastard! He just can't leave it alone, but it doesn't matter, I've had enough of him. I'm quitting his lousy job. He can find some other chump to look after his mine."

"Before you go off the deep end, I think you need to have a look at the rest of these pictures. When you two left the lot, my friend followed Elsina, as he didn't know who she was at the time. He took these shots at a cabin in Sun Lakes."

Jeremy's hands shook as he held the phone and examined the images.

"Who is the man? The shot isn't clear enough for recognition. Is there a clearer picture?"

"No, that was the best he could get. Is it possibly one of your Mexican partners?"

"It's not them. Both José and Javier are short, no taller than Elsina. This man is at least six feet. There must be some explanation for this, other than the way it appears. She wouldn't cheat on me. She loves me."

"I don't know. The Toyota was still there when my friend left around midnight."

Jeremy was quiet. He sat with his head in his hands saying nothing.

As Dusty waited for him to react, his cell phone rang.

"Where are you?" John asked. "I came over to your place to talk. Kellie said you and her husband had gone for a walk. I have a few interesting tidbits for you."

When Dusty described where they were, he said, "I'll be right over."

Jeremy was momentarily over his despair when John drove up, and they were introduced.

John looked to Dusty and asked, "Has he seen the pictures?"

"I just showed them to him. His mind is busy processing them. What have you got?"

"Well, I checked property files in Sun Lakes. The cabin lot is registered to an Arizona Company, El Centro Holdings, which is controlled by two hombres, José De La Pena and Javier Cruz. There are a few other goodies in the El Centro's basket, including one hundred percent ownership of East Arizona Imports, some California real estate, and a bunch of shares in Mexari."

"So, it all ties together. Did you know about this, Jeremy?"

"Pretty much," he replied. "I didn't know they owned the cabin in Sun Lakes, but it makes sense. Elsina took me there a few times."

It was John's turn to take the next step.

"Jeremy, this whole thing goes deeper than you think. Since Dusty told me of the limited value in your mining holdings, I've been wracking my brain as to the reason these two would want Mexari stock. The only answer I can come up with is they are using your Company as a cover for other illicit operations, like drug running."

"I don't believe that," he responded. "I know what's going on with Mexari. Sure, José and Javier set up an issue of preferred shares to cover the exploratory work they are doing at Chihuahua, but we are not importing drugs."

"Maybe, but John and I see a connection between this drug operation and the Company through Paul. Lonnie was transporting drugs. We know that for a fact, and Paul was his go-to guy. Paul was also responsible for raising your start-up money. Who is buying these preferred shares? Are they part of Paul's group? And, what happened to the money? Fred says there is no indication of recent work on the Chihuahua properties."

"No. These are investors mostly out of Michigan. This coincidence involving Paul doesn't mean there is a connection. If Paul was in the drug chain, it would be on his own. You'll have to talk to him about that. As far as work on the claims is concerned, I have progress reports and expense statements. I think Fred is losing it and probably looked in the wrong places. I'm driving down to Sun Lakes to the cabin. I don't believe your accusations about Elsina either."

John drove them back to Jeremy's house, where he immediately jumped into the Lexus and headed south to the Sun Lakes cabin. As they watched him pull away, John asked, "Do you think we should follow in case there is trouble?"

Dusty thought for a beat then replied, "I don't think so. He's riled enough about my delving into his affairs. If he caught us tracking him now, he would shut us out entirely. He's a big boy. As far as

I'm concerned, he's on his own. Hopefully, he will discover the truth and accept it."

"So, what do you do now?"

"I talk to Paul. I still think he may be the key piece in this puzzle, and I believe he is just frightened enough to unload. Other than that, I want to get together with Arturo. He was checking out the list of Mexican Directors. I'm willing to bet we already know the names of two of them. It will be interesting to learn the backgrounds for Cruz and De La Pena. I just don't know enough about Elsina's part in all this, and I doubt if he suspects her of being involved."

As Dusty climbed out of John's car, Kellie and Lara came down to meet him.

"Where's Jeremy? I thought you two were going for a walk."

"We did. He's gone to check on something. He didn't say when he plans to return."

"Dusty, you're not going to tell me what is going on, are you? I can sense when you are closing up."

"You're right. I'm not. It's up to him to tell you."

"Okay. I'll find out from him."

"Kellie, I'd like you to hold off a little longer before confronting him. We learned a few things, and I don't want him to clam up because he feels under attack."

"I can hold it for a couple of days, but Dad will be coming down here then and you know he won't back off."

"Well, all I can hope for is that I have the whole story by then."

44

Jeremy's mind was in turmoil as he headed for the cabin. That old insecure feeling he had experienced when he was first introduced to Elsina was starting to creep back in. He had been totally stricken from the moment Javier had introduced them. Every day he had gone to his office with the anticipation of seeing her. Their friendship had grown slowly until one day she had suddenly told him how deeply she cared for him. From then on they spent as much time together as Jeremy could manage without raising Kellie's suspicions. When Javier offered the use of his house in La Quinta, he jumped at the chance. The two weeks had been idyllic. By the time they were headed back to Sun City, he was convinced of her love for him and had reveled in the warmth of her presence.

Now the seeds of doubt had been planted by Dusty, John and their pictures, and they were beginning to germinate as he covered the miles to

Sun Lakes. When he pulled up in front of the cabin, his concern deepened. The white Toyota was sitting in the driveway. He pulled in behind it, got out and walked slowly to the front door, somewhat fearful of what he might find inside. The door was locked, but he retrieved the key from the under the ceramic lizard on the patio. Making as little noise as possible he unlocked the door and gently pushed it open. He walked slowly past the rooms at the front of the house to the back bedroom. The door was half open and he could see Elsina's naked body partly covered by a thin blanket. She was asleep. He debated whether to wake her, but he had to have some answers. He walked over to the bed, took her by the shoulders and shook her gently. She shifted her body under the cover and slowly came awake. The shock registered on her face as she regained consciousness.

"What are you doing here?" She asked. "Did you follow me?"

"No, but someone else did the other day. I didn't believe him when he told me where you went. Why did you lie to me, Elsina, and who is the man you met here?"

She didn't answer. She was looking past Jeremy. As he turned to see what had attracted her attention, everything went black.

John was almost to Scottsdale when he pulled into the service station just off 101 for gas, a coffee and a doughnut. He stopped in the parking area to enjoy the first thing he'd had to eat since noon. He couldn't get Jeremy's plight out of his mind. In spite of Dusty's assurance that his friend was capable of looking after himself, John had to admit to himself that he was concerned about the young man's safety. By the time his coffee was cold, he had decided to drive down to the cabin. He turned around and continued south to Sun Lakes.

He pulled up behind the bushes that had hidden him the previous day. There were no lights on in the cabin, but the white Toyota was still in the driveway and Jeremy's Lexus was parked behind it. John took his time approaching the house, continually listening for any sounds or movements from within. All was quiet. He stepped softly onto the porch and tried the front door. It was locked, as was the back door. John debated whether to force his way in. His concern for Jeremy won out over the possible embarrassment of breaking in on their love nest. He walked around the house, trying all the windows. Only a small window at the back of the building appeared to be loose enough to open. He returned to his car, dug a tire iron out of the trunk and eventually pried the window up far enough to slither in feet first. He landed in a small laundry room adjacent to a hallway, which ran the length of the cabin. The door across the hall was partially open. John pushed against it trying to gain access to the room, but it would only open far enough for him to slide in. Jeremy's body lay across the floor against the door.

He was not dead. John could feel a weak irregular pulse and detected shallow breathing. He struggled to lift the body up onto the bed. This sudden movement brought Jeremy slowly back to consciousness. He tried to sit up, but the pain in his head was so intense he just wanted to go back to sleep. John helped him to his feet, but he was too dizzy to stand on his own.

"What happened?" John asked.

"I don't know. I can't remember it all. Elsina was here. I think we talked, but I don't know. The pain in my head is blocking everything out."

"I think we better get you to the hospital."

They struggled out to John's car, where he got Jeremy strapped in before he phoned Dusty.

"Jeremy has been badly hurt. You need to bring Kellie to the Chandler hospital on Frye Road and meet us at Emergency. I'm headed there now."

The hospital staff loaded Jeremy on a gurney for examination. Dusty and Kellie found John in the waiting room working on his second cup of coffee.

"What happened to him? Where is he?" Kellie asked.

John patiently tried to explain to her that he probably had a concussion and the doctor would come as soon as they finished their examination. This seemed to pacify her for the moment, but the questions kept coming.

"What was he doing down here, and how did you happen to find him? Were you two together?"

"Dusty, I think it's time she hears the whole story, and you should be the one to explain it all to her. I've had a long day and am too beat to get into it."

"Okay. I have one question. Why did you go to Sun Lakes? When you left, I thought you were going home."

"I was, but I couldn't shake the feeling he was in danger. Anyway, this time I'm going home for sure. You two need to go over to the cabin and get his car before you go back."

He gave Dusty the address to plug into his GPS.

As he was about to leave, the doctor appeared to inform them that Jeremy had a severe concussion and was still in a coma. He needed to stay in the hospital until he was conscious and stable. They needed to conduct further tests to determine the extent of the injury and if there would be any brain damage. The doctor escorted them into the ward where Jeremy was asleep and suggested Kellie go home. He assured her he would phone if there was any change in her husband's condition.

On the way to Sun Lakes, Dusty related as much as he knew about Jeremy's antics to his friend's wife. Kellie was quiet until they reached the cabin.

"So, he told you he's in love with this Elsina babe and can't live without her, and all the while she's hooked up with someone else and is playing him for a sucker. Somehow, I don't seem to find much empathy for him. Dusty, why didn't you tell me all this before? I probably could have handled it bit by bit rather than have it all dumped on me tonight. I guess he and I are finally done, although in reality our marriage was finished long ago."

"All along I figured it was up to him to tell you, when in reality I probably knew he never would."

"You're right. He would have just taken off in the middle of the night with his little girl toy and eventually come whining back to me when she got sick of him."

"So, what are you going to do?"

"Probably nothing until he recovers from the beating. Then I will file for divorce and end this farce of a marriage. Beyond that, I don't know."

"Well, take it slow. Don't make any rash decisions guided by your anger. Do you have a set of keys for the Lexus? I hope so."

"I do, but I would like to go through the cabin. I don't know why; maybe it's just to see where some of this treachery took place."

While they were walking through the house, Kellie's cell phone went off.

"Mrs. Prince, this is Chandler Medical Center. You need to return to the hospital. Your husband has taken a turn for the worse."

When they got there, the doctor was summoned and met them at Emergency. He took Kellie by the arm and led her to a chair.

"Your husband has suffered an acute subdural hematoma from a severe blow to the head. The brain is slowly filling with blood. We are trying to stop the bleeding and relieve the pressure. This is all we can do at present. If this was the result of an inflicted injury rather than an accident, I am required to file a report with the police."

"We don't know how he received this injury," Dusty replied.

After the doctor had left, Kellie remained in the chair staring into space. There were no words; there were no tears. She just sat there until Dusty gently helped her up and led her to the Lexus.

"I'll drive you home."

When they got in the car, he put his arm around her as the tears started to flow.

"It's not fair. He fell in love; I understand that, and he cheated on me, but he didn't deserve to suffer like this. Dusty, we have to find out who did this."

"I plan to. We start with a visit to Elsina. If she thinks she is going to get all the blame, maybe it will frighten her into revealing the name of her boyfriend. Right now you need to go home and get some rest. I'll call Lara and tell her what happened."

They were both quiet on the trip back to Sun City, each lost in his own thoughts. Kellie was composed by the time she reached home.

Sunday morning was greeted by a warm westerly wind blowing swirls of dust along the streets of Sun City. By noon Kellie had notified Jeremy's relatives and friends of his condition and was making preparations to visit him. Dusty was still in bed when Lara came over and invited him to brunch.

A relaxed Kellie met him at the door.

"I want to confront Elsina as soon as possible before she learns about what happened. Can you contact her father and set it up? Besides, he must have some information on those Mexican directors. It probably doesn't matter now, except I will have to look after sorting out Jeremy's part of Mexari."

"I'll call Arturo and see what we can do. Do I need to make the call from my clean phone?"

"No. I had the house and phone debugged again last week. It was clean."

Dusty called Arturo's cell and left the message and number for a call back. Fifteen minutes later the old man was on the line.

"I was going to call you today. Some disturbing events have taken place."

"Can we come over and see you today? We would like to talk to you and Elsina, but I have one request, and I hope it will not offend you. I would ask you to have Elsina at your home when we arrive without telling her we are coming or that we wish to speak with her. I will explain fully and to your satisfaction if you will do this."

"I cannot do this. Elsina has left, and I do not know where she has gone. She was on holiday for two weeks, but returned home yesterday only long enough to pack all her belongings and leave in her little car. I am desolate. I don't know what has come over her."

"It is a long sordid tale. I believe I know why she left, and I will tell you the whole story. She is involved indirectly in the beating of a man and is probably running scared. I doubt if she will return to her home."

"I wish very much to hear what you have to say, but I must ask you, does the name Javier Cruz mean anything to you?"

"Yes! Absolutely! He may be an integral part of this."

"I thought so. I have much to tell you about Javier. I suggest we meet tomorrow. Hopefully, Elsina will have returned home by then."

45

In the middle of the night, Dusty's cell phone started ringing at ten to three. It quit ringing at seven to three, still hidden beneath his bed as he searched frantically for it through all the bed covers. He recognized the last number that had called. It was Anna's cell. She answered on the third ring and asked him to wake Lara and come down to the hospital. Misty was awake and wanted to talk to them.

"She's climbed out of her fog and is making a lot more sense."

When Lara and Dusty entered Misty's room, she was alone, sitting in an easy chair by the window. The ordeal had taken its toll on her body, especially her beautiful face. Instead of her normal buoyant, perky look, it was laced with lines and had lost that glow that made her unique. She wrapped her arms around her daughter, holding her tight as if she never wanted to let go. To Dusty, she held his face in her hands and whispered, "Thank you. I am so sorry to hear about Jeremy. I hope he will be alright. I have been trying to remember the events of that night, but not much is coming back. However. I believe that smell in the car was lavender."

"That was the perfume Aunt Janet used to wear," Lara observed.

Misty thought for a moment then said, "You're right. It was. I had forgotten that."

"Who is Aunt Janet?" Anna asked.

'She is the older lady I was telling you about. Janet Lorne is her name," Misty replied, trying to answer Anna's question without going into the details in front to her daughter. Anna caught the implications, but Dusty was confused.

"Is this the woman you …." he blurted out then suddenly stopped.

His realization was confirmed when Anna jabbed him in the ribs to keep him quiet,

"You guys don't have to go to all this trouble to hide Mom's relationship with Aunt Janet from me," Lara announced. "I've known about it since I was a kid and caught the two of you in bed one night."

Misty took her daughter's hand.

"I had hoped to keep the whole sorry affair from you, but I guess I was being unrealistic."

"It's okay, Mom," her daughter replied. "It's no big deal."

"So, do you think it was this woman that tried to kill you?" Anna asked.

"I don't know. I just remember that hint of lavender smell before I passed out."

"I think we need to have a talk with her and at least try and find out where she was that night," Dusty said.

"I agree," said Anna. "Misty, you told me she was extremely jealous of you with other women and threatened to kill you."

"I know, but I didn't take her as being serious."

"Maybe you should have. If she found out about us, that could have set her off."

"That's right. I had forgotten. She did know we had been together, got real angry and told me to get out of her house."

"Tomorrow we will go and confront her. Anna, if you and Lara will come with me, maybe we can trick her or get her angry enough to make a mistake. Other than that, we have nothing but the lingering smell of her perfume in the car to pin on her."

As they were walking back to the cars, Dusty said to Anna, "I'll treat you to an early breakfast and we can try and work out a plan to confront this woman tomorrow."

Kellie returned from the Chandler hospital just before noon...

"There is very little change in his condition. He is still in a coma, but his vital signs are stronger. The doctor seemed positive, although he believes Jeremy's recovery is going to take some time. He expects they will have to keep him there for a couple of weeks. I want to go to Arturo's home now and talk to Elsina, if she is there."

On the drive to Arturo's, Dusty described the events of the morning and their plan to talk to this Janet the next day.

"Are you talking about Janet Lorne?"

"Yes. Do you know her?"

"Oh yeah! She's a bitch. I met her about a year ago at some Association event. She disrupted the whole meeting with her big mouth. I remember I was tempted to go over and personally shut her up. Anyway, I heard her husband died all of a sudden a few months ago. It was a bit of a shock to those that knew them, as he seemed to be in good health and then he was dead."

"That's interesting. Maybe we'll bring it up when we talk with her."

"Good luck! She's a tough old bird. Who is going?"

"I'm taking Anna and Lara with me. We have a bit of a plan to put her off her guard."

Arturo was standing in the doorway when they pulled up in front of his house. He seemed agitated and hurried them out to the patio where a pitcher of margaritas was icing on the table.

"Your phone call was very troubling. I wish to know what trouble Elsina has gotten involved in. She has not returned and I am at a loss as to what to do."

Dusty described the events John had observed at the storage lot and the Sun Lakes cabin as well as Jeremy's reaction to it and his subsequent beating at the hands of an unknown assailant when he went to the cabin.

Arturo thought for a minute then replied, "This news is very disturbing. I was aware she was seeing someone for the past year. I asked her to bring him to our home, so I could meet him, but there was always some excuse why he couldn't make it."

Turning to Kellie, he asked, "Do you think it was your husband she has been with?"

"No," she replied. "There was another man who John saw at the cabin. He was probably the person who hit Jeremy. If we knew who he is, it would probably lead us to your daughter."

"We must endeavor to identify this man. This brings up the matter of Javier Cruz. This is a very dangerous man. He has come to my attention before. Mr. Sherant, you may remember me telling you about the kidnapping and murder of Elsina's father by a Mexican family involved in the drug trade. The leader of that family was Javier Cruz. We knew he was responsible; the Mexican police knew also, but they were unable to get enough evidence to bring him to trial. He was also indirectly responsible for the death of her mother. One of the reasons I adopted Elsina was to protect her from him and his family."

"It would seem he is still involved in her life. My friend discovered he is part owner of East Arizona Imports, the Company which employs Elsina and whose office is next door to Mexari."

"Yes," Arturo said, "and he is a director and the major shareholder of Mexari stock."

"It is becoming clear the only way we can sort out the story of what is going on involves Cruz and four people. Everything points to Cruz as being the ringleader, but somehow, to me, it doesn't fit. I think someone on this side of the border is calling the shots. If we can find Elsina and get her to open up to us: if Paul is willing to reveal his part in the operation: if Jeremy regains consciousness: and if we can find and question Elsina's lover, maybe we can get the whole picture. I know that is a lot of 'ifs', but we have to do something before anyone else gets killed or injured. Arturo, do you want to go to the police and report Elsina as a 'missing person'."

"No, I think she left on her own. If I send the police after her, she will be alienated and probably never return."

"Okay. I'll be talking to Paul. Hopefully I can learn enough to set our course of action."

Before returning to Sun City, Dusty and Kellie drove to Chandler to check on Jeremy.

"He came out of his coma for a short time this morning," the doctor reported, "but he was totally disoriented and had no memory of the events of the past few days. I see a long period of convalesce ahead. We can arrange for a transfer to the hospital in Sun City if you would prefer."

"Please do. My friend is a nurse there and can keep us apprised of his condition."

On the ride back to Sun City, Kellie asked, "Why did you tell Arturo you didn't think Cruz was the leader?"

"Just a gut feeling. All the bad stuff has taken place on this side of the border, and what really makes me wonder is that everyone I've talked to: Paul, Lonnie and that bozo Lucinda shot, all tell of getting their orders from the Arab, some guy with a strong mid-eastern accent. I think the answers will come when we find Elsina's boyfriend."

They found Lara at the house when they returned. Anna had given her a ride home and was still there, trying to calm her down.

"Mother is sure it was Aunt Janet who tried to kill her. She said that now her head is clear and it all fits. Paul was there. When he heard all this he said he was going to confront her."

"That is the last thing we want. He'll spook her for sure. I need to warn him off and let him in on our plan."

While Dusty was on the phone with Paul, Kellie asked Lara, "Did your mother say anything about Joel Lorne, Janet's husband?"

Lara didn't answer right away. The tears started to flow as Anna put her arm around the young woman. It took a few minutes for her to compose herself.

"It is strange you should ask that. Her husband died recently from a reported heart attack, but Mom has suspicions that it may have been induced. It had to do with medication she found in their medicine cabinet. She can't prove it, but she feels Aunt Janet killed him."

"Tell her the rest," Anna urged.

"Lara hesitated then went on, "Joel Lorne was my father."

·

46

The day of confrontation had arrived. Dusty had been successful in persuading Paul to hold off facing Janet Lorne. Anna and Lara were skeptical but ready to take her on.

"I want in on this," Kellie announced after breakfast.

Dust shrugged his shoulders then took her hand and sat her down beside him.

"Kellie, you have a lot of great qualities I admire, but when it comes to confronting people, you are a loose cannon. This is a sensitive situation, and we don't need your 'bull in a china shop' approach. Misty wanted to come also, but we felt she is too emotionally close to the problem to be much help. So, just trust us on this one."

Dusty made a couple of phone calls then they took off in Anna's car for the high-priced part of Sun City. Janet Lorne was home and met them at the door.

"Lara," she cried and moved to embrace the young woman. Lara automatically pulled back, causing the older woman to exclaim, "What's the matter? Aren't you happy to see your Aunt Janet?"

"Yes, of course," she stammered, "but we need to talk first."

"What is so important that you can't give your Aunt Janet a hug?"

"My mother believes you tried to kill her."

Dusty and Anna winced at this last statement. This girl was way off the script they had prepared.

"That's foolishness," Janet said. "I know your mother is still in a coma. Why would you think she believes that nonsense?"

"Because she told me. She is no longer unconscious and remembers what happened."

In spite of Lara rushing in with her accusation, Anna could see the words were having an effect on the older woman, who stepped back and cautiously invited them in to an elegant living room. Turning to Anna, she said, "I know you. You're the little slut Misty has been playing with, her little girl toy. And you," she pointed to Dusty, "you're the boy toy. What's wrong with you people? Misty and I have had a very loving relationship for years. Surely you know that, Lara."

"No. I don't know that. Maybe it was true in the past, but you told her to get out of your house and that you never wanted to see her again. How is that a loving relationship?"

"That was a misunderstanding. You're just too young and naive to understand what we have had between us all these years. Who do you think supported you two while you were growing up and paid for you to go to a good school? It was me, because your mother and I loved each other."

"Are you sure it wasn't because your husband was my father, and you felt guilty for pushing the two of them into the relationship? In fact, mother has the idea that you somehow caused his death by messing with his medication."

Anna had kept quiet. She could see that Lara was holding her own in the verbal exchange, but had decided to jump into the fray and help her out. She was also aware the older woman was starting to wilt as a result of Lara's last statement.

"The other thing you should know," Anna added, "was that Misty had grown tired of you. She and I had decided to move away from here and be together."

"Why would she want you and your ugly face?" Janet snarled.

"Because she was tired of looking at you and your wrinkled old body."

The older woman lunged at Anna. Dusty was anticipating the move and charged between them grabbing Janet, but he had underestimated the strength and anger of the woman. She pushed him back into a free-standing bookcase, tripping him at the same time. Dusty landed heavily and the bookcase fell over on top of him.

As the two women ended up on the floor, he shouted into his hidden microphone for John to come right away with police support. Hebrano and a Sun City officer had been waiting in a car listening and immediately rushed into the house. They pulled the two women apart, sat them on the sofa and tried to calm them.

"I'm taking you down to the station," the officer said to Janet. "I think it's time you answered a few questions. We also need to have a talk with Misty Carolli now that she is conscious."

He escorted Janet to the patrol car.
The next ten minutes were spent trying to
extract Dusty from the confines of the bookcase.
Short of a bit of bruising, he suffered little damage
from the event.

"That did not go as well as I had hoped," John
announced. "I don't think we have enough on that
tape for the cops to lay a charge. If she's as smart as
I think she is, she'll have her lawyer spring her out
of there before the day is over. Anna, you could lay
an assault charge and with all our testimonies, it
would probably stick. Other than that, it looks to me
like she's gotten away with attempted murder."

While they were walking out to the cars,
Dusty's cell rang: it was Kellie.

After hearing the results of the morning's
confrontation, she announced, "I went downtown to
Jeremy's office this morning to get his computer.
There was a new lock on the door; there was no
way I could get in. I tried the import company
office next door, but there was no one there, and it
was locked as well."

Dusty thought for a minute then replied, "It's
probably the work of this Javier Cruz. We know
that he and his partner actually control both Mexari
and East Arizona Imports, and Elsina runs the East
Arizona Import office. Since she is missing, I'm not
surprised their office is shut down. Kellie, this tells
me Jeremy's life may still be in danger. I suspect
Cruz doesn't want him back and is probably
concerned that Jeremy will come out of his coma
and will start talking about what is really going on.
We will be back in a few minutes, and we can
decide what to do next."

Before he got into his car, Dusty told John what
Kellie had discovered, "It tripped something in the

back of my mind that has been bouncing around. I believe this connection between Mexari and East Arizona, and between Jeremy and Elsina may be the key to the whole picture. Can you find out from the rental agency for that building the actual dates that the two companies took possession of their offices? I think we also need to know what the import company is bringing in and who their customers are"

"Getting the rental information shouldn't be too tough, but getting the lowdown on East Arizona could take a little longer" John replied. "The building management probably handles their own rentals."

Anna was emotionally distraught after her physical encounter with Janet Lorne.

"I need to go home and lay down for a couple of hours. I'll drive you two back then come over later, and we will go over to the hospital."

"That'll work," Dusty said. "One thing, will you phone the nurses' station near Jeremy's room and ask them to keep out any visitors. It may be an unnecessary precaution, but I'd rather not take any chances."

When they pulled into the driveway, Kellie was standing in the open doorway with the phone in her hand.

"John just phoned and wants you to call him back immediately."

"I'll use my cell. I still don't trust your land line."

His call was answered on the first ring.

"This is interesting," John announced. "First of all, I talked to an agent in the rental division. East Arizona Imports leased the original office. The signature on the agreement was 'Jose de la Pena'.

This was in August of 2010. There is no record of any office space leased to Mexari. This hit me as strange, so I contacted the building superintendent. He tells me that the import bunch built a divider wall down the center of their office, making two units, installed a separate doorway in the second office and sub-leased it to Mexari. As far as East Arizona's products and clientele is concerned, I'm not sure how to check them out short of breaking into their office, which is an option I don't want to think about."

"We'll put that on hold. I need to run something by you and Kellie. How soon can you come over here?"

"Ten or fifteen minutes, I'm not far away."

When John arrived, they gathered in the kitchen while Kellie poured coffee.

"Like I mentioned before, something clicked in my mind about the connections between the two companies and the Jeremy and Elsina relationship. Your information about the rental situation makes the connections even stronger. Since East Arizona remodeled their office for Mexari, and de la Pena and Cruz control both companies, the connection is obvious, but the way Jeremy was put in touch with this bunch intrigues me. Kelly, you said that Dan helped Jeremy form his company and find office space, and Anna later told me almost the same thing. It's making me wonder where Dan Seaborne fits in this whole mess, and who is Mr. Big, running the operation. I'm thinking one question answers the other."

"Are you saying Dan Seaborne is the Arab?"

"I don't know, but it explains a few things that have been puzzling me. I thought his concern for his sister's welfare, when we were out examining those claims, was a bit over the top, but it makes sense if he knew his boys were going to attack us."

"In that case," John observed, "we need to do a deep background check on him."

"Anna has related a few stories about him. Evidently she lived with Dan and Dolly in Detroit after her parents were killed. I can probably find out more, but I don't want to raise her suspicions that we may be investigating her brother, and I don't want him thinking we suspect him of being involved."

"You know, thinking back, I remember Jeremy telling me a couple of years ago of how impressed he was of Dan's knowledge of the mining business and how companies operate," Kellie said. "If he worked out Detroit, Dad should be able to find out what we need."

"I may be way off base suspecting him, and for Anna's sake, I hope I'm wrong, but it all seems to fit."

Before they could take the discussion any further, they heard Anna's car on the driveway. As Kellie walked to the door to welcome her, she said, "We keep this all to ourselves until we get some hard evidence."

All except John rode to the hospital in Kellie's Lexus. He was eager to get started sourcing East Arizona Imports: their products, clients, and possible warehouse location.

When they arrived at the hospital, they found Jeremy was still in a coma with no discernible change in his condition. Misty, on the other hand, was up and alert and ready to go home the next day. Paul was there and motioned to Dusty as he walked in. They stepped out into the hall and Paul suggested they go to the cafeteria, where they could talk in private.

"I'm getting her released and taking her home tomorrow. I've asked Lara to come and stay, but I am afraid I may be putting them in danger. Dusty, I need your help. I got into this mess, and I don't know how to get free."

"I will try Paul, but you need to level with me and tell me the whole story. I have an idea what is going on, but there is a lot of blanks that need filling, and now that Jeremy is out of it, you are the only one with the answers. I know about the drug smuggling and using Mexari as cover and have a pretty good picture of your role in the operation. I also know you are not the boss, or we would not be having this conversation. I want the big boss. You are never going to be safe until he is out of commission. Do you know who it is?"

"Dammit Dusty, if I knew, I would have had him killed in a heartbeat."

"Okay, to have this talk we will have to go somewhere safe. I want you to tell me the whole story from day one of how you got into this and everything that has happened since. If we can tie that in to what my friend John and I suspect, maybe we can end this nightmare."

47

John called Dusty the next morning.

"Two things of interest I need to pass on. Firstly, Janet Lorne has been released. As we predicted, she got her lawyer in right away. Unfortunately, my friends downtown don't have enough evidence to hold her, much less lay a charge. Then there is East Arizona. They have a small warehouse on Grand Avenue. I went there, but of course it is securely locked. As far as who their clients are, I can't get a handle on that."

"I guess I need to break into that warehouse, but I think I should do it alone. I've already gotten you on the wrong side of your friends."

"Yes, they are getting a bit hostile about me interfering in police business, but what about Carolli? If we could get his story and lay that in their laps, we would both be heroes."

"He wants to talk, John, but he's scared to death. We need to get him some place where he feels safe then maybe he'll open up."

"What about my home in Scottsdale. It's far enough away from Sun City he may feel better about it. I've had the house checked for bugs."

"That would probably work, but we're going to have to sneak him over there as I'm sure he's being watched."

That afternoon Paul made himself visible as he escorted Misty and her daughter from the hospital to his car and drove them to his home. With the car in the garage and the doors shut, as prearranged, he rushed through the house and out the back door to John's waiting vehicle. They immediately took off for Scottsdale. For the first few miles, they constantly checked for anyone following. By the time they had reached the Sun City limits, they were convinced no one was on their tail.

Paul started in, "I got a call from the Arab last evening. He's running another delivery tomorrow night. He told me it was my job this time to handle it, but something is out of line. First of all, the previous delivery notices have all been placed through the 'Help Wanted' ads in the Republic, and this time, delivery is not to a drop location, but I am to hand the packages personally to the night watchman at the Desert Museum down north of Tucson."

"That doesn't sound good," John replied. "I have this feeling you are being set up or your man is acting out of desperation, or both."

"Where is the plane coming in for you to make the pickup?"

"About two miles past the Museum gates, on the south side of North Kinney Road. It is supposed to happen at two in the morning."

As soon as he was out of heavy traffic, John pulled over to the curb and took a road map from the glove box.

"This is past the point of an evening's adventure. We need to bring in the police. Unfortunately, this is set to take place in Pima County, and all my contacts are here in Maricopa. I need to make a few calls and get the boys down in Tucson to send a couple of fellows to meet with us. I appreciate that bringing the police in would not be your first choice, Paul, but the risk not to is too great here."

Dusty took a turn at the wheel while John put through his calls. After he had explained the situation to his local contacts in the Sheriff's office, they had reluctantly given him names in the Tucson office. He called Tucson, explained it all and waited for a call back while they checked him out. They pulled up in front of his house as the return call came through. It was agreed they would drive to Tucson the next morning and meet with two officers.

John Hebrano's house was set in a small cul-de-sac on the north side of Scottsdale.

"We have the place to ourselves," John said. "I sent my wife over to her sister's. She got used to my secret meetings in my days on the Force, so it wasn't a surprised. First of all, I think you two should stay here tonight so we can get an early start to Tucson tomorrow."

"If we're going to do that, I need to let Misty know. The girls are expecting me back tonight," Paul replied.

"I'll set that up with Kellie. We don't want any calls going into your house," Dusty offered.

When he called Kellie, he asked her to go to the Rec. Center and call him back. Ten minutes later she made the call and informed him that her father was coming into Sky Harbor on an afternoon flight and had some interesting answers to their questions. She offered to drive over to the Corolli house before she went to the airport.

"Paul, we want to hear the whole story of how this operation is set up and how you got involved in it. Hopefully your willingness to cooperate can be used to lessen any charges laid against you."

"I need a drink for this," he replied.

Sipping on a scotch and water, he began, "Forty years ago in Chicago, I had a position as Chief Financial Officer of a Union. It was in bad financial shape when I took over, but in three years I put it in the black and the future looked bright. I was in charge of paying the bills, making collections and investing any surplus funds. I had gone along with traditional investments and we had done pretty well with them. One day these two fellows came to my office from a small brokerage house with an interesting proposal. They had underwritten a group of chemists who had developed a system of extracting gold from rock, which was too low-grade for traditional methods. They offered to let us in on the ground floor for a substantial investment. I checked out the story as best I could. Experts I talked to had not heard of the process, but said it was possibly feasible. I researched the brokers, Higgs and Norman, and found they were small but had been around for over three decades. When I contacted their office, I was told the original founders were dead, and the present owner was out of the country. Those two brokers were pressuring me for a decision. They assured me a twenty percent return on the investment within the year. I finally went ahead, signed the papers, invested half a million dollars of the Union's funds in this new company, and received the share certificates. At that point the whole thing fell apart. For four months, I heard nothing: no contact from the brokers, no company news, nothing. My worry turned to panic when I discovered the names of the chemists were fictitious, and there were no records of this Company that I had invested in so heavily. When I tried to contact Higgs and Norman, I found the office closed and the firm no longer doing business."

"Okay, at that point you were sitting there with half a million dollars of worthless stock certificates and some explaining to do to your Union members, but you hadn't broken the law. You had acted foolishly, but if stupidity was a crime, our jails would be overflowing," John said.

"I know," Paul went on, "but that's not the end of it. To cover the whole thing up, I created a false paper trail, indicating the money went to other acceptable investments and projects that didn't pan out. I covered all this with phony receipts, agreements, etc. Since our other investments were doing so well, no one spotted the discrepancy."

"So, what was the problem?" Dusty asked. "It sounds like you were able to cover yourself."

"That's what I thought until two years ago when UPS delivered this package to my door. Inside were photocopies of all the agreements, correspondence and payment cheques covering the bad investment. A note informed me that it would be appreciated if I performed a few simple tasks or the original documents would be forwarded to the proper authorities."

"Okay, so in essence, you committed fraud. The investment you made wasn't illegal, but your act of covering it up could have gotten you in trouble with someone, either the Union, the State or the Feds," John observed. "However, I'm thinking the Statute of Limitations comes into play. Any action against you would have to have been taken within, say a ten-year period. When you got that package so long after the event, you were probably in the clear."

Paul was quiet for a moment then said, "I remember thinking about that at the time, but I was too scared to follow through."

"This is beginning to make sense," Dusty observed. "This brokerage house, Higgs and Norman, where were they located? Was it by chance somewhere in Michigan? "

"Yes. They had only one office. It was in Detroit. How did you know?"

"We'll get to that. What was the name of this new owner who had bought the Firm?"

"I don't know. The only people I met were the two salesmen, and it was their names, which appeared on the documents. Oh, and I talked to a girl in the office."

"Have you got the names of those two salesmen?"

"Sure, I brought all the papers with me. Let's see," Paul said as he shuffled through the stack of document. "Here they are, Terrence Yancey and Thomas McCrae with some letters behind the names."

"Dusty, can you get in touch with Kellie and get her father to check on these two and locate them?" John asked. "It might be a challenge after all these years."

"I may not need to. The names ring a bell. Do you still have the download of all that stuff on Jeremy's computer? I'm pretty sure I saw those names in the Mexari documents."

While John was searching through the files on his computer, Dusty had Paul describe in detail how the operation was run.

"I found them," John announced. "They were part of the group out of Detroit buying shares. They were on that list we gave to Angleton."

By late afternoon, they had decided they needed to go back to Sun City and sneak Paul into his house.

"If the Arab's boys are watching the house, and I'm sure they are, we need to have them see you leave for the Museum area tomorrow, as instructed. Should they get suspicious, I have no doubt they will abort the delivery plan. Paul, you do exactly as they directed. Dusty and I will meet with the police in Tucson and try to convince them the whole thing is real. If they think it's a hoax and opt out, we will still be there to back you up."

They were almost sure Paul's house was under surveillance. When they drove by, keeping him out of sight, they tried to spot a suspicious vehicle, but everyone had a garage and there were no cars parked on the street. They covered a few other nearby streets with the same results.

"Maybe, we're getting too paranoid," Dusty said. "Chances are they may not have the house under surveillance."

"Possible," John replied, "but I'm not ready to take that chance. I did notice on our first run by your house there are a few places up for sale on the block, especially the one next door and another directly across from the entrance to your cul-de-sac. Paul, do you know if either of those houses is vacant?"

"Yes, they both are and have been empty for at least six months."

"That could be our answer. One person set up in each house with binoculars and night glasses would be able to spot any movement. It looks like chances of sneaking him in could be slim."

"Unless there's no surveillance, or if there is, we can create a diversion."

"Okay, here's what we do. I will walk along the street across from the cul-de-sac and act as an interested buyer in that house. I'll pick up a brochure and go in close, walk around and see if it looks set up. Dusty, you and Paul stay here in the car, but we keep our phones connected. If I see signs of anyone in there, I'll tell you and then start making a racket trying to open the back door. When I give you the word, you pull into the cul-de-sac quickly, let Paul out and drive away fast. Paul, you need to stay low. Crawl on your belly if you have to, but get in the house as fast as possible. Dusty, you can pick me up on the next street over, providing I get out of there alive."

Dusty and Paul waited for some sign from John to get under way. He gave a running account of his progress in a whisper so low Dusty had to turn his phone volume on full.

"It looks like a low-level flickering light on in the front room. It's probably coming from the TV," he whispered. "I'm going in close and see if I can spot anyone."

They could hear the rustle of the foliage and the sound of the gravel beneath his feet as he moved up to a large window at the side of the house.

"I can't see anyone, but something is making shadows move on the wall. Again, probably the television, or someone or something is in there. I'm going around to the back and try and go in. Be ready for my signal."

They heard the squeal of the door hinges and John's shout, "Go!"

Dusty raced the car into the cul-de-sac, practically pushed Paul out of the passenger seat and took off. He was half a block away when he heard the shot.

48

Jeremy wavered back and forth through various levels of consciousness. He knew who he was and that he occupied a bed in the Sun City hospital, but he had no idea how he had gotten there. Anna was working the evening shift and was the first to note his improvement. She phoned Kellie, who immediately came with her father to the hospital. Jeremy recognized them but was unable to communicate and didn't understand much of what they told him. They left at eleven. Anna checked in on him one more time before she went off shift at midnight.

The next thing he knew, a nurse was beside the bed. She bent down close, their faces almost touching. He had a brief vague flash of recognition before it all went black. His death wasn't discovered until the early morning rounds. His body had received a lethal injection of heroin.

The immediate police investigation was unsuccessful. No one had been observed entering or leaving Jeremy's room during the night.

Admittedly, the red-eye shift had been understaffed, and no one had checked his room until early morning. Only the surveillance camera set up near the elevator gave any clue. It had recorded a number of people coming and going, and all were recognized by the staff except one nurse. Since Anna was the last person to see Jeremy alive, she was called in and questioned. When shown the tape, she somehow felt she recognized the distorted image of the unknown woman. She racked her brain trying to fit the picture to a member of the staff.

Kellie was notified immediately, and she and her father were requested to return to the hospital for a few questions. Kellie was almost certain she recognized the woman on the tape as Elsina but was reticent to relay this information to the police, as she wondered if her hatred of her husband's lover was clouding her judgment. If she was wrong, she would probably be causing this young woman more grief than she deserved. In spite of the deterioration of their marriage, she was deeply saddened by his death. There was a time, she remembered, when she had loved him, and they were happy.

The police required the body for autopsy but informed her she would be notified when it was released. She tried to phone Dusty to pass on the sad news, but her calls were all dumped into voice mail. Finally she left the message that it was urgent for him he call her.

It had all gone exactly as planned. Surely, he would now believe she loved him, loved him enough to kill for him. Elsina took off the nurse's outfit as soon as she returned to her car, pulling on jeans and a tee for the trip to Sun Lakes. Along the way she dropped the uniform into a dumpster behind a convenience store. She drove directly to the cabin. She parked the Miata in the driveway, dug the key out from under the lizard and went inside. She headed directly to the small kitchen. She removed a panel from the back of a cupboard and retrieved her nickel-plated revolver. It was her most treasured possession, a gift from her father before he was murdered. On the day he died, she vowed to herself she would use this weapon to take vengeance on the man responsible, Javier Cruz. The gun was old, an Iver Johnson 32 caliber, but she had shined and oiled it regularly, waiting for the right time. She was eager to meet with her lover and go south. He had assured her he would help her in her quest, but there was one other matter to take care of before she went to him. Right now she needed sleep; tomorrow was going to be a busy day.

Arturo had been severely disturbed by Elsina's sudden departure. He had loved her as if she was his natural daughter and couldn't understand why she hadn't confided in him about her troubles. Sherant's explanation of her behavior was a shock, and he still didn't quite believe it. As he sat by the pool sipping his morning coffee, he was deep in thought when he heard a soft noise behind him. He turned to see Elsina standing behind his lounge. His immediate joy at seeing her again quickly turned to concern when he caught sight of the gun in her hand.

"What?"

"Be quiet. I will do the talking this time."

Arturo started to get up from the lounge, but Elsina brought the gun to his head and pushed him back down.

"Get comfortable before you die old man. I regret you won't suffer as much as my mother while she rotted in that jail. You could have used your power to get her out, but you couldn't be bothered, or were you afraid of what Cruz would do if you crossed him?"

Sweat was starting to form all over his body. He could feel the power of her anger and hatred. He knew she was partly right. He had tried to have her mother freed, and he had been haunted for years by the knowledge that he could have done more.

"I tried to have her released, but the charges were too serious. They would have gone easier on her, but she refused to tell who she was working for."

"You could have told them. They would have listened to you, but you were afraid, weren't you, afraid what Cruz and his 'matones' would do to you?"

Arturo did not respond. What she said was true.

"All I could do was take you into my home and raise you as my own daughter."

"So you wouldn't feel the guilt."

As Arturo started to stand up, Elsina hit him hard across the side of the head with the butt of her gun. The old man crumpled back into the lounge, barely conscious. Quickly she retrieved the syringe from her pocket and emptied the rest of the lethal heroine dose into his arm. He struggled against her efforts, but he was weakening. She calmly pushed him with the lounge into the pool and held his head under water until there was no further movement. Then she quickly collected the remainder of her possessions, emptied his safe and left.

After he heard the shot, Dusty drove quickly down the street behind the house John had entered. All was quiet, and there was no sign of his friend.

He made two more passes along the street, continually trying unsuccessfully to raise John on the cell. Finally, he parked on the street a block away and walked slowly, keeping in the shadows, back to their planned meeting spot. As he neared a group of cacti he heard a voice faintly calling his name. He waited while John crawled out from under some shrubs.

"We've got to get out of here fast. I think he's still out there looking for me. The son of a bitch shot me in the leg."

"Get out of sight," Dusty said. "I'll get the car and stop just long enough for you to get in. Have you got your gun in case he's still looking for you?"

"No, hell. I dropped it and the phone when I got hit, and I didn't have much incentive to look for them with him coming after me."

"Okay, just stay low, and we'll get you out of here."

Paul had jumped out of the car as Dusty stopped just long enough for him to get the door open. He hit the loose gravel, fell but kept moving. He crawled to the side door, dug the key out of his pocket and slowly opened the door. The motion light went on, followed by Lara holding his shotgun pointed at him. She put it down immediately and rushed to help him to his feet and into the kitchen where Misty was waiting. His first action was to caution them not to talk, explaining on paper that the entire house was probably one big transmitter. With the lights out, he looked out all the windows, checking the surrounding empty houses for any activity. Only the house across from the cul-de-sac had any lights on.

John was in pain. They had pulled over and Dusty was able to tie off the bleeding with a makeshift tourniquet. He would have liked to call Anna and have her look at the wound, but he was now hesitant to confide in her, since he was now convinced Dan was involved.

"Take me home," John demanded. "If we go to a hospital, the police will be notified and we'll have a whole bunch of explaining to do. My wife's sister used to be a nurse. I can trust her to take care of this and keep quiet. We have to get me mobile by tomorrow morning to meet those two officers down in Tucson."

John's sister-in-law was able to treat his wound successfully. The bullet had penetrated and passed through the thigh muscle a few inches above the knee. Except for dizziness from the loss of blood, he felt he would be ready to go the next day.

He was still a little woozy when they set off the next morning, but with an ample supply of pain killer, he felt he could make it through the day. A few minutes after noon they parked near the main Tucson police station on Stone Avenue. Two officers, Frood and Torres, met them at the front desk and led them to a small room. The two men were total opposites. Frood stood well over six foot and packed almost three hundred pounds of muscle. With a big booming voice and overbearing manner, he was obviously in charge. Dusty took an immediate dislike to the man, but realizing they needed his help, buried his feelings in polite responses to their questions. Torres was a small wiry officer of few words, but as John and Dusty each independently surmised, was probably the brighter of the two.

"What the hell is this all about, a supposed drug-running operation in our own backyard? Don't you think we would be aware of something like that?" Frood asked.

"I would think you should be," John replied, "but I'm sure you heard about the body found up in Superstition Mountains, and the little girl kidnapped in Mesa and the body of the Sun City man found in Lake Washington. And how about the two men who died when their truck exploded up near the Mammoth Mine or that fellow Atriba, who got blown away during a home invasion just west of here. "

Torres nodded in acknowledgment, "I heard of all of those, but so what?"

"Those events are all connected. The people responsible are the ones we are going after. You help us, and you get the glory of shutting down a major dope-smuggling operation."

Frood was the first to reply.

"I'm telling you I think this whole story is bullshit, and you have wasted enough of our time."

As he got up to leave, Torres said, "Hold it for a minute, Alex. You are probably right, but if any part of what they are telling us is on the level, we are going to look pretty stupid passing up the chance of breaking up an operation of this size. I'm willing to give up a night's sleep to find out."

Frood thought for a minute then replied, "Okay, I'm in. You've been right too many times for me to take the chance of missing this one."

The four men decided to meet after sundown a couple of hundred yards beyond the drop point on North Kinney Road. Dusty and the two officers would relocate and hide near the Museum entrance. John would wait for Paul to make the pickup then follow him at a safe distance. Torres made a call to alert other departments to be on the lookout for a small aircraft in the vicinity of the Museum early the next morning but to not intercept it until he radioed the word.

All that was left to do was wait until darkness.

49

The night was dark. At midnight the moon had illuminated the landscape, but two hours later the lunar light was gone, and a heavy cloud cover had taken over. They had not told Paul where they would be; they had only assured him they would back him up. Paul and John heard the drone of the small aircraft as it came in low over the desert. Although Paul was not aware of John's presence, John was close enough to see him move his car up to the pick-up spot, get out, and take the packages when the plane made its brief landing. As soon as the aircraft started climbing, John phoned Torres for him to give the word to have it intercepted.

Paul drove slowly back to the Museum parking area, got out and looked around. Dusty and the two officers had taken refuge behind some bushes near the gate. Paul walked slowly along the path toward them, searching his surroundings for some sign of movement. Seeing nothing, he began to worry he was on his own, but he knew he had to go through with the drop. As he approached the gate, it was opened slowly by a young man in a watchman's uniform. The man said nothing as Paul passed through the entrance and handed him the packages. As soon as he was inside, two other men grabbed him and forced him along a path within the enclosure. Dusty, Frood and Torres rushed the gate and grabbed the young man. Torres handcuffed him to a railing while Frood took off after the other two, who were by now out of sight.

"Keep an eye on this one," Torres instructed Dusty as he took off after his partner.

The sullen young man sat against the barrier. Dusty settled back on a bench across the archway with the packages beside him.

"I hope you realize the trouble you're in. You're probably going to jail for a long time. Do you know what's in these packages?"

"Hell, man, this dude said he'd pay me two grand just to take this stuff to him in Phoenix. I don't know what's in them, and I don't care. He gave me five hundred up front and agreed to pay the rest when I deliver."

As John hobbled up and sat down next to Dusty, they heard shots.

"Take my gun and go see what's happening," John said. "I'll stay here with sunny boy."

Dusty moved along the path in the direction Torres had taken. It was too dark to see clearly, but his ears picked up the soft staccato of someone running toward him. He stopped and stepped off the trail as the man emerged from the shadows.

"Stop," Dusty yelled and fired a shot into the air.

The man hesitated then slipped into an alcove beside a fenced enclosure. At the same moment Torres appeared and aimed his flashlight at the man.

"Stay where you are," the officer commanded, but the man quickly scaled the fence and jumped into the enclosure.

The silence of the night was broken by the snarl of a large cat, followed by the screams of the trapped man. Dusty and Torres rushed to the fence, where Torres' powerful light picked up the body of the man splayed on the rock with the cougar standing over him tearing at his form with its powerful jaws. The man wasn't moving.

"Are we going in and try and save him?" Dusty asked.

"Be my guest," Torres replied. "The guy is dead. Look at the gash in his neck. The way that cat is going after him, there won't be much left. They don't pay me enough to go in there. Besides, I have to meet the paramedics and take them to our casualties. The other fellow ambushed Frood, hit him in the shoulder before Alex could get off a shot. He let him have both barrels of his twelve gauge. There probably isn't enough left of that one to pick up with a blotter. Unfortunately, enough of the pellets hit your friend to drop him. I told them both to stay there until I could bring in some medical help. I called EMS. They are on their way and should be here in about a half an hour. I'm going to grab the First Aid kit from the car and go back and see what I can do for them. I want you to stay here and show the paramedics where to go."

Dusty agreed and joined John in keeping an eye on their prisoner.

After Torres had gone, John said, "Our young friend has some interesting stuff to tell us. He actually works here as a guard, started a couple of weeks ago, but was ready to quit when this fellow offers him a chunk of money to deliver the packages."

"Yeah man, all these wild animals were freaking me out. I was all set to pack it in when this dude comes up with this deal. I figured, what the hell, I was quitting anyway, why not pick up a few bucks to keep me going until I found another gig. Now you tell me I can go to jail. What the hell is in those packages that makes this such a big deal?"

"Cocaine."

"Oh crap, he never said anything about coke."

"I can't believe you are as stupid as you act. Didn't you suspect something fishy?"

"I didn't think anything; I just wanted the quick money."

"Okay," John said, "I think we can resolve something out of this mess. What were your exact instructions once you had the packages?"

"He told me to drive them over to an address in Phoenix. He would pay me the rest of the money when he had them. Oh yea, I was to call him on this phone when I was on the road and repeat a code so he would know I was clear. If I help you guys, can you ask the cops to go easy on me? I'm not a drug smuggler."

"Actually you are," Dusty said, "but maybe we can work something out. We want the address and the code for starters. Then we are going to take a trip to Phoenix, and you are going to make a phone call. I'm going to need your uniform, so we'd better go get your clothes. But first we have to get you unhooked from these handcuffs. I'll have to talk Torres into giving me the key."

"My clothes are in my locker, and the other watchman is tied up in there," the young man said as he dug the key out of his pocket. "Does this mean I'm making this delivery?"

"No, but you're coming with us in your car. I'm sure it's wired for transmitting a signal. He's not going to let you go wandering off with his packages."

As Dusty prepared to go search for Torres, the officer came up the path looking for the paramedics.

"There's no way I'm letting this fellow go along on your wild goose chase. You don't know, but he's feeding you a line. He's our prisoner, and he's going to stay that way, and we're hanging on to those packages; they're evidence. You two need to stay here also and give a statement back at the office after the EMS does their job."

After Torres had gone, John said, "I don't suppose you are going to do what he told us."

"I wasn't planning on it. We know where the boss is, and I'm sure he's not going to leave without his merchandise. Did you notice that address on Grand Avenue is the same one you found for the East Arizona warehouse? Why does that not surprise me?"

"Don't leave me here," the young man pleaded.

"Not much we can do about it," John replied. "At least, we won't be taking your car, although I don't think you are going to have much use for it for a while. I want you to make that phone call now, give whoever answers the code and tell them you're on your way. I doubt if you will be believed, but it's worth a shot. We'll put in a good word for you helping us."

The young man made the call. When he hung up, he said, "That was strange. It was a woman that answered."

Dusty and John were apprehensive as they made the trip from the Museum to the Grand Avenue warehouse in Peoria. The building was dark as they drove by and parked in the next block.

"I'm moving slow, so give me time to find a back entrance and get stationed. You take the gun and go to the front, and be careful. I have no idea what you're going to find, but I'm sure it won't be good."

Dusty waited ten minutes then assumed John was in place. He moved carefully along the front of the dark building, peering in each dirt-streaked window trying to determine what was waiting for him. He could see nothing. The front of the building had a loading bay with access from the street and a small door next to it with the word 'OFFICE' stenciled on the frosted glass. Dusty tried to turn the knob, but it wouldn't budge. While he was debating whether to put his shoulder to it, the door opened slowly. Elsina stood in the entrance with her gun leveled at his mid-section.

"Come in," she said. "I wasn't expecting you. Where are the parcels?"

"The Tucson police have them. They broke up your little party this morning. What are you doing mixed up in this? Does Dan have you doing all his dirty work?"

She didn't answer but motioned Dusty into one large room lit by a feeble light at the back. The front half of the room was filled with rows of metal tables stacked with an assortment of Mexican pottery, artifacts and figurines. Elsina kept the gun pointed at him.

"I know exactly what I am doing. We are going away together after this is over and start a new life. He loves me and I care very deeply for him."

GUY ALLEN

"It sounds much like the way you cared for
Jeremy. Smarten up, Elsina. Dan isn't going to
leave his wife, his sister and his way of life to run
away with you. Why would he?"

"Because he loves me."

"What other dirty jobs have you done for him
since he revealed his so-called love?"

She didn't answer, but Dusty had the
impression he had hit home with that last remark.
Elsina was so intent on him that she didn't hear
John sneak up behind her. He had given his gun to
Dusty, but had picked up a small piece of rebar in
the alley. He jabbed the end into her back as he
said, "Drop the gun. Now!"

His attack was so unexpected; her treasured
gun fell out of her hands. Dusty picked it up and
slipped it in his pocket.

"What do we do with her, Dusty? There's no
point in calling the cops, they'd have nothing to
arrest her for."

"We let her go. She deserves the chance to find
out what kind a phony bastard she's in love with."

"I want my gun back; it was my father's"

"Sure," Dusty replied as he took the bullets out
and tossed her the empty revolver. "You may need
it."

Elsina had parked the Miata a block away.
When she left the warehouse and walked toward her
parking spot, she saw two men getting into her car.

"Stop!" She yelled as she ran toward the
vehicle.

Dusty and John were discussing their next step
when they heard the explosion. They rushed out and
up the street where the flames were dying out.
Scattered around what was left of the small car were

350

pieces of metal and human body parts. Elsina stood in shock, unable to move.

Dusty walked up to her, put his arm around her and said, "That was meant for you."

Her body began to shake violently. She tore herself away from him and began to run down the street. Dusty and John watched her until she was out of sight. As a crowd began to form, they walked slowly in the opposite direction to John's car.

"She's going to find her lover," John observed. "You planted a whole bunch of seeds of doubt in her mind. I watched her face while you were talking to her. She didn't believe you until the car blew. Do you want to go after her?"

"I don't know. He's probably thinking his car bomb got rid of her, so he won't be going to their meeting place, which I suspect would be the East Arizona office or the cabin at Sun Lakes. I expect she will go there and wait for him until her suspicions take over and she will go seek him out at his home in Sun City."

"That sounds about right. Why don't we go settle in near his place and wait for the fireworks."

"Okay. I'm going to phone Kellie and get her to check on Misty and Lara and make sure they are safe."

When Dusty turned his phone back on, the first thing he saw was the voicemail notice from Kellie. He immediately called her and learned of Jeremy's murder and Kellie's suspicions of Elsina as the killer.

When he hung up, he said, "We have a change of plans. Jeremy was killed early yesterday morning. We apparently screwed up by letting Elsina go."

50

Elsina hailed a taxi, which took her to a rental agency, where she leased a car. She was excited, but troubled by the destruction of her Miata and Dusty's words. He was obviously wrong about Dan, but why had things not worked out as they had planned. She drove to the cabin at Sun Lakes to wait for him and spent the day getting ready for the escape south and their new life together. As the day wore on she became more concerned, and memories of Dusty's words and the events of the morning started to drift back into her mind. By dark she was beginning to believe she had been used. She had tried to phone Dan at least a dozen times, but all her attempts were directed into his voicemail. She could see no course of action other than go to his home. He had strongly forbid her visiting his residence, but she was desperate for answers. She decided to wait until morning in case he came to see her during the night.

John dropped Dusty at the caseta and said, "I'm going over to the East Arizona office to see if she ended up there. What do you plan?"

"After I talk to Kellie and her father, I'm going over and stake out Dan's place and see if she show up there. I want to talk with Angleton and see if he discovered anything up north that definitely ties Dan to this mess. As it stands right now, we have nothing solid enough to get him arrested."

When Dusty went to the house he was surprised to find Misty and Lara.

"I called Kellie after Paul left and asked her if we could stay here. I thought we would be safer. Is Paul okay?" Misty asked.

"I don't know," Dusty said as he went on to describe what had happened. "I'll call the Tucson police and find out. Unfortunately, his call was answered by Torres who spent the next ten minutes reaming him out for leaving them with this moron, who knew nothing, and three neatly-wrapped empty packages.

"Are you saying the packages contained nothing?"

"Well, not totally. There was a note. It said 'Better luck next time, suckers.' We're looking pretty stupid intercepting a plane that was smuggling empty boxes. Your friend is in the Tucson hospital. They picked a bunch of shotgun pellets out of his hide, but he should be clear to get out tomorrow. Obviously, we can't charge him with anything, but if you or your buddy show your faces over here again, I'm going to try real hard to find something to charge you with."

When he hung up, Dusty handed the phone to Misty, suggesting she call the hospital and arrange for Paul's release.

While Misty was on the phone, Dusty repeated Torres' story.

"It sounds like this Seaborne fellow has been playing you all along," Angleton observed. "He has covered his tracks well. As you asked, I investigated this block of shareholders, who have been buying up the Mexari stock. It appears they are a bunch of nobodies organized by a couple of Detroit brokers."

"Let me guess," Dusty interrupted. "The brokers' names are Terrence Yancey and Thomas McCrae, and their company is called Higgs and Norman."

Angleton's surprise and annoyance was evident, "You could have saved me a lot of work if you would have told me this earlier."

Dusty explained what Paul had told him and added, "He also said Higgs and Norman were both dead, and the Company had been bought by someone else, but he didn't know the identity of the buyer."

"I couldn't find that information either. The Company was still registered to Higgs and Norman, but from what I've learned from you and Kellie, I'm willing to bet our mystery owner is Seaborne."

"I agree. He has covered himself from day one, but his two mistakes may come back to haunt him. He has tried to eliminate the two people who might be able to finger him, Paul and Elsina, and failed."

Dusty took his Landrover for the stakeout on Dan's house although he knew it would be recognized by anyone who knew him. He was especially concerned that Anna might spot him, as that would take some explaining. As he settled in, John called, "I checked out the East Arizona office. She's not there. I thought I might take a drive out to Sun Lakes."

"Okay. You can come out here and spell me off tonight if you get bored."

Elsina was wide awake at 5 AM. In fact, she had hardly slept, her mind kept racing. No longer did she feel confidence in Dan's promises. She had risked everything; there was no turning back. The car was packed, and she had decided to resolve it all today. She drove to Sun City and parked near Dan's house. Dusty noticed the car go by, but had no idea who was driving. On the other hand, Elsina immediately recognized Dusty's Landrover from his visits to Arturo. She was puzzled as to why he was there, but assumed it had something to do with Anna. She parked out of his sight, but within view of the Seaborne house. She had decided to wait until she saw some signs of life in the house then call Dan's cell. If he didn't answer this time, she would knock on the door.

Dan Seaborne was feeling good. He was up early, preparing for his regular golf date and had asked Anna to take Jeremy's place. Everything was working according to plan. He felt his superior intellect and organizational powers had created the perfect scenario. He had eliminated those who could immediately tie him to the events. Paul would be nourishment for the desert animals by now, and the beautiful Elsina would be out of the picture. He somewhat regretted the loss of his lover, but she was expendable. He missed her simply because she had been so useful in helping him carry out his plans. Now the only loose ends were the boys in Michigan and Cruz. He believed neither would risk their own safety by exposing him. His only other concern was Dusty Sherant and his ex-cop buddy, but they were just irritants, who knew nothing about what was going on.

He was loading their gear into the golf cart when his cell phone went off. A quick look at the screen was his first shock of the morning. The call was from Elsina. He quickly turned the phone off and tossed it into his golf bag. Elsina had a clear view of his actions. As far as she was concerned, it was the final proof, and she was convinced of his deception. Her anger knew no bounds, and she had to restrain herself from going over there and settling it once and for all. As she was vacillating on her decision, Dan and Anna pulled out of the driveway and headed east. She started the car and was about to pursue them when Dusty's truck appeared following in their tracks. She waited a couple of minutes then pulled out to join the procession.

Sunrise was at 7:38. It was a beautiful day. It was the kind of morning when avid golfers would dip into their repertoire of excuses for why they would be unable to take part in the workaday world.

The boys were on the course, ready to go at 7:40. Dan and Anna were the first to arrive. Dan was always the first. He paid special attention to sunrise times and precise calculations of the exact time interval it would take the sun to completely clear the horizon, thus providing enough light to proceed with their game, which was actually more than a game to Dan; it was one of the main reasons he enjoyed his life in the retirement years. . This was a good day for Dan; everyone had showed up at the proper time. He was pleased to see Tim and Louie were suitably attired with a complete compliment of expensive clubs. Anna was filling in for Jeremy, and was beautifully attired in a tennis skirt and top.

Elsina followed Dusty into the Club lot, but parked her car at the opposite end. She followed him at a distance as he walked along the rough area beside the first fairway. When Dan's group reached the first green, Elsina had to duck into a copse of bushes when she saw Dusty turn and walk across the fairway toward her and the clubhouse. She continued to follow the foursome to the third hole where Dan flubbed his drive, hooking the ball toward her hiding spot in the brush off to the side of a large sand trap. As he walked over to take his second shot out of the trap, she had to duck down to stay out of sight. He came closer, and the rage she had taken control of earlier was unleashed. As he lined up to hit the ball, she stepped out of the bushes. At the last minute, Dan lifted his head and looked straight at her, the shock and fear registering immediately on his face.

"What are you ...?"

She fired twice. The first shot hit him in the center of his chest; the second penetrated his forehead. Dan Seaborne was dead before he hit the sand.

The other three were waiting on the fairway for him to finish his shot.

Anna yelled, "No!" and ran to him and cradled his body in her arms.

"Daddy! Don't die! Don't leave me, Daddy!" she sobbed.

Louie called 911. The paramedics arrived half an hour later, and the police were close behind. Anna had recognized Elsina and gave the police a description

Dusty had followed Dan and Anna as far as the first green. He had half expected Elsina to show up, but with no sign of her, and hunger overtaking his intention to remain, he headed to the clubhouse for breakfast. He heard the shots as he was approaching the golf cart area. He immediately turned back and had only gone a few yards when he caught side of a figure running through the brush toward the parking lot. He changed direction and reached the lot just as Elsina emerged. He moved to cut her off, but she turned and pointed the gun at him.

"Leave it, Dusty. I will shoot you this time. I have nothing to lose."

He said nothing and stood there watching as she got in her car and drove away. He then walked back to the scene of the shooting. Dan's body was stretched out in the sand trap with Anna sitting by his side. Dusty walked over to comfort her, but she pushed him away.

"What did you have against my father?"

"Your father?"

"Yes. I am his daughter. He told me you were out to get him. I want to know why."

"Because he was a crook and a murderer. He killed Jeremy and was smuggling drugs."

"Those are lies," she screamed. "Elsina killed your friend. My father was an honest businessman."

Dusty could see the futility of talking with her any more in her present state. He turned and walked away.

When the police arrived he told them the make and model of Elsina's car, her tab number, and a description of the clothes she was wearing.

He drove back to the caseta, told Kellie briefly what had happened, phoned John with the news then went to bed and slept for the rest of the day.

Kelly's Epilogue

This whole mess is finally over; at least I hope it is. Two weeks has passed since Elsina shot Dan, and a week ago Jeremy's body was released for cremation, and we had a 'Celebration of his Life'. Dusty and I are convinced it was Elsina that administered that final injection, as she probably did to Arturo, her adoptive father, but no killings can be proven to be attributed to her. Dusty tried to get access to Dan's personal papers through Anna, but she has refused to help, blaming Dusty, in part, on her father's death. He finally had a look at the documents with Dolly's help while Anna was at work. Dolly was devastated by her husband's secret actions, but had suspected something was going on for some time. She told Dusty the facade about the relationship between Dan and Anna started when Anna was born, the product of a teenage romance between Dan and his high school lover. Dusty found nothing incriminating in Dan's files. The Arab had covered his tracks well.

Paul and Misty are back home helping each other recover from their ordeals. Lara returned to Seattle, and my father flew back to Toronto, leaving me to sell the house. He also wants me to take over the management of the Amyot Mine, a task I will try very hard to dump on someone else. So, I guess I'd better clean this place up, get it listed and get out of Arizona before it turns into an oven.

Dusty's Epilogue

I continue to be impressed by the attention to
detail and the care exercised by Dan Seaborne in
creating and operating this whole exercise. It would
appear on the surface that he had anticipated
everything, but as in any endeavor, it is those small,
unexpected events that cause failure. He had
counted on his thugs getting rid of Paul, and the car
bomb eliminating Elsina, and hence his downfall
and demise.

John, Paul and I spent one afternoon sketching
out what we knew about the operation. In the
beginning, Jeremy had indicated his desire to form
and run his own mining company. With Dan's
guidance, he had set it up and opened an office
through Dan's connections with Cruz in East
Arizona Imports. Although we couldn't substantiate
it, we figured Dan owned the Higgs and Norman
brokerage house, and used the documents from

Paul's past to have Yancey and McCrae force him to recruit a group of his old Union friends to put up seed money for Mexari. Jeremy then staked a bunch of claims in Arizona and paid Mervyn Chipman to write bogus reports. Cruz and his partner de la Pena vended prospects in Chihuahua County for control of Mexari. Jeremy resisted giving up control but was persuaded by Dan, who also introduced Jeremy to Elsina with the purpose of her keeping him busy and under control. The scene was set to initiate the drug operation with Mexari as cover. The packages were flown in by aircraft to drop points and delivered to pickup spots by runners. Paul was coerced into guiding this phase and had recruited Lonnie Trame until he ran off with a delivery. Mildred did a couple of runs until she left town. Paul was left to make the final delivery to the Museum. The merchandise eventually landed in the hands of suppliers in Michigan. They paid for it by buying Mexari stock through contacts of Dan's. Cruz and his buddies had formed contracting companies in Chihuahua and submitted invoices to Mexari for work on the silver claims, which was never performed. They were paid from the Mexari treasury funds that had been collected from the sale of the shares. The operation began to falter when Fred and I discovered the claims were worthless, opinions, which were passed on to Dan by Jeremy, which led to attempts on the lives of both Fred and myself. I am surprised but convinced that Jeremy knew what was going on from day one.

John and I had considered presenting what we knew about the operation to the police for investigation, but we realized we couldn't substantiate any of our knowledge, and to do so would have implicated Paul. We felt he had suffered enough. John was curious about the Mexican pottery when we were in East Arizona's warehouse. He took a ceramic doll and later broke it open, spilling cocaine all over the interior of his car. The police raided the warehouse, but the only persons identified with the Company were Dan, Elsina, and Cruz. Before they could request the extradition of Cruz from Mexico, I received a letter from Mexico City. All it contained was an article from the local newspaper. I had John translate it;

'Mexico City police report this morning the gunshot death of one of the City's business leaders. Javier Cruz was gunned down as he emerged from his residence. Neighbors reported seeing an unidentified woman in the area prior to the shooting.'

There was no accompanying note, but Elsina had signed her name at the bottom of the clipping.

I am saddened by the end of my relationship with Anna. I truly did care for her, but her attitude and accusations toward me regarding her father's death soured whatever feelings I had.

John and I developed a solid friendship and mutual respect. He made me promise if I ever got into any other wild situations, to give him a call. It was the most excitement he had in years.

Fred, on the other hand, informed me that if I ever got into any more of these messes, he'd rather not hear about it. At his age, all he was interested in was good news.

Where do I go from here? Home. I kind of miss Lucie, but I find my feelings for Kellie have steadily grown stronger over the winter. It's been almost six months in the U.S., and they will put me on the tax rolls if I stay any longer, besides with my tendency to get into dangerous situations, I had better return to Canada where I can afford the health care. Angleton offered me a job managing his mine up north. Kellie and I had a good laugh over that one.

Two weeks have passed since Elsina shot her lover, and a week ago Jeremy's body was released for cremation, prompting us to hold a 'Celebration of His Life'. We are convinced it was Elsina who administered the final injection as she probably did to Arturo.

Kellie promised to come and see me on her way home after she sells the Sun City house, hopefully before Arizona turns into an oven. I am looking forward to her visit. Somehow she has crawled into my mind and taken possession of my fantasies.

Maybe now I can go home and have that holiday I was expecting when I drove down here.

To The Reader

I hope you have enjoyed reading Sun City as much as I enjoyed writing it. My request is that you take a few minutes and jot a review of the book and post it on Amazon.com
Just Google 'Amazon books' then type
'Sun City Guy Allen' in the search bar

I welcome your comments and opinions on Sun City. Please email me at:
guyallen3303@gmail.com

Guy Allen
New Westminster, B.C.
August, 2019

Guy Allen is a retired geological engineer with many years experience in mineral, and in oil and gas industries

Also by Guy Allen

Available as an Ebook and in
Paperback

Talisman
A historical adventure set in the
goldfields of California in the 1850s

Amyot
A mystery in a Northern
Saskatchewan wildcat drilling setting

Bush Camp
A party of mine hunters deal with
danger in the wilds of Northern British
Columbia

Website
http://www.guyallen.ca

email: guyallen3303@gmail.com

www.ingramcontent.com/pod-product-compliance
Lightning Source LLC
Chambersburg PA
CBHW061309170626
46817CB00001B/111